THE CALLOWAY SISTERS

ALSO BY THE AUTHOR

NON-FICTION

Unto the Skies: A Biography of Amy Johnson
(Book Guild, 2017)

FICTION

The Rules of Engagement
(Book Guild, 2019)

To Beryl and Tony

Karim

THE CALLOWAY SISTERS

K. A. Lalani

The Book Guild Ltd

First published in Great Britain in 2022 by
The Book Guild Ltd
Unit E2 Airfield Business Park,
Harrison Road, Market Harborough,
Leicestershire. LE16 7UL
Tel: 0116 2792299
www.bookguild.co.uk
Email: info@bookguild.co.uk
Twitter: @bookguild

Typeset in Aldine401 BT

Printed and bound in Great Britain by 4edge Limited

ISBN 978 1914471 483

British Library Cataloguing in Publication Data.
A catalogue record for this book is available from the British Library.

Printed on FSC accredited paper

I dedicate this novel to all the Allied troops who fought in the Gallipoli campaign, but especially those from Australia and New Zealand and to the plucky nurses, "the Anzac Girls", who followed their men to the Front and served them so loyally.

PRELUDE

Melbourne, Australia – December 1913

Agnes Maria Calloway sat in her bedroom suite at the family home in Toorak, an affluent suburb of Melbourne, trying to temper her anticipation for the coming party. Charlotte, the family maid, who was currently running a comb through her hair, smiled at her mistress, sharing in the sense of excitement, although Agnes wished the butterflies which had been fluttering in her stomach would go away.

Agnes smiled back, but only slightly, having chastised the girl, firstly for eavesdropping and then for gossiping to her about what she had overheard. She felt a little guilt believing that she was going to benefit from the news, but she always tried to discourage Charlotte from her habit of listening to private conversations as she knew her mother wouldn't tolerate it if she were to catch her in the act. Agnes still wanted to know what she had overheard two nights ago.

'So what exactly did you hear my father, Mr Calloway, say?'

Charlotte frowned as she formulated the words in her mind. 'That he found the terms of betroth…'

'Betrothal,' supplied Agnes eagerly.

'Yes, that, most satisfactory.'

'So what did Mr Landseer say in response?' asked Agnes.

'Can't recall, Miss, as I thought I heard something and left.'

'You did the wise thing, Charlotte, and I have told you before that eavesdropping is disrespectful and Mrs Calloway would take a dim view if she caught you.'

'Yes, Miss Agnes, but do you think an announcement will be made tonight?'

'It would seem a fair assumption to make, and it would be an opportune time.'

'Do you really like him, Miss Agnes?' Charlotte asked, blushing a deep crimson in fear that she had overstepped the mark. Of them all Agnes was the most generous and patient with her, but Charlotte knew that even Agnes's tolerance had its limit.

Agnes smiled reassuringly. 'It's a reasonable question to ask in the circumstances, and yes, I *do*. Mr Landseer can be a difficult study to some and he has a tendency to appear arrogant sometimes, but I believe we are well matched. I have known him many years, so I feel there is an understanding between us. A mutual respect for one another's views, which for me is vitally important. I couldn't commit to a man who didn't respect what I think and merely wanted a pretty girl to hang on his arm. A trophy! No, I couldn't accept that. Besides, Mr Landseer is very well regarded within the business community in this city. His father helped to establish the bank he works for, and the Landseer name is very well established in Melbourne.'

Agnes looked at the effort Charlotte had put into styling her hair, and she smiled, giving the girl an encouraging nod; her amber eyes, which people said were one of her most attractive features, shone brightly as she held a piece of jewellery against her chest.

'You had better finish, Charlotte, as Miss Sarah will need your help.'

Charlotte smiled as she ran the brush through Agnes's hair once more before inserting the tortoiseshell comb. She felt a tinge of anticipation on her mistress's behalf, about how the night's events might unfold and thus, she could understand her excitement.

Michael Landseer blew heavily on the cigar, which had been lit for him by his host, smiling broadly as he lifted the snifter in salute.

'You have fine taste in cigars, Jensen, and an exceptionally good cognac. I trust these indulgences to which you have become accustomed will remain within your means. I have to say, the terms I've laid out, to which you have agreed, are acceptable.'

Jensen Calloway perched on the edge of his rosewood desk, smiled slightly, feeling more relaxed than he had in a long while, although far from as satisfied as Michael Landseer believed he should be. He had never anticipated having to take out a loan, and although the terms being offered were heavily in the bank's favour – as he would expect them to be – he had been assured of Landseer's discretion on another private matter, which for him was vital.

'Yes, and I'm sure that Agnes will also be overjoyed – I daresay ecstatic – at the news.'

'Agnes, why so?'

'The betrothal? The one I will be delighted to formally announce at the Christmas party.'

'I am aware of the plan regarding the announcement, Jensen, but I fear you are harbouring under an illusion, as I have no wish to marry Agnes.'

Jensen stiffened. His complexion darkened as his eyebrows pleated in a deep frown. 'I don't understand. Have you gone back on your word?'

Michael took a long gulp of cognac. 'No. I simply mean to clarify that I have no wish to marry Agnes. My interest lies with Sarah and that is the only betrothal I shall agree to.'

'What? I naturally assumed that it was Agnes you were referring to when you mentioned marriage. There has been an understanding over the years, as it's always been Agnes who has expressed an interest in you. Besides, Sarah is still very young!'

Jensen felt the panic in his voice as he spoke, to which Michael shrugged nonchalantly as he took another long sip of cognac, his gaze fixed on his host's face.

'That is Agnes's dilemma, or perhaps it will also become yours, given the predicament you are currently in, which has been the purpose of our recent discussions. Please forgive me, however, when I say that whatever interest Agnes may have had in becoming my wife hasn't been shared by me. I never considered Agnes, attractive though she is. My interest lies solely with Sarah.'

He lifted the brandy snifter to his nose, taking in the aroma, while Jensen, visibly paler, absorbed the enormity of his words and what they might mean for their arrangement.

'Is the bank's sanction of my loan application dependent upon her agreement?' Jensen asked tentatively, after a short silence.

Michael blew heavily on his cigar, smiling like a man who knew he held a winning hand. He shook his head slowly. 'The loan will have to be agreed by the other directors, but my opinion will be sought and, of course, should my engagement to Sarah be formally announced, that will influence any *bias* on your behalf.'

He reached for the decanter, helping himself to more cognac as once again Jensen absorbed the ramifications of the terms he had laid out.

He wasn't convinced that Agnes was *so* interested in *him* to be left heartbroken by the news that his preference lay with her sister, but he accepted that it would feel like a humiliation to be usurped by her younger sibling. Agnes Calloway was never going to make for him a suitable wife. Her combative views on political issues would be wholly detrimental to him career-wise, and he knew she held them too fervently to hold them back. Why that obsession with Women's Suffrage thousands of miles away in England? No, he could never countenance that nonsense under his roof – or, more accurately, his mother's roof, and Honoria was key in this. He was doing this for her. A good, respectful marriage was beneficial to him in terms of career advancement and he knew his mother was keen to see him climb the ranks in the bank that his deceased father had helped to establish and which still bore his name. He smiled, conscious that Jensen had suddenly become very quiet – almost *morose*.

To Michael's thinking this arrangement gave him the best of both worlds. An engaging wife and every opportunity to continue to indulge his lustful appetites where they currently lay – albeit after a respectful period of abstinence to convince his new bride of his devotion – and unlike Jensen, he would be sure to keep any vices he had under his own roof; had his host been like-minded, he wouldn't have appeared as *vulnerable* as he now was. The letter that was sent to Jensen, of course by a reliable source of *his*, had been the trump card, as it had pushed Jensen Calloway into requesting a loan. A situation that he had *so* subtly encouraged. He looked at his host, blowing heavily on his cigar, to create a blue-grey cloud of smoke between them.

'How do I persuade Sarah of your interest in her, when she has always believed it was her sister who wished to become your fiancée? Especially as she has no particular interest in you.'

'Again, Jensen, that is not my problem. I am offering you a solution to your current problem – by way of a loan – the sanction of which would be heavily influenced by my input, and in return for that I have expressed a wish, a desire to marry your youngest daughter. I have no doubt you wish to continue to live in this fine mansion and to present a confident, affluent lifestyle to your clientele which they have become accustomed to you displaying. Alas, that comes at a price, which, I am sure – once it has been explained to her by either yourself or Marguerite – Sarah will be prepared to pay. Please convince her that it *is* for the best, Jensen, for all your sakes.'

Michael stubbed out his cigar in the ash tray provided and, standing, took the last two mouthfuls of cognac in a single gulp, sighing as he set the glass down, offering Jensen his hand. For almost a nanosecond Jensen hesitated about accepting the gesture, but antagonising Michael Landseer at this delicate juncture in their dealings would do him no favours. So he shook Michael's hand.

'The funds you seek by way of a loan will guarantee that you retain the status that your hard-won reputation within the business community of this city demands. My father had a great respect for you, Jensen. He admired your acumen and your judgement.'

'Strange that you should mention Ernest at this time, because I always believed you to be an honourable man, just as he was. I trust I wasn't mistaken in that assessment.'

The words felt like a jibe to Michael, and he was certain Jensen had intended them as such – perhaps as a last brazen act of defiance – but he was prepared to let it go. Let the man, who, if all went to plan, would become his father-in-law in a matter of months, have *his* moment.

A man who had made himself vulnerable due to his vices and his lack of discretion in controlling them.

'I shall endeavour to convince the bank when my opinion is sought that you are a risk worth taking and all I ask in return is that your beautiful daughter *Sarah* acquiesces to become my wife. To what extent she knows that the fortunes of the Calloway family are resting upon her shoulders is entirely up to you.'

Jensen half-turned, unable to stomach the smug look in Michael Landseer's eyes, for a moment longer as he took his leave.

Were it not for the fact that he *needed* Michael on his side to secure the loan, he would have *struck* him. He had been ready to accept him as a husband to Agnes and would have suffered him thus, but now he had to convince Sarah to take the hand in marriage of a man that he simply couldn't afford to have as an enemy.

The Landseer Home – Melbourne – Same Evening

Honoria Landseer was considered by many who knew her to be older in her demeanour than her fifty-three years, and the last five years which she had endured as a widow had contributed to that perception. Nobody, however, doubted her steely resolve or the determination to protect her husband's good name and his legacy in the business community in Melbourne, which to her mind was at risk of being compromised by what she saw as her son's worst excesses, the nature of which she knew her husband would not have tolerated. Michael revelled in trying her patience to its limit and to rejoice in his unequivocal right to her disapproval.

He arrived home from the Calloway mansion in Toorak via his club, where he had indulged in several more cognacs, and flopped into the chair opposite her, lighting his cigar – despite her disapproval of the habit being indulged in her drawing room.

'Evening, Mother. You will be delighted to hear that I have sealed the deal with Jensen. He has formally signed the loan application that I had drawn up. So the next phase in our plan of revenge – I'm sorry, retribution – upon the house of Calloway is in motion!'

Honoria scowled, treating her son to a withering stare. 'Look at you! Your father would be ashamed!'

'I daresay that he would, Mother, given he had expressed no interest in bearing your long-held grudge against the

Calloways. He was certainly against dragging the bank into your murky plans, especially after you had become aware of Jensen's weakness for the flesh of Melbourne's finest whorehouses.'

Honoria closed her eyes, taking a deep breath to compose herself. Pursing her lips, she sighed wearily. 'Michael, it is late and I wish to retire, so if you could manage to spare me the vulgarity and come to the point. What exactly has been agreed?'

Michael stumbled to his feet and made his way to a drinks cabinet. 'As you wish. I have indicated to Jensen that the bank will be inclined upon my recommendation to agree to the terms of a loan and that in return, I shall have the hand in marriage of his daughter. Of course the crucial factor – that you insisted upon – is that the deeds to the Calloway mansion be secured by the bank as collateral in the event that he defaults on the repayments.'

Honoria shook her head slightly, as she hadn't insisted upon that clause, but she agreed it was likely the bank directors would have inserted it into the contract themselves. She nodded slightly. 'It is perhaps harsh to involve the girl in our plan but no more than what my poor mother suffered at Cyrus Calloway's hands, and I am sure Agnes will *endure*. She is made of stern stuff, and who knows? She may yet become a good influence upon you. Dare I say it, she may succeed where I have evidently failed in curbing your excesses.'

Michael turned to her again with decanter in hand. He smiled mischievously. 'Ouch, Mother! I am wounded by your censure. You are, however, mistaken as I have no wish to become betrothed to Agnes. I have expressed an interest in taking the hand of her sister Sarah.'

'What? That is not what we agreed. You were to become engaged to Agnes.'

'I am aware of what you thought I was agreeing to, but on further consideration, I decided the prospect of marrying Agnes didn't suit me, so I amended the plan and have set my hand at winning Sarah.'

'He'll never agree to it!' snapped Honoria, fuming.

'He has no choice. Jensen also remarked how delighted Agnes would be and sadly I felt compelled to inform him that I had no interest in marrying Agnes.'

'Why?'

Michael resumed his seat and took a long slow gulp of cognac. 'It's the fixation she has with that Women's Suffrage issue, that factor alone put me off. Sarah is younger – I'll admit only slightly more attractive – but biddable. Agnes, by contrast, is combative by nature. I have no wish to see that quality in a wife.'

Honoria was struggling to retain her even temper. She felt the plan they had been forming for weeks was in jeopardy and all to indulge her son's ego. 'Sarah is *too* timid. She looks like a delicate flower. That's why you have switched your allegiance. All that you want is an obedient, pretty wife that you can have on your arm to parade around this city like a filly on Melbourne Cup Day.'

Michael nodded, as if that prospect, exactly as his mother described it, was his ideal.

'Well, I hope that she flatters to deceive! I hope she proves more than a match for you from the moment you place the band of gold on her finger.'

'On the contrary, Mother. I think Sarah will prove to be as biddable as I want to her to be. On my arm, at social functions and in *my* bed...'

Honoria stood to confront him and Michael recoiled, his hands raised in mock surrender.

She shook her head in disgust at him, although she knew that when inebriated he was immune to her censure.

'If you ruin that sweet young girl, you'll be damned in hell, Michael Landseer!'

'Oh, I think our places in hell are already booked, Mother. Have no fear of that, but please remember, revenge – and yes, I use the word deliberately, because that is what has been in your mind all these years and what your husband tried to counsel you against. *Revenge!* It isn't painless. It cannot be a victimless act, not if it's to be successful. So if you are baulking at the finer details and you want to throw in your hand, now is the time to say so. I daresay Jensen may still get a favourable hearing from the bank, but it will still want the Toorak mansion as collateral, and he will have to forego my personal recommendation.'

Michael paused to look at Honoria as she stood at the bottom of the stairs, her hand on the newel post, as she took several deep breaths to marshal her anger.

He wanted to laugh, but he contented himself with a gleeful smile, adding, 'We both know what a poisoned chalice that recommendation will be, don't we? Although he doesn't know it yet.'

Honoria looked at him and she couldn't conceal her disgust at the glee with which he contemplated another man's ruin, but for most of her life she *had* wanted to see the Calloways punished. Retribution, she called it, for the humiliation that Cyrus Calloway had caused her mother Louise, with his breach of promise and the pain *his* rejection had caused her. She had been forced to keep her counsel throughout her marriage, given Ernest Landseer's opposition, but now was the time for Jensen Calloway to feel her *wrath*, and yes, maybe she had turned Michael into a vessel of her anger, but he had adhered willingly, and she could see now that he relished the prospect of revenge all too much, but she couldn't back out now.

'Well?' he prompted her.

'Do it!' she said.

Michael smiled. 'Thank you, Mother. I bid you good night.'

He staggered on his feet as he treated Honoria to an overtly theatrical bow.

In her bedroom suite Honoria sat on the edge of her bed, taking a moment of silent reflection. She was fuming, but her instincts were right.

She pulled on the cord to summon the maid, but when she didn't come Honoria screamed out her name. 'Yolande!' The sound echoing throughout the house, but what she couldn't see was the conspiratorial wink that passed between Michael and Yolande as he clumsily ascended the stairs.

1

After she dismissed Charlotte to attend to her sister's needs, Agnes took a moment to compose herself and look forward to the evening. She didn't want to think about why Michael had sought her father's permission – or consent – to marry her, without first having asked her formally. Was she so obvious in revealing her wish to become his wife? Perhaps he saw no point in proposing if he wasn't confident of gaining her father's agreement? And wasn't it more than a little odd that her father hadn't told her of Michael's plans?

She could only hope that Charlotte hadn't overheard what she imagined her mistress wanted to hear. The girl was hopelessly clumsy in her eavesdropping and should she ever be caught Agnes doubted she could save the girl from her mother's wrath. She would have to keep her counsel at the party and temper her anticipation until the announcement was made. To display the dignified demeanour of contented surprise.

The *kudos* that she could claim, however, from being publicly announced as Michael Landseer's fiancée would wipe the smug smile from Leticia Crozier's face, and she wasn't going to conceal the pleasure that prospect would give her.

She had to admit there were aspects of Michael's character that she didn't find appealing. His lack of understanding for the cause of Women's Suffrage in the mother country didn't impress her, and the fact that she had seen his mood change considerably for the worst when heavily imbued with cognac was also concerning, but she had cultivated the prospect of a union with him for so long now that she hadn't given serious consideration to the possibility that she might refuse him, but it remained a prerogative she kept in reserve, so that he believed she had an alternative to accepting *his* proposal.

She looked at her reflection in the dressing-table mirror and the smile which briefly lit her eyes. There was a knock on the door and, squaring her shoulders, she took a steadying breath before commanding the person to enter. The door opened and her sister Sarah walked in. Agnes could see the pensive look on Sarah's face, but she didn't want her mood spoiled, however much she was erring on the side of caution that an announcement would be made until the moment came.

'What is it?' she asked.

'It's that wretched girl Charlotte. She has been eavesdropping again and has revealed that an engagement announcement is going to be made tonight. She has to go! Mama has given her too many chances.'

Agnes shook her head. 'You're too hard on her. I agree she can be hopelessly indiscreet sometimes, but she has a good heart. I would be sorry to see her go.'

'You're not concerned by what she is claiming to have overheard then?' Sarah asked tentatively.

Agnes looked at her sister in the mirror and shook her head. Sarah's pleated frown wasn't the reaction she had anticipated, but she didn't pursue it.

'Charlotte *is* a romantic at heart and I wouldn't be surprised if she has imagined some of what she had overheard.' Agnes stood, offering Sarah her arm. 'Shall we?'

Once again Sarah's smile was slightly awkward as she nodded and Agnes decided not to press her. Sarah had been nervous on Agnes's behalf since their father revealed to her what was being planned, as she had expected he would have spoken to Agnes first. So she couldn't understand how her sibling remained *so* neutral.

She may be right about the maid having a kind heart, but *if* Charlotte had got what she had overheard wrong the portents for Agnes would be disastrous and she wouldn't wish that on her elder sister for anything.

Sarah nodded warily and they descended the stairs together, Sarah looking more radiant than she felt in the turquoise silk gown. She saw Michael Landseer, with brandy snifter in hand, which he raised in salute and she realised it was *her* that he was staring at, just as she recognised the arrogant sneer behind his smile, which unnerved her even more. What was it about this man that made her feel so uneasy?

Marguerite Calloway appeared to greet another arriving guest, and Sarah could see how nervous their mother – who usually exuded serene calmness – looked tonight, although the pre-Christmas party was an annual event and Marguerite was an experienced hostess. Agnes noticed too, as she whispered something to that extent as they reached the bottom step in unison and their mother arrived to swiftly whisk Sarah away.

Marguerite couldn't help wondering, with all that her husband had confided in her following Michael Landseer's ultimatum, how tonight would pan out.

Her reaction had been incendiary and they had barely spoken civilly to each other until the first guests had begun arriving. Putting on a show for Melbourne's finest was, however, something she was accustomed to, but forgiveness didn't come easily to her and she doubted she could ever forgive Jensen for the dire predicament that his vices and the woeful lack of discretion had put them in, along with the impact that it was going to have on their daughters' lives.

She no longer believed Michael Landseer to be the honest man she could have welcomed as a future son-in-law, but now that his *betrothal* seemed inevitable and the confirmation of it would be shared with their assembled guests according to *his* dictating was a bitter pill to swallow, as she knew that in order to accede to Landseer's demands and retain their fragile reputation within Melbourne's business community, they would have to sacrifice one daughter to this wretched man and potentially break the other's heart in the process.

Sarah greeted her mother with a kiss on the cheek as Marguerite shepherded her into a corner out of earshot.

'Have you spoken to Michael?'

'I was putting it off until I had to. He is *so* arrogant! So sycophantic and assured of his self-importance. I can't imagine why Agnes has been so *enamoured* of him.'

Marguerite smiled. She would have done anything to spare her youngest this ordeal and yet even in that simple task she had failed. She had no worries of Agnes, as her eldest was very strong-willed and she knew her own mind, but Sarah was different.

'Well, after tonight she won't have to. She will have had her eyes opened to the kind of man Michael Landseer truly is. As we all have.'

Sarah nodded grimly. 'Some more than most.'

'Your father needs to keep him on side. So *be* nice to him.'

Marguerite turned to greet one of her friends and Sarah slid into the throng of mingling guests. Agnes had also disappeared, for which she was thankful, and Michael approached her with a lascivious smile upon his face. She imagined he would have been the sort to rip the wings off butterflies as a child, and she wondered if the spite ran right through him. She smiled uneasily, fearing what he was going to say, but another guest called out to him, and when he turned, Sarah fled.

4

Jensen Calloway had not been looking forward to the party as he generally did, having always viewed the evening as his opportunity to shine among the elite of Melbourne society. Tonight, however, he roamed among his guests, conscious that Michael Landseer's gaze was fixed upon him, waiting for any deviation from their carefully choreographed plan.

Wielding as he did the power with which to bring the façade of Calloway respectability crashing down around him, there were sufficient members of the city's business community among the assembled guests with whom he regularly did business and he would not wish to know his private business – one of the least auspicious of which Michael Landseer had somehow managed to acquire knowledge of. It had never occurred to him as a wise strategy to simply bluff his way through when Michael had first confronted him about the contents of the letter – and should Michael yet choose to be indiscreet, Jensen knew it would spell *his* ruin.

It was bad enough Michael held his fate with the bank in his hands.

With sufficient influence with the board, he held the leverage and Jensen couldn't be sure of securing the loan with another financial establishment and still trust Landseer to remain silent. Then there was the less palatable fact that he would have the man as his son-in-law in due course, but not in wedlock to the daughter he had expected, who could, he knew, hold her ground with a man like him, but to Sarah, his youngest, which he had only agreed to under *duress.*

Jensen caught a fleeting glimpse of himself in the mirror as he moved among his guests. His expression was grim as he turned away and it was no surprise that he didn't like what he saw, nor the fact that he only had himself to blame.

He made a swift escape to his study, pouring himself a large cognac. His favourite libation. Champagne would only leave a bitter taste in his mouth tonight, as he had nothing to celebrate.

He looked at himself in the mirror again, cursing under his breath. 'You fool, Calloway! You *utter* fool!' He finished the cognac in a gulp and was poised to pour himself another snifter of courage when there was a soft knock on the study door. 'Not Marguerite! Please not her,' he muttered under his breath. He didn't want it to be Landseer either, which he knew was more than likely. He really couldn't stomach the smug smile the man had been displaying most of the evening.

'Come,' he said tentatively; as the door opened ajar to reveal Sarah, his shoulders sagged with relief.

'What is it? Why aren't you out there being nice to Michael? I have told you how imperative it is that you keep him engaged! It is vital, Sarah!'

'It's so unfair! That's what it is! The man is a snake! Why has he developed an interest in me? I've never encouraged him. It is Agnes that has held a mild interest in him these years, and she will be devastated by this turn of events.'

Jensen put the snifter on his desk and placed both hands on Sarah's shoulders. 'I have explained to you why it has to be thus and I wish your sister's feelings could be spared, but, harsh though it may sound, I fear she has overestimated Michael's interest in her. He has an unpredictable streak to his personality and I fear he may yet change his mind and give a negative view of my reliability to the bank, should he feel antagonised. I cannot *stress* enough how vital it is for us all that I secure those funds, and as much as I hate having to admit it, Michael holds the winning hand.'

'With me as your trump card?' Sarah asked glumly.

Jensen pulled her to him so that she couldn't see the tears that he could so easily have surrendered to, but he wouldn't appear weak in her presence or more *vitally* show Michael how vulnerable he had become.

He let her go and she looked at him as he nodded encouragingly for her to leave, and although she held no realistic expectations, she hoped he may yet offer her a means of escape.

'Answer me this before I go. Marriage to a man that I cannot stand, at the expense of my sister's happiness, how can that ever be right?'

Michael Landseer was enjoying himself immensely. With a cigar in one hand and a large brandy snifter in another, he watched his hosts and the other guests with sufficient interest with which to appear outwardly polite, but he was eager for the announcement to be formally made so that he could escape the tedium of small talk with those in whom he had no interest and take his leave.

He saw Agnes walk past him, smiling shyly and he couldn't help speculating on what she might have been told. Was Jensen keeping his card close to his chest? Is that why Agnes looked hopelessly deluded that an announcement involving her was going to be made this evening?

Jensen must think he was doing a deal with the devil and Michael smiled, as he liked being compared to the devil, whether it be from another's estimation of his character or whether it was a view he held himself. Then Sarah came fleetingly into his line of sight. Beautiful, biddable Sarah who looked every inch the sacrificial Calloway lamb, who would become his fiancée by the evening's end. Her elder sister would doubtless be shocked, perhaps even feel humiliated, once the reality of it had sunk in, and he felt no shame in delighting at the prospect. It would mean the crucial phase in the Landseer plan would have been executed, and he recalled Honoria's words, even though she was baulking at the sudden change in seeking Sarah's hand in marriage.

Perhaps she should have heeded his father's advice and left the whole thing alone, but from the first time she had fed *him* the scraps of his grandmother Louise's sorry tale, he had bought the idea, and having taken his mother's tacit instruction 'do it' as her approval that she wasn't backing out, now she would have to accept that her long-hoped-for plan to wreak retribution on Jensen and his family for the sins of Cyrus Calloway would be followed, according to his means and with *his* ends in mind.

Jensen Calloway gently tapped the side of a crystal champagne flute to command the attention of his guests, as anticipation of what was to be announced fizzled around him. He tried to calm his nerves with a long deep breath. The cognac he had consumed in the privacy of his study for once had not had the desired effect, for he felt sick to the stomach at what he was about to do, and the fact he saw no alternative served only to make him feel worse. He was grateful that Marguerite remained loyal and that she appeared so resolutely strong as always, but he didn't know how she could project a demeanour of such glacial calm given the circumstances. His wife was a survivor by instinct, he realised that; however, the price they were asking both their daughters to pay for his act of reckless folly was high.

'Friends, business associates, I would like to thank you all once again for accepting our invitation to what has become an annual event in our home. This year, there is another reason for us to celebrate, aside of Christmas, as I formally announce the engagement of Michael Landseer to my daughter…' He paused, his voice faltering slightly, as assembled guests exchanged confused glances, wondering what possible reason there was for delay.

Marguerite nodded at him to continue and suddenly Michael was fidgeting, pushing his way through to stand alongside his host. *Don't falter now, Jensen, or all will be lost.* He heard a voice inside his head as Michael looked at him with barely concealed warning. Jensen squared his shoulders and added, 'My daughter Sarah Calloway!'

There were murmurs of shock mingling with the applause as Michael accepted the warm-hearted pats on his back and words of congratulation.

Jensen looked across at Agnes and he could see her expression frozen in a mixture of shock and anger. She was conscious of the gloating smile of Leticia Crozier in her peripheral vision, and for her sense of self-preservation, she forced a smile onto her face, but it hurt and the *rawness* inside her was real. In that moment, she didn't know who she felt most betrayed by – her father? Sarah, the sister in whom she had confided most of her dreams of becoming engaged to Michael Landseer?

Michael! The obvious source of her pain. He had rejected her in favour of Sarah, her younger sibling, and he had done it to cause her ultimate humiliation. It was written all over his smug face. That events tonight had been organised *thus* to suit him and to inflict hurt upon her, she had no doubt. Worst of all her family had been complicit in his plan. She took a steadying breath, turning her head away from the curious glances of guests, through whom she pushed her way, ignoring her father's plea as she found the relative safety of his study.

Michael had watched Agnes make a hasty retreat to the study with a look of gleeful satisfaction on his face. Then he looked across at his host whispering in his wife's ear. Of his new fiancée he saw nothing, but Sarah could wait. He would give her time to absorb the enormity of what had been announced. He looked down and saw that a scrap of paper had been pushed into his hands, and when he read its contents, his smile diminished. Cursing under his breath, he went to the study.

'Come,' came the firm female voice in response to his knock, and he pushed at the door, which she had left unlocked.

'Agnes.'

'You're not worthy of my sister's hand in marriage. You were only just about worthy of mine, and I had the measure of you. I knew what I *should* expect.'

'Yet Jensen has formally announced our engagement, so

9

your father evidently doesn't share your opinion – which for him is fortunate, given his current predicament.'

'I have had my eyes opened about the kind of man you are and I'll ensure Sarah sees you for what you are.'

'Really? Or does all this just amount to bravado from a spurned sister, not deemed quite as attractive as her younger sibling? Jensen thought it was you I was interested in securing as my future wife and I was *forced* to put him right. I'm sorry this is going to come as a shock to you, Agnes, but I was never interested in having you – I can tolerate you as my future sister-in-law, but that is as far as my interest goes. You are too brittle by nature and overly opinionated, and as prospective wife material goes, your priorities are all wrong. You can, I am sure, attract the attention of a reasonably eligible young blade around town, but unless you temper this fixation you have with Women's Suffrage, I fear your options may yet be limited to some feckless dullard.'

Michael drew heavily on his cigar, filling the now-putrid air of the study with a cloud of blue-grey smoke, which momentarily obscured his view of Agnes. 'Unless, of course, you find the prospect of a long spinsterhood under your parents' roof palatable?'

'Save your advice. I have no use of it.'

'As you wish.' Michael nodded, raising his hands in mock surrender.

Smiling again, he made for the door. 'Is that it? We're done? Because I *would* rather spend the rest of the evening with my fiancée than be hidden away trading verbal blows with her *bitter* older sibling.'

He left with his characteristic sneer that she had come to know so well and Agnes gripped the side of the rosewood desk as the door closed behind him. She couldn't face going back to the party. She didn't want to hear any lame excuses from her father for what she could only see as his betrayal. Or her mother's worn platitudes that all would be well and that she would get over the disappointment.

Her concern now was for Sarah. She wanted to know when her sister had been informed of what was being planned. She reached for the decanter, pouring herself a handsome measure of cognac. She finished it in two gulps, wincing at the burning sensation it caused in her throat and then, turning to her right, she gazed at the portraits on the wall.

The first was of her paternal grandfather whom she had never met, Cyrus Calloway! Often described as a likeable "*larrikin*" and then she looked at her father's portrait.

He was not blameless in this tawdry affair. She didn't know the details of the predicament that he was in, to which Michael had referred, but *he* could have warned her that Michael had turned his attentions to Sarah.

To have spared her the humiliation of discovering it was her younger sibling he wanted to marry and yet her father had chosen not to. Surely Michael couldn't have dictated that decision? It had been a cruel act and one she would never have expected from the father she adored. Raising her arm, she shook her head silently as she flung an empty snifter at his portrait, watching it smash against his smiling face.

2

It took Agnes a few moments to recover her composure. She took several deep breaths, gripping the edge of the desk until her knuckles were white.

She was surprised but also relieved that the smashing glass hadn't alerted anyone to enquire about her well-being, as she wasn't ready to see anyone yet – least of all her parents, either one of which were the most likely to come looking for her – although she suspected their attention would be focused on their guests, sipping champagne and accepting congratulations from those eager to express their delight at the news of Sarah's engagement to an eminent banker. Agnes sighed heavily.

Her sense of weariness at her situation reinforced itself. How could she have been *so* deluded in thinking that Michael Landseer coveted her as his wife? Had she always been the foil for where his true feelings lay?

Could Sarah be offered to him against her will or was it possible her sister was acquiescent in the plan to usurp her? She had no doubt that Michael had revelled in her sense of humiliation, but she could never believe that of her sibling. Her feelings now were of concern for *her*, although she suspected in due course it was likely she would feel relieved at not becoming Michael Landseer's wife. What did the future hold for Sarah in that capacity? What bleak outcome had their parents subjected their youngest daughter to, by accepting this proposal of marriage? To what extent had their father needed Michael's discretion in the matter of the loan application and what if the bank still declined to offer the funds?

Could it possibly be that Sarah's hand was being offered in a bleak marriage for nothing?

All the questions swirling around in her head required answers and Agnes was determined to get some of those from her father in due course, although she suspected her sister might be the best source for others. As sisters, they had always been very close, despite the differences in their demeanour and in what Agnes readily acknowledged was her *zeal* in respect of political issues. She was conscious that she couldn't remain in the study for the rest of the evening and the annual December soiree their parents hosted usually dragged on past midnight, but for her the prospect of returning to the party held no appeal. She wasn't sure she could stomach the gloating smile of Michael Landseer and she wasn't prepared to let Leticia Crozier have the satisfaction of goading her as the spurned older sister.

She knew Leticia well enough that her *instinct* for spitefulness would compel her to just that conclusion, and what if she wasn't alone in that vein of thinking? Suppose all her parents' friends and associates had come to the conclusion that Michael Landseer had been offered the hand of either Calloway sister in marriage and that he had opted for the younger, more biddable Sarah?

Agnes knew she couldn't escape to her room without forcing a path through assembled guests, although there was no other option. Squaring her shoulders, she took one long deep breath and opened the study door.

As the evening was drawing to a close, Michael Landseer, heavily imbued from all the champagne he had consumed followed by several cognacs, was approached by Leticia Crozier, the sister of his best friend Aaron, who couldn't keep the look of glee from her face. He would have readily escaped to avoid her company had she not boxed him into a corner at the foot of the stairs, as he didn't particularly like her.

It was – and he smiled at the realisation as it struck him – the one thing that perhaps he and Agnes still had in common. Although unlike Agnes, he felt the need to *err* on the side of politeness to Leticia, for the sake of his friendship with Aaron.

'I can't say that I blame you for tossing over Agnes in favour of her younger, more attractive sister, but I still *don't* understand why you are limiting your choice to either. A man of your standing can surely do better.'

Michael smiled, puffing heavily on his cigar; he leaned into Leticia as if he were going to kiss her, which, he knew from Aaron, she longed for him to do, and whispered, 'When I can have you, perhaps?'

'Exactly! A better choice all round, given the long history of our families and your friendship with Aaron.'

Michael smiled, exhaling smoke into Leticia's face. 'Because as much as I value my friendship with Aaron, I find the prospect of committing myself in wedlock to you unpalatable!'

Leticia looked at him with narrowing eyes, and with her pride wounded, she lifted a hand to strike him; however, Michael predicted her move and he swerved away from the blow, gripping her arm as she let it fall by her side.

'Look at you!' she hissed. 'Drunk as usual. Your status at the bank – which you owe entirely to your father – aside, you're no great catch, Michael Landseer!'

Michael rocked slightly on his heels, but he retained his balance and his dignity. Raising an eyebrow at Leticia, he moved closer to her with an air of menace in his demeanour. 'In which case you can be thankful that you've had a lucky escape, Lettie.'

He paused to smile mischievously, knowing just how *much* she hated the childhood shortening of her name. She wanted to spit her venom at him, but Michael, who had always enjoyed a love-hate relationship with Aaron's sister, infuriated her further by laughing, as he had known for years she would surrender herself to him instantly if he ever showed the slightest hint that he wanted her. He added, 'Because I was no more interested in you as my future wife than I was in being betrothed to Agnes.'

Leticia struggled to break free of his hold on her wrist, and he looked around him at the diminishing throng of now-departing guests as Sarah came into his line of vision. 'Once I've had my fill of the alluring Sarah, and *I* have fulfilled my need, she also will be begging me to set her free.'

Leticia smiled, thinking he had fed her a tasty morsel of gossip, but she knew him well enough not to be fooled. 'Why, what is your plan for the Calloway ingénue?'

'Unburden myself to you, Leticia? Given your reputation for being *so* indiscreet? I don't think I should be so reckless. I prefer to trust Aaron with my confidences.'

'Damn you to hell, Michael!' As he released his hold, she lifted her chin defiantly and said, 'What's to stop me from telling Sarah what a miserable life she has in store as your wife?'

Michael shrugged. 'Because they wouldn't believe you. Your reputation for spreading spiteful gossip precedes you, Leticia! Besides which, I know that Jensen cannot afford anything to go amiss as he is relying upon my favourable input at the bank to secure the loan he has requested.'

Leticia smiled and moved closer. 'So how much trouble is he in?'

Michael looked at her, preparing himself for what he was certain would be shared widely around the city, and suddenly he relished his opportunity for indiscretion as he had no inclination to spare Jensen's reputation.

'More than he ever knew, and very soon all of Melbourne will bear witness to the spectacular fall of the house of Calloway!'

The Landseer House, Melbourne – Later

Michael sat in an enamel bathtub smoking heavily and, despite the lateness of the hour, enjoying a long luxuriating soak. He felt blissfully happy at the events this evening. His marriage to Sarah had been formally announced to most of those who mattered in Melbourne society and he had put Agnes Calloway firmly in her place as the now-redundant older sister.

He had also seen Jensen practically fawning in his bid to be accommodating and that had to be the *most* satisfying sight of all.

Things really couldn't be better. Life couldn't taste sweeter. He had even been given the opportunity to put Leticia Crozier's latent ambitions to the fire and he had extinguished them. Although he had been forewarned in that regard by Aaron. Leticia was as notorious in Melbourne for setting her cap at every eligible young man who caught her eye as she was for her woeful lack of discretion, and Michael smiled, recalling that he had also taken advantage of that weakness in her character.

There was a slight knock on the door that he barely heard but was expecting, and on his command it opened further as Yolande the maid entered the room. He had his back to the door but saw the stealth with which she moved from the mirror with a bucket of hot water to replenish the bath in both hands. She slowly filled the bath and, on Michael's nod, she untied her dress, letting it fall in a heap at her feet. He didn't know much detail about Yolande's parentage, but it hadn't ever mattered as her nakedness always aroused him, and in the muted light, it was almost beyond his endurance, as she looked irresistibly alluring with her caramel-skinned curves as he inclined his head for her to join him in the bathtub.

She took the sponge in both hands and, with a look of desire-induced menace in her eyes, she lathered his genitals beneath the bubbles and watched as he convulsed with desire. Lifting a cup, he sluiced soapy water over her shoulders, watching it cascade, her skin glowing luminous in the candlelight. He winced as he felt her hands around his throbbing manhood, tormenting him on a knife edge of arousal as she bit gently on her bottom lip. Nodding her encouragement, he spat out his cigar, seeking her mouth to devour her with the fervour of his kisses as he surrendered completely to the reality of his most *carnal* desire.

The Calloway Mansion, Toorak

Three days passed before Sarah was received by her sister, days in which she was made to fret anxiously about how her older sibling would act towards her now that she was engaged to be married to Michael Landseer. Her main concern was that Agnes might have reached the conclusion she had known Michael had made it clear to their father that his allegiance had switched to *her* and that she had been too scared to tell her, or that she had been complicit alongside their parents in a bid to deceive her sister.

Marguerite Calloway was willing to play the long game by allowing Agnes time alone in her room to come to terms with the arrangement, adding when Jensen encouraged her to show some mercy that they couldn't have *forced* Michael to take Agnes as his wife, adding that her patience with their elder daughter had a limit and that Agnes would be wise not to test her *endurance* on the issue of her sister's engagement. Whenever she thought Sarah might be wavering, she took her firmly by the shoulder, reminding her that her father needed to secure the funds from Argate & Landseer, and that it needed to be approved swiftly.

Thus Sarah was informed that her forthcoming nuptials were an alliance rather than a love match and that they were based on solely on necessity.

Although Marguerite was squarely on her husband's side in their determination to ensure they maintained their social status within the city, she did lay the blame for them needing to secure the loan entirely upon his shoulders.

For a time Agnes was cut adrift from the family in her suite, taking all her meals there; despite her mother's mild censure and a futile bid in refusing to let Charlotte wait on her, she sent a message through the maid that she was ready to see her sister. Sarah knocked tentatively, waiting for the command to enter. While their mother had accused Agnes of sulking, both Sarah and her father had been conciliatory, believing Agnes deserved time to become accustomed to the fact that she had lost the hand of Michael to Sarah.

Agnes could see the apprehension etched on her sister's face, while to Sarah's eyes she looked strangely serene.

'Thank you for agreeing to see me.'

Agnes laughed slightly and Sarah's expression relaxed. 'You are talking like an old school friend who has arrived unannounced and is unsure whether she will be admitted. You're my *sister*. I was always going to see you once I'd had time to process all that happened at the party and come to terms with Michael's betrayal. Whether I *still* wished to view it as such.'

'Do you?'

Agnes shook her head. 'No, Sarah. I am, however, concerned for you at the prospect of becoming his wife. I had to come to terms with the possibility that Michael probably never intended to formalise matters between us, that it may have been a fantasy, I had indulged for too long and I view him in a renewed, less favourable light, and I must *urge* you not to commit yourself to him. You can do so much better, and you deserve to be happy, which I fear no woman will be when bound in matrimony to him.'

'I have to marry him. I cannot back out as our father needs to secure the loan and *he* is depending on Michael's recommendation.'

Agnes shook her head. 'That is untrue. Our father is a safe risk for any loan at any bank and if he were deemed otherwise do you believe that the word of Michael Landseer alone would sway matters to such an extent? There has to be more to it than just a loan application. He must know something about our family and our parents are trying to buy his silence by bonding you into marriage. We will have to find out what.'

Agnes took a deep breath and, standing, she put her hands on Sarah's shoulders. 'If there were a way out of this marriage, wouldn't you take it?'

'There isn't.'

'But don't you want to try? I thought you would baulk at the prospect of marrying Michael. You never sounded encouraging about me committing myself to him whenever we speculated on it, but perhaps you do.'

'There's no point in hoping there is a means of escape when there isn't one and I refuse to risk our father's... our family's ruin by failing to commit. I can *endure* this marriage. I am stronger than you imagine me to be. The question for you to answer, Agnes, is can you *endure* the humiliation our parents will suffer *if* Michael does his worst – assuming he has anything to bring it about – when you have the power to prevent it?'

Agnes flopped down onto the stool in front of her dressing table and glanced in the mirror. Sarah glimpsed the almost imperceptible shake of the head and then she heard Agnes whisper, 'No.'

'A date hasn't been set as yet, but I don't expect it to be long. Michael is keen for us to marry in March. So if you're going to find a way out that keeps the Calloway reputation intact you have got to find it soon.'

Agnes nodded. Her brows pleated in a frown she turned to her sister. 'I wonder what would happen marriage-wise if the bank declined Father's application?'

'That doesn't bear consideration. Besides, Father is convinced that Michael's input will allay any doubts.'

Agnes shook her head. 'If he is *so* reliant on that man's word then he must be in trouble.'

Sarah stood by the door, ready to leave. 'They wanted me to assure them that you're OK, that you have come to terms with Michael's decision, that you're not, as Mother says, sulking?'

Agnes smiled, as they both knew it was exactly what their mother would think. Marguerite Calloway hadn't indulged their sulking when they were young girls and she would surely be far less tolerant of it now. Agnes smiled. 'You can tell them that I have come to terms with the reality. Truth be told, I have come very swiftly to *loathe* Michael. He attempted to imply that my support for Women's Suffrage was the deciding motive that forced him to switch his allegiance. My sole concern now is for you to find an honourable way out. One that is right for us all but ultimately will spare you the humiliation of marriage to that man.'

Sarah smiled wanly, wishing she had Agnes's strong mind and her belief there could be a way out of the mess. So she left and Agnes alone was in a reflective mood as she gazed at herself. Sarah had voiced sufficient doubts about the forthcoming marriage for her to be motivated to find a way out, but it was like being temporarily lost in a maze as every conceivable exit led to another dead end. What was it that Michael really wanted that he would be prepared to risk his reputation at his father's bank should Jensen default on the repayments?

What did they have that the Landseers, with all their wealth, could possibly want? Then it came to her. The Toorak mansion! Their family home.

Michael had always admired it, and he had articulated his admiration to her countless times. The Landseers had always lived modestly in comparison, as that was Ernest's character. So maybe Michael coveted it for himself, so that he could lord it over his peers and show off in that *crass* way that was so uniquely *his*. That was the real prize, she was convinced of it. More than Sarah's hand in marriage or hers. She still didn't know the details of why her father needed to secure the funds *so* desperately, and the only way to find out was to confront him directly.

Which she would if that was what it took to save her beloved sister from a nightmare marriage.

3

Within days of his engagement being announced, Michael was flexing his financial muscle and exerting whatever influence he had with the directors at Argate & Landseer to heap pressure on his future father-in-law while basking gleefully in the knowledge of the strain that it was placing upon him. He made it clear to his mother that he wasn't inclined to show the Calloways any mercy and he resented any attempt Honoria made to sanction him for what she described as his gratuitous sense of satisfaction.

'Lest we forget, you wanted this outcome, Mother. It's a little late now to start salving your conscience. I grew up on the stories you spoon-fed me of poor Grandmother Louise and her sense of humiliation because of Cyrus Calloway's betrayal.'

At this Honoria snapped as she watched Michael pour himself another cognac. 'OK, Michael, you have made your point. I haven't been the perfect mother. Your father said that I indulged you and perhaps he was right, but do not attempt to imply that the pleasure you're gaining from making Jensen squirm is something you inherited from me. Because it isn't!'

Michael looked at her for a moment, grimacing. 'It's too late now as I have tendered the loan application to the directors and if my recommendation amounts to anything it will be approved in due course and Jensen will get his funds. Then...'

He paused to take a long sip of cognac, shrugging slightly as he added, 'Whatever happens is in Jensen's hands, and whether he prospers and repays the loan or founders is down to his own good fortune and business acumen.'

Honoria sneered derisorily, looking at Michael directly. 'As if it were that simple. You don't intend to spare Jensen, and as for what you have planned for your fiancée, God only knows.'

'All *you* have to do is hold your nerve and spare me your platitudes and enjoy the demise of the Calloways, which you have craved for so long. Be grateful – yes, grateful – Honoria, that you owe it all to your wayward and godforsaken son!'

'So it is blasphemy that you throw at me now, is it? Go away, Michael! You are being especially vile this evening! The lengths you will go to provoke me are unbelievable! Your own mother! I have made a rod for my own back indulging you as I have, I will admit that, and I probably should have dismissed you years ago. You have the means with which to put a roof over your own head and yet I have allowed you to stay and *torment* me with your vulgar excesses under mine.'

If Michael was shocked by the vehemence behind Honoria's words, he didn't show it; he wouldn't give her the satisfaction. An hour later he was sat opposite Aaron Crozier in the lounge bar at his club.

Aaron was still slightly piqued with his friend, as his sister Leticia had relayed the details of Michael's caustic attitude towards her at the Calloway party.

'I shouldn't have anything to do with you, after I felt the force of Leticia's *ire*.'

Michael laughed slightly, shaking his head. 'I daresay only Leticia's pride was wounded, and I know your sister isn't shy in issuing a barb or two of her own.'

Aaron smiled ruefully as he summoned the steward with a raised hand before returning his attention to the hand his friend had dealt him. He knew he should know better than to agree to a game of cards with Michael as he rarely ever got the better of his friend and invariably paid the price.

He showed his hand and Michael blew heavily on his cigar as he conceded defeat. Aaron smiled. 'You can't be lucky in love and at cards.'

Michael shook his head, taking the glass of cognac from the tray of the steward stood beside him.

'Who said anything about being lucky in *love*? The Calloway-Landseer marriage is a business arrangement. Nothing more. I have no doubts that the pleasure I can derive from having the younger Calloway girl on my arm is far preferable to her sister and her wretched political views. That aside, there is an end to which my marriage is a means and that is where *my* priorities lie.'

'The details of which you're keeping close to your chest?'

Michael nodded. 'Jensen is entitled to the bank's discretion regarding the details of his loan application and the directors will expect nothing else; however, if the plan goes as intended, all will be revealed in due course. I don't know how much of Jensen's difficulties he has chosen to share with his offspring, but I imagine he would have wanted to spare some details, so that he can still look them in the eye and not have them be repulsed.'

'So you don't think she has any romantic feelings for *you*?'

Michael shook his head. 'It's probably better that she doesn't. I would expect her loyalty to remain with her father when the fallout begins. Whether he'll be deemed worthy of her loyalty is down to him.'

Aaron Crozier shook his head, smiling. His grey eyes dazzled as he blew on his cigarette and laid down another hand, but this time Michael was the winner.

'I don't begin to understand this *feud* you have with the Calloways, but I trust it's all going to be worth it?'

Michael nodded. 'Oh yes, Aaron. Before too long I will be able to entertain you under my own roof! Which you currently refer to as the Calloway mansion in Toorak!'

Aaron stared at his friend, trying to gauge whether he was joking. He spat out his cigarette and blanched when he realised that Michael meant it. 'You're serious? Jensen *must* know the bank will demand it as standard collateral and he's prepared to take the risk?'

'He believes that I will try to get the best possible deal for him and I will present the bank's terms as an *affait accompli* to him when we meet on Christmas Eve, convincing him that I have done my best. A kind of poetic justice in reverse.'

Aaron shook his head, not understanding Michael's meaning but reluctant to probe further. His family had never been as well acquainted with the Calloways, although he was aware that his father Eugene had business dealings with Jensen Calloway while he was in college, although no personal relationship had been established, just as he knew the nature of his father's business relationship with Ernest Landseer had altered very abruptly and for the worst, for reasons that were never discussed, and that their personal lives had subsequently diverged completely. Although he had never been told why, he had been forced to resist all attempts by his father to drive a wedge between him and Michael to the point that he had found the courage to tell them *his* friendship with Michael Landseer was non-negotiable.

Aaron whistled loudly, ignoring the disapproving looks of several patrons who turned their heads towards him. 'So he understands the implications of defaulting?'

Michael shrugged. 'As a businessman of some acumen, I imagine he does, but the letter I sent shook him badly. I also fear he may have misconstrued the extent of my influence at the bank or that by agreeing to my marrying Sarah, he has acquired an ally on the board and that my primary objective is to assist *him*. I fear on that alone he is *deluded.*'

'He could refuse the terms of the loan and look elsewhere?'

Michael shook his head. 'He wants to keep it quiet. He will sign and thence he will have participated in his own downfall!'

Michael blew heavily on his cigar, creating a blue-grey cloud between them, but Aaron could still see the menace mixed with glee behind Michael's smile. Realising his friend was totally absorbed in *the* plan to ruin Jensen Calloway, who may have unwittingly entered into an arrangement with his *nemesis*, Aaron shivered with genuine fear for a man he barely knew.

Agnes was biding her time about when to confront her father about what she feared were Michael's true motives. She waited until her mother and sister took a planned trip into central Melbourne. Plans for a formal engagement party had been abandoned by mutual consent, which was a huge relief to Sarah, because Jensen was reluctant to flaunt his daughter's nuptials in his current circumstances. Marguerite was determined to prepare for her daughter's wedding trousseau as tradition demanded, despite half-hearted efforts at discouraging her on Jensen's part because she was adamant they make a show of normality to their friends and his clientele that all was well.

Agnes knew she had no worries regarding Charlotte's indiscretion as it was the maid's day off. She took several steadying deep breaths and knocked on the study door several times before Jensen issued the terse command for her to enter.

'Agnes,' he said in a flat tone, as he knew it could only be her.

'May we speak candidly… about the loan you are seeking from Argate & Landseer?'

She had rehearsed in her mirror several times how best to broach the subject, as she feared her father would regard her query as having crossed a line, and she could tell from the deep frown pleating his brows that he was far from pleased at her intrusion into his business affairs.

'I am intrigued by your sudden interest in my business, Agnes, or that you assume I should wish to discuss such matters with you! Especially when your mother has the good sense to leave such matters to my good judgement.'

'Has your judgement always served us so well? In which case, why do you need Michael's influence at the bank and why is Sarah being sacrificed to grease the wheels of this deal and to flatter his ego?'

Jensen stood suddenly; his complexion deepened red. 'How dare you? Kindly remember who you are speaking to. Your sister hasn't been sacrificed for anything. She has agreed to a betrothal and she led us to believe you had reconciled yourself to the fact that Michael was no longer interested in pursuing a relationship with you.'

'I have!' Agnes replied with the same vehemence in her tone.

'Really? Because it looks like jealousy from my point of view. I was genuinely surprised and a little disappointed on your behalf when Michael stated his preference for marrying Sarah. Now I am relieved, as I can see your combative nature was a factor in his decision and that it wouldn't be conducive to my securing the loan.'

'What price is he demanding for his discretion and his leverage with the bank? *His* father's bank? I think it's this house. The roof over our heads!'

'Don't be ridiculous. He has made no such demands regarding the house.'

'Can you be sure that he won't? It's standard practice to demand collateral in the event of a default and the deeds to this mansion would cover it sufficiently.'

'The contract is still being drafted and I have every confidence that there is no need for concern. I don't anticipate defaulting. Now I have *tolerated* your rudeness long enough. I want you to leave.' Jensen turned his back slightly and Agnes reached out a hand, but he remained aloof and she feared she had overplayed her hand and had got nothing from him.

'As you wish. I just hope for all our sakes that your faith in Michael Landseer is justified!'

Jensen turned to face her again and Agnes was left in no doubt regarding his *wrath*.

'This is outrageous, Agnes, that you should have no respect for me under my roof! That you dare to judge me like this is *insufferable*. I suppose I have my sister-in-law to thank for this, encouraging you to speak your mind so openly, to flaunt the convention of respect. How typical!'

'What I fear has got nothing to do with Aunt Lillian. If anyone has encouraged me to be bold and confident, it is you, but I guess it's only acceptable when you're not being challenged.'

Jensen took several deep breaths. His fists clenched and held against the rosewood desk. He knew Agnes was no fool and that he hadn't managed to allay her fears through bluster or with patrician authority.

He needed to change tactics.

'Agnes, I know you are shrewd and I *am* imploring you not to put everything we have at risk by upsetting Michael. I need his support. I know there are other financial institutions in Melbourne I could seek out for a loan, but I have put my faith in him and everything we have depends on Argate & Landseer signing off on my application, and I mean everything. The brokerage. My business reputation in this city and the status that affords us. Although I don't think we are in danger of losing the roof over our heads, if I don't secure funds from Michael's bank and word circulates that I am considered a bad risk, then your fears regarding this house may yet become reality.'

Agnes looked deep into her father's eyes and she could see the heartfelt plea hidden in their depths. She knew that was as far as he could go.

Jensen Calloway was not the type to beg, nor would she expect it from him. He half-turned from her again and said, 'We are welcoming Michael into our family as your sister's husband

and that is final. Your sister is reconciled to that and you *must* come to terms with it!'

'I have. Believe me! I still fear, however, that he has the means to bring us down, should he choose to do so. I have no delusions when it comes to his character. He is spiteful, arrogant and avaricious, and I hope we don't all pay the price of underestimating his motives!'

Jensen retained his position with his back turned and Agnes could see that his demeanour had stiffened in resistance to her fears and what he saw as her intrusion. She had done her best or her worst and so she left without another word. The door closed behind her.

Jensen turned at the click of the study door and slumped into his chair. Agnes had been right about so much and she had voiced the fears that he was yet to reconcile himself to, although he had *urged* his wife to trust Michael Landseer, in spite of her own misgivings. The man knew too much about his vices, but thankfully nobody as yet – aside from his wife – knew of the gesture he had made almost twenty years ago that had potentially saved a pregnant woman from a backstreet butcher and almost certain death. It was an act of kindness that had carried such an enormous risk to his reputation, which bore no comparison to the vices that Michael Landseer had somehow become aware of. He remembered the words he had uttered to Marguerite when he had decided to seek Michael's help – 'Trust him' – although there were so many reasons why he shouldn't, but he had to hope that his future son-in-law or any of his business associates would not discover the nature of his greatest vice and right now he knew that hope was all he had to cling to.

4

Christmas Eve 1913

When the draft contract for Jensen Calloway's loan application arrived, his worst fears were confirmed just as Agnes had predicted and which he had *so* strenuously denied. The stark reality of the crucial and damning clause was in front of him in black and white on Argate & Landseer headed paper. He was relieved Agnes wasn't here to see the pinched look on his face, as she had accepted an invitation to stay at her Aunt Lillian's house in Fitzroy and neither he nor Marguerite had attempted to dissuade her. Although he had been surprised by his wife's acquiescence, as she always had a competitive relationship with Lillian, whose influence over Agnes she viewed with deep distrust.

It was still all too *easy* for them to attribute Agnes's attitude to a lack of acceptance at Michael's choice, but Jensen knew instinctively that his eldest daughter held no lingering hopes for a future with Michael.

Her paramount concern now was for the future well-being of their family and for what marriage to Michael would mean for her sister. Marguerite's patience with him had finally snapped after Agnes's departure, as she feared Agnes would return emboldened with Lillian's encouragement to question their judgement and authority ever more vigorously. This was why Marguerite didn't like either daughter being under Lillian's influence for too long and she could only blame Jensen for this outcome as the task of allaying Sarah's fears regarding Agnes's decision also fell to her.

Christmas would be difficult without her and nobody felt Agnes's absence more keenly than Sarah. She began to worry about what her life would be like once she was Michael's wife living under the Landseers' roof. She barely knew Honoria Landseer, who she had met only a few times, and yet it was likely she would spend more time after marriage in the company of her mother-in-law. For Jensen there was only the stark reality that he had bartered Sarah's future happiness for what remained of his self-respect and he didn't need Marguerite to tell him that he would likely be damned to *hell* because of it.

'What do we have to celebrate, Jensen? One failed repayment, from one bad month trading, and we *could* be destitute. I have a little money set aside, but it won't last long if the bank raises the interest on our loan, and Michael has little influence to stop them. What then? Throw ourselves at Lillian's mercy? Do you think my sister would willingly come to our aid? Not without constantly reminding us of our failure, as the price for her generosity. She has always thought I could do better in my choice of husband. Her gloating would be unbearable. Now we have Agnes under her roof, prey to her *influence*. Have you considered the alternative? Some drab tenement in a less salubrious part of the city!'

'We must retain a united front. You have assured me of your loyalty up to now and believe me, I doubt that I am *worthy* of it, but one chink of doubt could alert our friends, my clients of the peril we may find ourselves in and then all will be at risk, and I have no faith that our future son-in-law will come willingly to our aid!'

'Of course he won't! Michael is a businessman and you keep reminding me that this is all *about* business. We have already offered him our *trump* card! Our youngest daughter's virtue on a plate, thanks to your failure to control your male *urges*!'

Marguerite left without another word or backward glance, because she refused to submit to tears, however much she felt like shedding them.

Jensen flopped into the chair behind his desk, his eyes drifting momentarily to the decanter of cognac. He never indulged during the day. The fact he was even tempted was a sign of his desperation, because however much he was unworthy of Marguerite's loyalty, he doubted he could survive this crisis without her.

The Landseer Home – Christmas Eve

Michael was half asleep, but he knew the space beside him was still warm from Yolande since she had left his bed. Discretion was key to their relationship continuing, but it concerned him just how much she relished the danger of discovery. It hadn't been urgent tonight for her to leave his room so soon after they had sex as Honoria was at midnight mass and wouldn't be home for a while, but he knew Yolande liked to push against the boundaries he had set, however much he insisted upon their necessity. She didn't have as much as him to lose, of course, should knowledge of their physical relationship become public. None of his friends at the club would understand the importance of their relationship, and he wished that it could still just be about the sex they enjoyed, as no woman had ever been as skilled in arousing him as Yolande had become, and he didn't even want to confront the jealousy he would feel if he knew any other man had induced her to the orgasm that she had experienced in his bed tonight. Truth be told, however, the worst she could experience was dismissal from her role, although he would resist his mother's attempt to be rid of her as strongly as he could without arousing her suspicion. What set him apart from Jensen Calloway was that he hadn't left himself vulnerable to blackmail, but he freely acknowledged that indulging in his primal excesses under his own roof was fraught with danger, especially when the object of his affection was keen at best, or worst, determined, to invite exposure upon them.

He had warned Yolande that it would spell the end of their meetings should she be so reckless, but she didn't seem to care. He had planned to put a temporary halt to their rendezvous once he was married, as he wanted to enjoy the pleasures that his biddable young wife had to offer in the marital bed, but for how long he could resist Yolande's lure he was unsure and what made it worse was that she knew how hard he tried to resist her temptation. There had been numerous occasions when his mother had been on the brink of dismissing Yolande, on the grounds that she could be insolent and that Honoria considered her too prone to idleness to be relied upon, and whenever his mother discussed the issue he *urged* caution – albeit as neutrally as he could, to allay any suspicion. He had always managed to dissuade Honoria on the grounds that breaking in new domestic staff wasn't easy and this advice had always bought him time, but he feared there would come a time when his mother wouldn't tolerate Yolande's insolence any longer and the pleasure he derived from having those caramel-skinned curves against him in bed would be lost forever.

So he *urged* Yolande to find a working relationship with her mistress that worked for them both, however much he knew Yolande was by instinct mischievous and that she might one day goad Honoria into dismissing her just so that she could reveal the truth of their relationship as her trump card. He could only imagine the look of *contempt* on Honoria's face at the knowledge he was bedding a servant under her roof and someone she held in such little regard as Yolande. So such a confrontation had to be avoided and it required all the deftness he could lay claim to.

He looked at his reflection in the mirror as he dressed for his mother's return, wishing he wasn't *so* weak when it came to his *lust* for the family maid.

He half-turned, smiling ruefully, as weakness was the vice that he threw at Jensen's feet and soon he would enjoy the conjugal rights that came with his marriage to Sarah Calloway. He could only imagine how adventurous his wife would be in their bed, but it was a match that Melbourne society would doubtless applaud him for – and that was the most important aspect of it – but *still* he couldn't resist the *frisson* of danger that his liaisons with Yolande gave him and which made them so *enticing*. He lit a cigar and sauntered downstairs to await Honoria's return.

She was usually in a better mood after church and he imagined a small libation to mark Christmas Day might further lighten her mood, but his thoughts drifted back to Jensen. In three months' time he would commit himself in marriage to Sarah. Who knew how long her father could cling to all that he had? He hoped he would have dealt the crucial blows long before next Christmas, to have Jensen reeling. It was what Honoria still wanted despite her recent hesitancy. Besides which, it was too late now.

The loan application had been approved. As far the directors were concerned Jensen Calloway was in debt to them, but he had seen the extent to which Jensen had become a desperate man, although he made a good attempt at concealing it, but desperation led to mistakes and that element compared to his liability to the bank was nothing when set against the one Jensen had to him, as that, Michael considered with a broad grin, would form the foundation of the Calloway's demise.

He poured himself a cognac and gazed at his reflection in the mirror.

Ernest, his father, would be *appalled* that the bank he had helped to establish was being compromised for his satisfaction and there was the danger that Jensen might not default swiftly and so alert the directors, but he was confident it wouldn't come to that. The fear of defaulting would be the crucial factor, and he dismissed Honoria's belief that he was doing this for his maternal grandmother, because he hadn't seen Louise more than a couple of dozen times growing up. His mother wanted the Calloways to pay and for years she had *chafed* at her husband's censure and his advice not to embark upon a path she might come to regret. She was *right* about him enjoying the prospect of revenge – not retribution – or even *justice*, as she would prefer to call it. He was prepared to accept that a *lust* for revenge was part of his nature, one of his vices, and it wasn't something that he was prepared to be ashamed of. It was too late to repent now anyway, as Honoria was right to say he would be damned to hell for his sins, according to her faith's teaching. So Hell *be* damned! He could succumb to that if it were his fate, and there was a twinkle in his eyes – let all the furies fall upon Jensen Calloway's head as well. Let him pay for the sins of *his* father.

Agnes looked around the bedroom suite that had been allocated to her and she was thankful her stay was only temporary. She had become accustomed to the comforts her suite at the family home in Toorak afforded her and it was so *galling* to remind herself of the apparently easy manner with which her father had responded to her fear of them losing it to Michael's greed. It had also shocked her at how easily her parents had taken the news of her decision to come and stay with her Aunt Lillian.

She had become aware of the animosity between her mother and Lillian Frazer as she had grown into adulthood, that her mother's resentment stemmed from Lillian's poor view of Jensen Calloway as a prospective husband, how she had never accorded him the respect that Marguerite felt he warranted. It was to Lillian's credit that she had never shared her dim of view of Jensen to either her or Sarah, whenever they visited the house in Fitzroy – which wasn't often as their mother usually resisted Lillian's invitations vigorously. Agnes knew that for her part, her mother had never approved of Lillian's resistance to marriage and that the house she owned had been bequeathed to her by a wealthy married *lover*. She had also asserted that Agnes's passion for Women's Suffrage had been directly inherited by Lillian, and this Agnes had forcefully resented as it suggested she didn't have a mind of her own.

Lillian had also been horrified by the news of Sarah's engagement, insisting her younger niece had to live before she succumbed to marriage, and everything Agnes told her aunt about Michael Landseer made Lillian – to whom independence of mind and spirit was the greatest virtue of all for a young woman – even more *incensed*. Agnes was conscious she was taking an enormous risk in sharing the details of Sarah's engagement with her aunt as her parents would resist any interference on Lillian's part, and although she felt emboldened by Lillian's assurance that she had a room in Fitzroy for as long as she needed it, she was still wary about risking her father's *wrath* further.

Lillian Frazer, a smartly attired woman in her late forties, with sable hair and keen grey eyes, waved these concerns away. 'You're worried for your sister and I always tried to give your mother the benefit of my wisdom; sadly she didn't see it thus. She even suggested once that I was putting her off getting engaged so I could steal your father for myself. As if… Sorry, I didn't intend to disparage him, but I wanted the same options for her that I am now encouraging for Sarah, what little good it will do me. I don't know this Michael Landseer and I don't like much of how you describe him, but that apart I *insist* that Sarah is yet too young to marry anyone! She *needs* to experience life! You both do.'

Agnes couldn't help smiling sheepishly, as a few nights ago, she had been contemplating an engagement to Michael

Landseer. However, his change of heart had been integral to her seeing him for what he was and the mystique had vanished almost immediately. Alas her chance of freedom had come at Sarah's expense and that she deeply regretted.

She retired to her room that night having accepted the invitation to spend Christmas with Aunt Lillian in Fitzroy, convinced that for the sake of them all, some distance between her and her parents was the best policy, as she feared the more she endeavoured to question his decisions and challenge his authority, the more her father would dig his heels in, convinced that the arrangement he had made was the surest way of safeguarding the Calloway fortunes, while she feared it was an alliance that would prove the swiftest route to his ruin. She believed her father had *succumbed* far too meekly to this fate at Michael Landseer's hands.

5

March 1914

The wedding day came around far too swiftly for Sarah and she was as nervous on the morning of the ceremony as she had been the night of the party the previous December, when her engagement to Michael Landseer had been announced. That night she had feared her sister Agnes's reaction to the news that Michael had chosen her, when many of their friends had anticipated his engagement to Agnes was pending. Sarah was still in awe of her elder sibling but knew Agnes didn't support her decision to proceed with the nuptials, and Sarah's primary fear that morning was that Agnes might not attend. Her sister's opposition had hardened since her return to Toorak from Aunt Lillian's and she had lost count of the amount of times her sister had pleaded with her to change her mind. Their parents were aware of Agnes's efforts to dissuade her and their mother laid the blame for that on Lillian's shoulders. For her part Sarah had no illusions about what marriage to Michael would be like and what he expected from her as his wife once their vows had been exchanged.

He was accustomed to being the master in his home, nor did she anticipate much in support from Honoria. On the few occasions she had met her future mother-in-law she had been strangely reticent in expressing any opinion about her son's forthcoming marriage, but she had been very frank in expressing her surprise that Michael's preference had switched to her when *she* had always believed that his interest lay with Agnes. For his part Michael's moods were much harder to gauge. He was such a complex man, as he veered from melancholy introspection to an exuberance that Sarah found frustratingly difficult to anticipate. She didn't like that her loyalties were being divided between their parents and her elder sister, and she panicked when Jensen had threatened to banish Agnes from the Toorak home, if her efforts to weaken Sarah's resolve in the weeks up to the ceremony continued. Agnes perceived it to be an idle threat as the only viable option she had was to return to Aunt Lillian in Fitzroy. An arrangement their mother would find *abhorrent* and which she was liable to resist at all costs. Knowing this Agnes remained emboldened in her beliefs, but she agreed to soften her stance slightly as Sarah gave no indication that she *wasn't* inclined to marry Michael, but Agnes couldn't be swayed from her conviction that Michael meant them all to suffer considerable ill will at his hands and that Sarah was merely a pawn in that plan. She increasingly feared her father had led them to be trapped. She had ceased caring whether their father chose to heed her concerns or not.

Agnes's choice of future career path also raised eyebrows in the Toorak mansion, even though it met with tacit approval – her Aunt Lillian's encouragement in this regard notwithstanding. Nursing was a solid, positive choice for a young woman of her class and Jensen was confident that the aptitude required to apply herself to her studies would sufficiently divert her attentions from the issue of Women's Suffrage, of which, he admitted to Marguerite, his tolerance had been tested to its limit.

Gazing at her reflection in the cheval mirror, dressed in her wedding finery, Sarah wished she could play the role of a happy blushing bride with conviction, but she feared it was beyond her. She half-turned, hearing a knock on the bedroom door; she commanded whoever it was to enter and the smile that lit her face went to her eyes as Agnes stood hesitantly in the doorway.

'Shouldn't you be getting changed?' Sarah asked.

'I will. First I wanted to see you. Are you nervous?'

Sarah nodded silently, biting her bottom lip; she took the hand Agnes offered her. 'So if you're planning a last attempt to dissuade me from going through with the ceremony… Please *don't*. It will only make me feel worse. This is my fate and I am resigned to it. Besides, this could have been your day. *Remember.*'

Agnes shuddered slightly. 'If I hadn't been such a wilful political firebrand? No, I think Michael had already made his choice. Besides, I don't see him as I might once have done as a potential husband. My only concern now is that he treats you *right*. With respect!'

Sarah nodded. 'He *will*. I'm certain. I think a lot of what he says is for show. Bluster to appease his circle.'

'Well, I hope you're right, because I wouldn't want to rely upon Honoria Landseer as an ally. Anyway, I brought you this. Something borrowed and blue in one.' Agnes smiled mischievously as she revealed a powder-blue silk garter which she stretched to test its elasticity, and when it made a pinging sound they laughed in unison –something they hadn't done in a long time.

'I miss this, Agnes. *Us!* Being together, as we are now. Today I shall leave this house for the last time as Sarah Marguerite Calloway and become Mrs M Landseer. This has always been our home, but it shall not be mine after today.'

Agnes couldn't help wondering how much longer it would remain the Calloway home if the man destined to become her sister's husband had his way. For a moment she wanted to share her fears about their future with her sister, as she had ever since she had voiced them to their father, but she held back and then within a nanosecond the moment had gone.

Agnes took her sister's hands in hers, squeezing them tight. 'Listen, I *will* always be on your side, Sarah. No matter what the circumstances. If you have any doubts about Michael, if he hurts you any way or that he falls short of abiding by the vows he will utter in church today, you *must* seek me out Sarah. I will *do* whatever I can to help.'

Sarah couldn't help smiling at the earnest way in which Agnes had spoken. 'You would risk his *wrath* by intervening?'

Agnes couldn't mistake the sceptical look in Sarah's eyes, but she had meant every word, and although she knew Michael didn't like her and that he would loathe any intervention by her into his marital affairs, she wouldn't be deterred nor *cowed* by him to protect her sister.

'If I had to, *yes!*'

Agnes let go of Sarah's hands, moving backwards to the door. She had said her piece and didn't regret a word, although she knew their parents would be aghast at her latest attempt – before vows had been exchanged – to influence a change in events, but she didn't care. She gave Sarah an encouraging nod and took her leave. In Agnes's eyes her sister still looked too young to marry anyone, especially a man like Michael. 'Good luck!' she whispered as she took her leave. It was a sentiment meant for all of them and she feared they would yet *still* come to need it.

Michael Landseer looked very smart in his morning suit of dove grey as he stood at the altar in the oldest church in Melbourne. He could admit to feeling a little nervous, but unlike his best man Aaron Crozier stood beside him, it didn't show. He had no doubts that Sarah would come to exchange their vows, as he was confident Jensen wouldn't risk any misstep in their agreement, and therefore he had no fears of being *humiliated* by his bride failing to show. He was aware that some of the assembled guests on his side didn't understand the urgency in his marrying. Their three-month engagement had been short and his mother had warned him that some would leap to their conclusions as to why.

Well, *damn* them had been his typical response, which he knew had incurred Honoria's wrath as he knew that protecting their good name in Melbourne mattered to her, even if she had given up hope that it *still* mattered to him. He had even smiled politely when Aaron had made a few coarse jokes about him exerting his conjugal rights that evening, but rather than focusing on Sarah's alluring curves, his mind had rested on Yolande, whose bed he still intended to grace, but not tonight as he had adhered to his mother's suggestion that they spend the night at the bridal suite of a central Melbourne hotel. He knew his attention should be focused upon his wife-to-be, but as Sarah was as yet inexperienced in the art of giving and receiving sexual pleasure, he knew he was going to crave Yolande's assured skills in seduction even more.

Tonight she would have to wait, knowing that he could not join her, but they had made up for that the last two nights, and the memory of it brought a lewd smile to his face, and he bowed his head to conceal it, as Yolande had been more adventurous in the skills she had applied to arouse him, and in her post-coital bliss, she had been more daring, taunting him about whether he believed his wife was sufficiently skilled to pleasure him as she had. Yolande always knew how far she could push him and he wondered if Sarah would be so brave. He didn't know whether he could tolerate it so easily from her, as he had told his mother that he expected her to be biddable to his whims, but he had no such expectations when it came to Yolande. She was already too practised in the dark arts of seduction to suddenly play at coyness. She couldn't convince him even if she were to try, but he knew that where Yolande held the upper hand was that she knew that Michael desired her too much to walk away for good, while Sarah's abilities to arouse and maybe frustrate him were yet to be proved and he doubted she had what it took to play him at the game that Yolande had thus far mastered as her own.

As he looked around the church, with the cream of Melbourne society in their finery, he was intrigued by what they would think of his physical bond with the servant girl Yolande. How horrified and outraged would they be? Sadly for Yolande, he wasn't going to test their tolerance.

Sarah adequately fitted their expectations of what a wife for a man like him should be, and Michael was prepared to settle for adhering to their expectations of him. Honoria might have abandoned her hopes that he may yet show himself to be a man of virtue and decorum, as his father had always been, but he had learnt from his father that some risks were worth taking. Some habits could withstand the harsh glare of public scrutiny while others carried too large a burden to be shared and his *lust* – because that was what it basically was – for the servant girl Yolande could never see the light of day.

He knew that he didn't care now, as Honoria claimed, that he was beyond the point where she could bring him from the edge of callous revenge and into the habit of pursuing reasonable business practices as his father always advocated them. Besides which, what did he care for the opinions or approbation of the sallow-faced old matrons that Honoria was prepared to tolerate as friends? It was a conversation they had returned to many times, but she could baulk all she wanted; the fact remained she had set him on this path and she would reap as she had sown while he would enjoy the pleasures of Sarah Calloway's flesh and in due course rejoice in the humiliation of her father.

The wedding ceremony went as smoothly as could be expected for Sarah, who looked beautiful, although she was pensively tugging on her bottom lip worrying about what the future would hold, admitting later that her stomach was in knots about the reality of marriage to Michael Landseer now that the moment of reckoning had come. She wasn't overly late, as the bride's privilege dictated, nor did she make any slip in saying her vows, but she wasn't a happy blushing bride. She looked to Agnes for moral support. A gesture that didn't go unnoticed by either Michael or her mother, who she knew had expressed an opinion – albeit quietly and without too much conviction – that it might have been best if Agnes had stayed away.

Jensen took his daughter to the altar with a sombre look upon his face, as he felt like he was taking a lamb to slaughter giving this woman to this man. He knew, however, there was no choice. Sarah's freedom was the price he was paying to save himself from humiliation and it tore at his heart to do it. For her part Agnes was determined to share Sarah's day as a supportive sibling, but her attempts to avoid Leticia Crozier's barbed comments at the reception later failed, as her old adversary approached her.

'So you are the bridesmaid again, Agnes? Still on the shelf! Don't you ever fear your options are running out? There was a time when Michael Landseer was your best bet, but then he saw you for the source of conflict that you are and switched his allegiance to Sarah.'

Unable to conceal her smugness Leticia moved away but felt a hand rest gently on her arm. She looked down and found it was Agnes restraining her, and she raised a quizzical eyebrow.

'Unlike you, Leticia, I *will* never need a man to define me, nor will I ever be defined by whoever I marry. What about you? Are you sufficiently single-minded to remain true to yourself after you have a ring upon your finger? To assert the best version of yourself on whoever claims your love? I can see there is room for improvement, but will it be improvement on your terms or his?'

This time it was Agnes who raised a quizzical eyebrow as she slowly removed her hand, treating Leticia to a saccharine sweet smile.

'I should stop all this Women's Suffrage business, as no man worth having will want an activist for a wife.'

Agnes smiled, surprised that she had stayed long enough to give Leticia the opportunity of a comeback. Each had relished their verbal sparring over the years, but there was no grudging admiration of the other. They both readily confessed to *loathing* each other.

'I am surprised that Aaron's wide circle of friends hasn't proved a rich hunting ground for you, Leticia. Perhaps you should ask him to make your case as a future wife to one of his loyal circle? Unless that simpering *"come hither and get me, boys"* demeanour of yours is equally off-putting as well?'

Agnes walked away at that point, noticing the pointed stares of several guests at the sound of raised voices. She left Leticia feeling exposed slightly, flushed with embarrassment and seething with barely concealed rage.

Bridal Suite, The Windsor Hotel, Melbourne

Michael Landseer sat indolently with a cigar between his teeth and a cognac on the arm of the chair, waiting for Sarah to emerge from the bathroom. He understood she needed time to prepare herself for their first night together as a married couple and he was willing to be patient, to make allowances for the fact that she might be apprehensive, as many a bride was on her wedding night. There was something endearing to him about her virginal innocence, which he would divest her of before the night was out. He had seen the dagger looks that his mother had sent in his direction at the reception and at one point he had to reassure Sarah that it wasn't her who had incurred Honoria's *wrath*, although he was certain she hadn't yet reconciled herself with his choice. She continued to describe Sarah as timid. Which she was, but *he* wasn't so concerned that she might consider herself unworthy of his demands in the marital bed, as the marriage was a means to an end. While Sarah expected him to be a man of experience in such matters, he couldn't help speculating on what her reaction would be if she knew where most of his sexual experience had come from, and with whom?

That brought a broad smile to his face. The thought of how she would react. Would she just be mildly disappointed at his choice, or would it be disgust bordering on revulsion at the idea of him sharing a bed with the family maid? It didn't surprise him that he rejoiced at the prospect of both his wife and mother being confronted sometime in the future with the reality of his infidelity with Yolande, especially when the realisation hit that they were powerless to stop him. He took a long sip of cognac and sighed. So she was making him wait. So be it. He would tolerate that tonight, but she would be wise not to test his patience too much. He had chosen her as the more biddable of the Calloway sisters to wear his ring and share his bed, and he expected her to meet his expectations in that regard. Tonight he would be the gentleman. Considerate, virtuous and as patient as she *needed* him to be, because he didn't intend to disappoint her.

He stubbed out his cigar and went to the bathroom door. A gentle knock, by way of mild query, could do no harm. He was rocking on his heels, feeling a burgeoning arousal. Smiling lasciviously, he realised suddenly how much he wanted her. Her soft milky curves, which were such a contrast to the delights that Yolande's caramel nakedness offered him, were driving him further to the edge of need and towards a precipice of desire that was like nothing he had previously known and he felt the hardness in his groin. The door opened and Sarah smiled wanly. It was the uncertain smile of wariness that came from innocence. That she was submitting herself to the man that she had consented to have her as her husband. The vows she had made in church that very afternoon now had to be honoured. It was too late now to resent how much she felt she had been duped, that her father had sacrificed her for his good name and their standing in Melbourne. Tonight it was only about her and

Michael, about what he would offer of himself and what she was expected to submit.

He had extinguished most of the lights, so only one remained, and in that moment she looked more alluring than he had ever imagined. He lifted her nightdress up and she shuddered at the reality of him seeing her so exposed, but he urged her to trust him with a look and then a whisper that was barely audible. They were on the bed; she knelt at his side as he lay supine, and when they touched the heated softness of her skin against his made him shudder slightly, but he didn't notice the slight smile that curved at her lips because the last thing she wanted was to incur his displeasure and she was certain any hint that she might be *mocking* him would surely inspire anger. She had seen his temper and heard how cruel he had been to Agnes with his jibes. He nodded gently as she lay down beside him and removed the last barrier to her nakedness and with it her virtue, which would be sacrificed by dawn to a husband she knew she didn't *love* and whom she shouldn't trust.

6

March 1914

In the weeks that followed Sarah grew more accustomed to the physical aspects of marriage, which Michael saw as his right, but she remained a passive participant in the sexual act at best and would never claim to enjoy their clumsy nocturnal couplings – invariably due to Michael being too heavily imbued with cognac to bring her to orgasm with any deftness – and she prayed she wouldn't fall pregnant for many months yet.

It was a great relief that Michael seemed to be in no hurry to sire an heir. He viewed sex as greedily as he did his other appetites, and his were voracious, but she was invariably embarrassed by his capacity for vulgarity, as his mother was appalled.

One night after a particularly vigorous attempt to invoke a passionate response from her, he pulled away, falling onto his back, his breathing heavy; he cursed loudly, wanting to provoke a response, but Sarah ignored him. Turning away, she fell swiftly into a deep sleep. When she woke hours later, it was to find the space beside her in bed empty, and as Michael wasn't inclined to rise before he had to, curiosity overrode her relief and, climbing out of bed, she went in search of him. Where could he possibly be at this hour? Had he gone to one of his clubs in the city, his anger piqued by her lack of response in bed? He never seemed to understand that the stale odour of cigars on his breath was hardly romantic, but she had learnt quickly that expecting him to curb his excesses post-marriage was a forlorn hope, as Honoria had witheringly told her. Of course it was *her* fault in his eyes and maybe his mother also blamed her, but Sarah didn't care. She wanted to be satisfied about his whereabouts, and if she found he had sought satisfaction for his primal urges in another's arms she would be bruised by the rejection just weeks into their marriage but, knowing Michael as she now did, sadly not surprised by his insensitivity.

As she made her way onto the galleried landing she heard the click of a door and Honoria emerged from her room. Her brows knitted into a deep frown as she saw Sarah, looking at her suspiciously. 'What are you doing up? Return to your room, please, Sarah.'

'I will not be dismissed as if I were a child. Where is Michael?'

'How should I know? I am not my son's keeper. His whereabouts should be more concerning to you, as *his* wife!'

Honoria had placed an emphasis on the word wife and Sarah took it for the barbed comment it had been intended.

'Your son is a law *unto* himself, Honoria, as you know. I was woken and surprised to find his place in bed empty. I am merely curious as to whether he has gone out.'

'If you cannot claim his attention in bed, Sarah, then perhaps it's your failure as a wife that's the issue. I knew you were the wrong choice as such and I told him so. You are a nice girl but too timid and willing to placate him.'

'Ssh.' Sarah held up her hand to silence Honoria and was treated to a snort of disdain.

'Did you hear that?'

'What?'

'Noises coming from Yolande's room upstairs.'

49

'So the wretched girl has sneaked someone into the house after we have all retired. Nothing that girl does would surprise me.'

Sarah pushed past and mounted the first step to the top floor, then she felt Honoria's straining hand on her arm. 'I advise you not to go there!'

Sarah shook her off. 'Why, Honoria? What I am likely to find? If you suspected Yolande of smuggling strangers into this house you would dismiss her immediately regardless of how long it took to find a suitable replacement and we both know it.' Sarah paused; pulling her arm free she saw the darkened expression on Honoria's face and froze.

'Whose up there with her? Is it Michael?'

'Don't be absurd. That is the most ridiculous and insulting suggestion that could have come from your mouth. You must be depraved.'

Sarah smiled and knew Honoria was covering something up, but she couldn't disguise her disgust at what Sarah was implying. Sarah continued to the second floor and knocked three times on the door. She could hear noises from within, and she knocked again and said, 'Michael, it's your wife!'

A moment passed and then the door was opened, and Sarah's suspicions were confirmed as Michael stood indolently against the door frame.

Honoria pushed past them and saw Yolande naked in the bed her son had just left and she rocked on her heels, almost falling until Sarah offered a hand to steady her. It struck Sarah suddenly that maybe *she* had misjudged Honoria. Had she discouraged her because she knew what her daughter-in-law would find or because she suspected it and wanted to hope against all evidence that she was wrong?

'This is why I didn't want you to pry. Because I wanted to spare you this! The reality of them together. I feared it but couldn't accept that my son so recently wed could demean himself to share her bed.'

'So you knew?'

'Of course she knew. My mother would have to be a fool not to and we all know that Honoria Landseer is no fool!' Michael spoke with evident contempt for them both.

'So dismiss her!' Sarah shrieked, struggling to keep her tone neutral and not appear desperate. 'I have tried. He won't hear of it!'

Sarah took a long deep breath, fighting the wave of nausea which threatened to assail her. She could feel the bile rising in her throat but wouldn't submit to it. Her husband didn't betray a hint of guilt. It was as if he had wanted to be caught and he revelled in Honoria's sense of outrage.

'I always thought you were in charge of this household, but by letting that girl stay you show your weakness, and that's not something I ever expected from you, Honoria. You acquiesce to his adultery by failing to act. I can see that you are disgusted, as I am, but it *torments* me that I don't expect any better from the man that I married!'

Honoria nodded. 'Good, because now you have no romantic delusions about him. I have tried to curb his excesses, to hope that he might yet demonstrate the decorum his father always showed, but *he's* a lost cause and maybe it's better you found that out sooner rather than later, because I can live with his vulgar excesses. Can you? Because if you're not and he has a mind to, he will break you. Not just your heart but whatever is left of your spirit as well.'

Sarah shook her head, but she wasn't confident that she could prove her mother-in-law wrong about her strength of character, because Honoria was intuitive.

Michael looked at her, his head slanted sideways, his eyebrows raised questioningly, as if she were an object of pity. 'So, my dear wife, you have caught me in *flagrante delicto* with the staff! So what is your next move?'

She heard Yolande's snigger from behind the door and Sarah pushed past her husband into Yolande's room. She had covered her naked form with a single sheet, but her pose and demeanour as she lay supine lacked any modesty and Sarah held the same opinion as Honoria that the girl was no more than a *whore*.

She sneered derisorily. 'I shouldn't be surprised that you would be an unfaithful husband, Michael – although perhaps not in a matter of weeks following our exchange of vows, but I am surprised that you are *so* limited in your choice. You couldn't have gone cheaper if you had tried!'

Yolande half-rose to strike Sarah, but a warning look from Michael deterred her.

Sarah moved to push past him again, but he held her firm, his arm snaking possessively around her waist. She felt his burgeoning arousal as he pulled her to him, but she pushed him away.

'Would you have preferred it if I had taken my pleasure in a city brothel as Jensen preferred to do?'

Sarah lashed out to strike him, but he parried her move, bringing her arms to her side. 'Comes as a shock, does it? You thought your precious papa was above having primal urges that your mother can no longer satisfy?'

'How dare you insinuate such rubbish about my family? Have you no shame at being caught with that *slut*?'

Michael shrugged and, smiling, he said, 'Sadly your high opinion of your father isn't justified. Jensen is as weak as any man when it comes to his vices and it is fear regarding the potential exposure of those vices that brought trouble to his door.'

Sarah looked at Michael and she saw the depth of the contempt in which he held her. As if the evidence of his infidelity under his own roof wasn't sufficient. She felt the sting of unshed tears but refused to submit to them.

'Don't worry. This changes nothing in regard to our marriage. I shall still expect my conjugal rights in the marital bed.'

'You're wrong, Michael, *because* this changes everything.' She turned and walked slowly down to their first-floor suite.

Honoria looked at her son with more disgust than she ever had before, but he shook his head.

'Don't, Mother. Just *don't*! The moral high ground you chose to stand on is quaking beneath your feet. Remember how much you wanted this. Justice for Grandmother Louise has always been your driving ambition and the Calloways have always been collateral damage.'

'This has nothing to do with that. Justice for my mother never demanded you sharing a bed with a servant whore! That is solely due to your depraved urges.'

'I meant what I said as well. Despite Sarah's little show of bravado. I will insist upon my needs being met in bed and perhaps it isn't too soon to start thinking about producing an heir! Being with child will give Sarah something to focus her mind on!' He looked at Honoria with brows raised, challenging his mother to refuse him. Had he still been looking at Yolande as he spoke, he would have noted the look of horror on her face at the prospect of her lover becoming a father. That was a situation Yolande would do anything to destroy.

Michael had always relished the impression that he held all the cards in their relationship, and until his recent marriage Yolande had never felt threatened in their illicit couplings as long as he could trust her to stay on the right side of discreet. It wouldn't hurt him to realise she knew how to be a survivor. She had learnt that much from her mother and she would emerge and their relationship could *endure* if she played a few trump cards of her own. Michael gently closed the door, but not before he heard Yolande's long, deep sigh. So he was returning to his wife's bed? Her fun had ended for the evening.

Honoria gripped his arm at the top of the stairs and squeezed tight. 'If you have compromised our plan to slake your *lust* for that girl, I will never forgive you, Michael. I warned you to

53

clean up your act before your nuptials, but you couldn't even manage that.'

'I would have thought by now, Honoria, that you would have accepted I don't have what it takes to live up to the saintly Ernest Landseer! I lack my father's virtue and maybe his character as well. Luckily for you, though, that I have what it takes to bring down Jensen Calloway and ensure that he pays for his father's sins where Louise is concerned. If anyone is to blame for what Sarah discovered about me tonight it is Jensen, who was more than willing to sacrifice his youngest daughter on the altar of his precious reputation to save his own skin, leaving her prey to – what do you call them, Mother? – my vulgar excesses.'

'So be it. Have her! Continue to satisfy your sordid needs with the servant girl, but remember, your grubby secret is out now. So perhaps Sarah doesn't think she has much to lose but something potentially valuable to trade with.'

Honoria pulled free of her son and returned to her room. If Michael was worried he didn't show it, believing as he did that Sarah lacked the courage to go against him, especially when she didn't know the full extent of how it could damage her father, but he was a little concerned that Yolande would not take kindly to the news whenever it came that he had sired an heir, but he returned to his suite convinced now that a child was the best way to keep Sarah as the biddable wife he needed her to be.

7

In the weeks that followed as autumnal rains lashed down on Melbourne life became significantly less tolerable for Sarah, as Michael was ever more determined to exert his belief that the sooner she was with child the better.

He shared his desire to become a father sooner than he had intended with his friend Aaron Crozier, one evening at their club over several cognacs, striving to impress upon his friend that it was entirely natural to want to consummate his marriage, although in the back of his mind he had Yolande's intensely jealous impulses to contend with, and despite all his assurances that his wife's future pregnancy had no impact on them, she was not to be placated. He knew for himself that a child was no indication that he wanted the marriage to be a success, nor did he intend to prolong it beyond the point he had got what he wanted from Jensen.

As Yolande ran a soapy sponge across his shoulders and down his back, he smiled in that lascivious way that he had which motivated Sarah to despise him all the more, while Yolande, by contrast, saw it as a turn-on.

He took the sponge from her hand and, in a sudden movement, tossed it into the tub and grabbed her hand, thrusting it beneath the foam in the direction of his groin. Yolande smiled as she felt her hand encircling his aroused manhood.

'When she is with child it will limit her options. Besides which, her father cannot hold out forever. He is bound to miss a loan repayment, as the brokerage is suffering and he's showing signs of strain. When the plan reaches its climax, the marriage will exist in name only. Providing the child is a boy, of course, in which case I will *not* need try again. Be sure of one certainty, though, Sarah Calloway will not occupy the role in my life that she might have expected when we exchanged vows. Our union was always a means to an end and my mother – *your* mistress – knew that was the case. So Yolande when I tell you my plan to become a father changes nothing between *us*, I mean it.'

Yolande was on her haunches now, lathering his chest and shoulders with her free hand. 'You are sure you don't *love* her?'

'In the way that I desire you? No!'

Michael smiled; lifting her hand from beneath the foam, he kissed it and then he sought her mouth, kissing her hungrily as their tongues meshed. He smiled.

Yolande was definitely emboldened in her position since their relationship had been exposed, and he regretted that as it had boosted her confidence. He had preferred when their liaisons were illicit and he had been spared Honoria's icy contempt. But it was done. He would manage it, as he managed so much else in bringing the plan to a satisfied conclusion, but he was as equally determined to exert his authority with Yolande and be assured that however much he was supplicant to her skills in arousing him, his mistress would know that *her* import in his life was also within his gift to bestow.

While the relationship between Michael and Sarah slipped gradually towards indifference and quiet submission on her part, the one between Michael and his mother found a new low. The plan to wreak retribution upon Jensen Calloway sparked less interest with her since she had discovered Michael's infidelity as fact, her determination to curb Yolande's influence commanded a greater hold. Honoria no longer sought to dismiss her as it was a futile aim. She intended to control her. Without Michael's knowledge she placed an advertisement in the Melbourne classified pages for a housekeeper who could assume responsibility for running the household. She knew Sarah wasn't up to it and she wanted to devote more of her time to various associations and municipal good works. A housekeeper with sufficient seniority was the best solution and Yolande would be answerable to her, and if the wretched girl couldn't obey orders, she would free to leave.

Honoria felt some empathy for her daughter-in-law, encouraging her to spend time with her sister Agnes, who was now actively pursuing a career in nursing. Sarah appeared to be making a reasonable effort of accepting the shift in her marriage to Michael, but they both had to suffer the brazen way he sought Yolande's company after dinner each evening.

Honoria knew it must hurt, however much Sarah endeavoured to conceal her humiliation, and she was glad that Sarah wasn't as yet pregnant, as she feared a child would only *bind* her to Michael for perpetuity and that could only lead to her heartache as Michael had no intention of giving up his obsession with the servant girl.

'Choose carefully your path to freedom,' she had urged Sarah. 'I shall support you where I can.' Sarah had shook her head, fearing that sadly there was no way out, and Honoria wondered how much she had been told of her father's current difficulties. Not for the first time she had questioned whether it was worth pursuing the retribution she had for so long wanted from the Calloways. She had never sought absolution from it, although she wished now she had listened more keenly to her husband's warning. It wasn't the only time that he had advised against indulging rash action, that caution was sometimes the best course.

It had once cost them a valued family friend who had come to Ernest seeking help for a grave lapse of judgement and Ernest had rightly sent him on his way. How she wished now that she had stood firmly with him over her desire for retrospective justice for Louise, because it may just have saved Michael from a slow descent to his own damnation. Now, she realised sadly, he had passed a point of no return.

Reaching for the cord she pulled and waited. Not for the first time Yolande ignored her mistress, and Honoria's face contorted into a grimace, as she knew the wretched girl's most likely whereabouts. She went to the stairs, shouting, 'Yolande,' but again there was silence, and the reality of the girl's increasing contempt for authority, underpinned as it was by Michael's sordid desire for her, caused bile to rise in her throat.

Agnes met her sister in a coffeehouse in central Melbourne one morning three weeks after Sarah had uncovered the truth of Michael's infidelity.

Agnes could see the shadows under Sarah's eyes, reaching the sad conclusion that marriage to Michael Landseer must be turning out to be the very hell that she had always feared it would be. She was, however, encouraged that Sarah's spirits remained buoyant but was horrified when she revealed that she was determined to uncover the truth of whatever hold Michael had over their father.

'He won't tell you, Sarah. Believe me, I have tried. I wanted to save you from the torment that I knew your marriage to him was going to be.'

Sarah smiled wanly. If only she knew. 'It would have been a hell for you too, Agnes, if he had taken you despite your politics, which he wastes no time in mentioning again were a contributing factor. He states they had the potential to make him a laughingstock among his peers. Although he could manage that by himself.'

She blushed suddenly, fearing she had said too much, although she was too ashamed to reveal the facts of his lust for Yolande. So, head bent, she took a long gulp of coffee and looked around her. The uniform of a trainee nurse suited Agnes. There was a colour in her cheeks that she hadn't seen in a while, although Sarah knew she didn't have to glance in the mirror for confirmation that it had vanished from hers.

'He hasn't mistreated you? Physically, I mean.'

Sarah shook her head. 'No, but he does want me to be with child. It will be something to focus my time on, he says, but I am not keen. He isn't an appealing lover or a considerate one, as I daresay you can imagine, and marital relations are an ordeal to be *endured*.'

Agnes reached out for Sarah hand, but she shook her head. She didn't want her sister knowing how desperate she felt, so she was determined to keep her emotions in check. 'It would help if he didn't come to bed so inebriated with alcohol. The aroma of cognac and stale cigars are hardly an aphrodisiac. How could our father had subjected either of us to such a torment? Has he no sense of honour? To give me away so willingly to such a vulgar man. Because that sums Michael up, Agnes! His vulgarity!'

Agnes shook her head sadly. Why had it come to this?

'This is my fate. Whatever mistakes our father has made that meant he had to seek financial help from Michael of all people must have been serious. How do we find out what price he is prepared to pay? Surely it can't be so high as the price I will be expected to pay in a marriage that is akin to purgatory!'

Agnes smiled uneasily. She had tried once to get their father to open up to her, to share his burdens, but he had refused. She couldn't see him being any more candid with Sarah, as he believed it was his responsibility to get them all out of their current difficulties and not burden his offspring with the details. It was a matter of honour with him. But what price was his honour if it had been traded for Sarah's happiness? The last time her efforts had been in vain, but that was before Sarah had married, and Agnes was convinced she wasn't hearing all the details that amounted to her sister's marriage being a hell to be endured. Whatever sin their father had committed, whatever error of judgement that required financial rescue from Argate & Landseer, couldn't be so awful that his daughters had to be spared from knowing it, and she had decided the time for dithering out of respect for their father's code of honour was over. If Sarah fell pregnant with Michael's child, she would surely be trapped. As the eldest sibling she would not stand aside and let that happen. For her part Sarah was equally determined to discover the nature of the leverage Michael held over them. Trust him was all that he had offered. She was cautious about telling Agnes too much, but she had to know what payment for the sins of their father Michael Landseer had secured her hand in marriage.

Sarah knew she had to choose the right moment to gain entry to the Toorak mansion and her father's study. It was possible that what she needed to see might be filed away at the brokerage for safekeeping, in which case her mission would be doomed, but she remained hopeful that there would be something in the wall safe at home that she could confront him with.

She arrived on one of the days she knew her mother would be attending one of her various charitable associations like the ones Honoria was involved with. Marguerite Calloway had been keen to continue attending them to demonstrate normality. Her daughter had become engaged to and then married an eminent banker, so why would she hide away? That had been their mother's *rationale* and their father had agreed.

Sarah was grateful for that now as she rang the bell and waited for Charlotte to answer, confident she could convince the silly girl the visit should be their secret. Thankfully their hired help was manageable in ways that the wretched Yolande wasn't. Knowing her mother's routine by heart, Sarah knew she had half an hour at most, and as her father would be at the brokerage, she could act swiftly and be back in central Melbourne before anyone knew she had been home.

Charlotte beamed excitedly as she answered the door, treating Sarah to the usual nonsense which Agnes was so much more adept at tolerating from Charlotte than any of them, but as Sarah had less time to indulge her, she assured Charlotte that there was nothing her parents needed to know and made her way to the study. The wall safe was concealed behind the portrait of her paternal grandfather, Cyrus Calloway, who beamed down on her, and she wondered whether from all the stories they had ever been told about him whether he had ever been compromised in business, as his son *insisted* he had fallen prey to? Somehow she doubted it, but squaring her shoulders she set to remembering the combination that would let her into the safe. It took several attempts, but eventually it opened and Sarah smiled to herself. Because there among various documents she recognised the bank's embossed insignia on cream paper and she pulled it out, gasping with shock at one image of a young-looking man, evidently her father, in a compromising position with a young girl, who was scantily and provocatively dressed like a prostitute.

Thinking of Yolande, she felt nausea rising in her throat and thrust the images aside to concentrate her attention on the contract. She froze in fear suddenly at a click, fearing her mother's return was imminent, but as the door opened slowly she sighed with relief at the sight of Agnes in the doorway. She tried to conceal the images but given the lack of shock on her sister's face, Sarah guessed Agnes was aware of their existence. They were proof of their father's sin and socially very embarrassing for how their parents strived to portray themselves to friends and clients, but were these sepia images the extent of what her husband had on their father and what possible price could he realistically extort from Jensen by threatening to publish them? Or perhaps more shockingly could they represent the milder tip of a much bigger sin that could lead to their father's unredeemable shame and were his efforts to avert that outcome the catalyst that had thrust them all into the merciless orbit of Michael Landseer?

'Show me, Sarah.'

'What?'

'The images that you are doing a poor job of concealing.'

'What do you know of the photographs?'

'Only that it was probable they existed. Not the content. Although judging how deathly pale you look, I suggest they are pretty damning!'

Sarah still hesitated to show her sister the images of their father in another woman's arms, and in that moment, Sarah was surprised by the force of an *urge* to spare their mother the humiliation of these images.

Agnes held out her hand and Sarah, half-turning, put the creased images into her sister's hand.

Agnes struggled to keep her expression neutral, but she understood why their father wanted to keep the images hidden from them. Whether he had been able to spare their mother, she was uncertain, but had she demanded to see them, they both knew she would get her way. Their mother was too independently minded not to offer her unqualified support without knowing what was involved.

'If only our father had found a different way out of this mess, without having to *coerce* you into marriage to that man! I know I have had a lucky escape after all those years of foolishly coveting an engagement to him, but I never contemplated that *my* freedom would come at the expense of yours.'

Suddenly they heard a noise and, fearing their duplicity was going to be exposed, Agnes nodded at the safe. 'Put them back. If we decide to play our hand in acknowledging their existence, I suggest we do so on our terms.' Agnes crept to the door and looked out, hoping only to see Charlotte, and was relieved to see the girl doing her chores. Agnes half-turned and saw that Sarah had replaced the images and closed the safe behind the portrait of Cyrus.

They crept into the hallway, where Charlotte joined them, and Agnes placed her hands on Charlotte's shoulders, insisting she kept their visit a secret. She nodded her agreement, but as usual Sarah was sceptical that the girl really grasped the importance, and in that moment they turned sharply as a shadow appeared at the front door. As the key was inserted in the lock, they fled.

Without the damning images Sarah was forced to accept she had no other viable plan with which to confront Michael. She knew that if Agnes had been aware of what she intended her sister would have advised her against such a tactic, and Sarah swiftly came to realise that it was fraught with danger. Honoria was also growing frustrated at the lack of response to her advertisement in the classified pages, as nobody remotely suitable had thus far applied for the role of housekeeper, so for the time being Yolande remained safe in her position.

An incident which may have presented them with a valid reason to dismiss her occurred when a piece of jewellery belonging to Sarah went missing. Both were convinced Yolande was the culprit, but they had no tangible proof, and when Michael was informed, he suggested Sarah may have misplaced the item and that it would turn up. When she found it had been replaced the next morning, informing Honoria after Michael had left for work, they knew he must have told Yolande as he also suspected her and thus had given her the chance to put it back. Sarah had previously caught Yolande in her bedroom putting Sarah's clothes against her and twirling around the room. Sarah had snapped, angrily grabbing the dress and demanding to know what the servant thought she was doing.

Yolande's pathetic defence was that Michael had told her he wanted her to have something pretty to wear.

'So purchase something with your wages or cajole your lover to buy you something!'

Yolande had laughed mockingly. 'Really? When we both know that *my* lover is your *husband*?'

Sarah shook her head. She no longer cared that Michael found his sexual appetites were more satisfied in Yolande's bed than in theirs. He was welcome to go there if only he would leave her alone.

'You have been a lousy wife for the master. Why else would he rush to my bed each night?' The look of taunting contempt from a servant whore was too much for Sarah and she lunged at her angrily. Grabbing Yolande's hair, she had dragged her out of their bedroom suite, and on that occasion she told Michael when he came home, which had resulted in Honoria disciplining Yolande in front of him. She had relished watching the wretched girl squirming in guilt and hoping for forgiveness, knowing that Michael would offer no words of defence, as he, like his father always had, found the domestic details irksome and so gave his mother a free hand.

Although Sarah was careful not to show visible signs of it, she enjoyed every minute of Yolande's humiliation, rejoicing in Michael's angry departure for the club afterwards.

It was after Michael's departure that Honoria looked again through the handful of applications she had received via the employment agency after her advertisement failed to inspire interest. She found one and handed it to Sarah.

'Sadly none of the applicants the agency have sent me particularly stand out as especially remarkable, but she is the worth interviewing. We could see her together.'

Sarah looked at the sheet Honoria offered and nodded. For the moment Michael remained ignorant of their plans, but Honoria doubted he would demur too strongly. They agreed that Yolande's actions had gone too far, and Sarah knew she had enjoyed far more freedom than her mother would ever have indulged from Charlotte. It was time to curb those freedoms, and forcing Yolande to report to someone who had been hired to supervise her was the first crucial step.

'I doubt my son's patience will last if he comes home to have Yolande whining about how unfair her life is. He may not be able to resist her charms, but he won't want to be bothered with petty domestic squabbles, and if that factor alone sours his interest in her, so be it!'

They interviewed Grace Metcalfe together and within half an hour of her departure Honoria rang the employment agency and informed them Grace had been hired as housekeeper. Honoria poured Michael his cognac that evening and told him she had hired additional domestic help.

'Really? Is it necessary?'

'I think so. Yolande evidently struggles to accept my authority and I plan to spend more time at my various associations and become engaged in charitable good works, so Mrs Metcalfe, who has the relevant experience, will be in charge from now on, and Yolande will be reporting to her!'

Michael blanched, spluttering on his cognac, as he knew just how much Yolande would hate the new arrangement, having served them on her own for so long, but he was not inclined to intervene. *She* had overstepped recently and he had been embarrassed by her conduct.

She had to understand the limits of her role in the Landseer household regardless of how much he desired her in bed, and by having acted *so* rashly she had played directly into his mother's hands.

'As you wish, Mother. I take you *will* inform her of the new structure?'

Michael sipped his cognac, stretching out his legs. He dared not look at Sarah, but with his gaze fixed on Honoria, he nodded.

'It will be my pleasure, Michael!'

He mumbled something obscene under his breath but had to acknowledge the power dynamic had shifted back to his mother and she had exploited it brilliantly. It reminded him of how his father used to relish the moment in their chess duels when Michael, as an adolescent and novice at chess, would make a move which left himself cruelly exposed to Ernest, who was a superb player. This was Honoria's checkmate and he winced visibly, reminding himself why he *never* played chess anymore.

8

July 1914

With the winter rains came the heart-wrenching reality for Sarah that she *was* expecting. Michael's wish that his wife should be with child had been realised after numerous cognac-fuelled fumbled attempts that were not even remotely romantic, even though she had prayed that she wouldn't be expecting right to the moment that it was confirmed by her physician. She found Michael's gloating arrogance nauseating, as he had viewed her pregnant state as yet another means to an end which suited him perfectly, hoping that she might overwhelmed with morning sickness and then too preoccupied with the reality of expectant motherhood to *resist* his will. The timing, however, could have been better, as Jensen appeared to be holding out against the threat of default far longer than Michael had ever anticipated and his resilience thus far at meeting monthly loan repayments was infuriating. Michael was baffled because his most reliable sources told him that the Calloway brokerage was struggling, and although he believed Marguerite had some savings, he didn't anticipate they were sufficiently substantial for them to have survived for this long.

Thus it frustrated him that his dream of claiming the Toorak mansion for himself was not yet close to being realised

The new housekeeper Grace Metcalfe had settled in remarkably well and he was impressed that Honoria's increased activities in the city were having no impact on domestic arrangements. He discovered that he liked the new set-up. He still resented slightly that his mother's sleight of hand had caught him off-guard, but it bore no comparison to Yolande's outspoken resentment of Grace Metcalfe's presence which he was subjected to most evenings. Her whining was wearing very thin and her belief that, as his lover, he would take her side against Honoria simply hadn't been proved right and she felt more isolated than ever within the Landseer household. He told her bluntly in a heated exchange that she simply wasn't experienced enough to command the kind of role that Grace Metcalfe could and that she would have to live with and make the best of new arrangements. Nor was he troubled by her threats to leave, as they had never materialised into anything serious and she knew him well enough to realise that he *just* wouldn't succumb to blackmail.

Honoria had heard the exchange and couldn't resist a slight triumphant smile as Michael left for his nightly trip to his club after Yolande had been ordered to return to her duties in the kitchen, prompting Honoria to say, 'I wish now that I had appointed someone like Grace Metcalfe years ago.'

Although Michael was able to detach himself from what he considered trivial domestic arguments at home, the political situation in Europe was much harder to ignore. The ticker-tape machines were frantically busy amid speculation about how the tense diplomatic brinkmanship which had grown and intensified since the end of June was rife. Would the nations of Europe be plunged into war, and how might Australia be involved in any conflict that Britain found itself dragged into? Questions like these had swirled around the Melbourne business community on a daily basis ever since Archduke Ferdinand's assassination, and the directors at Argate & Landseer, among many financial institutions, had convened several emergency meetings throughout the month to discuss the worsening situation and agree their strategy. The hope was that diplomacy would win and the sheer madness of war could be averted, until the moment came when reality dictated otherwise.

One day when Honoria was not attending one of her association meetings she enquired about how Sarah was feeling. Relations between them had improved and they had found a new understanding by working together in appointing Grace Metcalfe as housekeeper without Michael knowing and consolidating their mutual dislike of Yolande. Sarah was not yet ready to look upon her mother-in-law as a trusted ally, but it was a welcome change not to be treated to her withering looks and barbed comments of disdain. It did surprise her, however, that Honoria was not enthused about the prospect of becoming a grandmother and that she had reacted with concern to the news that Sarah was pregnant.

'I am as well as can be expected, thank you,' she responded, treating Honoria to a wan smile. She hadn't shared the news of her pregnancy with her parents, nor had she yet confided in Agnes, as she knew her sister would view the news negatively.

Honoria reached out and patted Sarah's hand. 'It can't be easy. Michael hasn't made marriage the joy that it should be in the early months. I think you have endured an ordeal.'

'You mustn't blame yourself. Michael is an adult, and as such he should take responsibility for his excesses.'

Honoria nodded. 'Yes, but it's his appetite for cruelty that is particularly alien to me. I fear his excesses will be his undoing eventually, that one day life might present a bill to Michael that he will find impossible to pay. Penance won't ever be easy for him. You, however, must find a path to freedom for yourself and I will do all that *I* can to assist you.'

Sarah looked at her mother-in-law with incredulity, her brows pleated into a deep frown. She didn't know what to make of what Honoria had said, but she was sure it must have been a careless slip of the tongue, although she didn't doubt that Honoria was being sincere. 'Divorce, you mean? Michael wouldn't countenance it. He won't let me go, especially once the baby has arrived.'

Honoria shook her head. 'I have no idea what the path to his destruction will look like, only that it must come and that Michael will be the author of it. His dalliance with Yolande is such a huge risk and I know from Grace that the wretched girl is sounding increasingly reckless. It will only take a wrong word and he will be ruined, socially speaking. Backed into a corner, she will find a route out that will ensure her survival and *because* Michael is *so* besotted, he cannot see the threat she poses to his career and our good name.'

Sarah nodded, smiling to herself. The last remark sounded just like Honoria, with the kind of barbed comment that *she* had been subjected to in the early weeks of her marriage. Michael had informed her in one of his most conciliatory moments of sobriety, which were becoming rarer, that Honoria was the keeper of the Landseer name.

Her devotion to her husband was as strong in the years she had been mourning him as it had been when his father was alive, that nothing would stand in her way of vigorously defending it.

'So there are no circumstances in which you think he might give her up?' Sarah hoped she had kept any note of hope out of her voice, as she really didn't care anymore.

'Not unless he is pushed too far. Yolande has learnt how to be a survivor, but with Michael, however, it is *instinctive*. He can put up with her whining by walking away from it, but should she challenge him to lay his cards upon the table and make some declaration of commitment to her, that may prove her weakness…' Honoria's voice trailed off and Sarah was unsure of how to respond. It was clear she still wanted her son to be the husband that she had been throughout her marriage to Ernest, and although it went against her character, perhaps Honoria still hoped Michael had the capacity within him; sadly, even after four months of marriage, Sarah no longer clung to such a hope. There was little that Michael could do for her to repair the damage. Honoria looked at her again and reached for her hand; Sarah gave it to her.

'I am genuinely sorry for the humiliation he has brought to you.' Honoria didn't doubt that Sarah was a victim; it was why she had berated him for switching his allegiance to her from Agnes and for diverging from the original plan, but Sarah was not the only young woman to have suffered.

Two generations ago there had been poor Louise, whose own hopes had been cruelly dashed. Honoria could not forget the plight of her poor sweet mother and the humiliation that she had suffered at the hands of the man she had loved. So while she regretted what Sarah had been forced to endure these last four months due to Michael's inability to control his primal lust, Honoria wasn't prepared to forgive Cyrus or Jensen Calloway for their sins.

Sarah half-turned from her mother-in-law and indulged herself with a secret smile. It was telling that Honoria, who loathed Yolande with such intensity, still described the girl as a survivor and conferred the same instinct upon Michael, but she didn't evidently have the same confidence in *her* survival instincts. They definitely existed, because without detection she had managed one night, a few weeks after first discovering the truth of Michael's infidelity with Yolande, to take two images of them in bed together. This was *her* insurance policy, along with one of the images of her father in a compromising position with a prostitute that she had taken from the safe without Agnes's knowledge. Together they represented her survival plan, and if she needed to play them to secure the freedom that Honoria spoke of, then so be it!

Sarah continued to be buoyed by Honoria's moral support

in the days that followed even though they never spoke so candidly again.

Michael came home heavily imbued with cognac one evening in early August and was behaving in his *most* obnoxious way. Sarah prepared herself for a quarrel; she knew when a fight was imminent and it was usually Michael who instigated it. Although heavily in his cups and rocking on his heels, Honoria and Sarah could see that his mood was more melancholy than belligerent. He poured himself another cognac and turned to look at them, raising his glass to propose a toast.

'To my dear mother and beautiful wife, I urge you to prepare yourselves for an almighty bust-up! For I have it on good authority that this evening His Majesty's Government has sent a telegram to Berlin demanding that Germany respects Belgium's neutrality or that a state of war will exist with the might of the British Empire!' He lifted his glass and fell slightly forward until Sarah moved to first steady and then help him into a chair.

Honoria scoffed. 'Is it the cognac talking?'

He shook his head. 'No! I admit that I am heavily imbued with my favourite libation; however you may sadly discover in the morning papers that unless Germany takes the demand seriously there will be war in Europe! For now I intend to retire... Wife, do you plan to join me?'

Sarah looked at him, barely able to conceal her disgust, and said, 'Is it me you really want, Michael? Your pregnant, biddable wife or do you intend on abandoning our bed for that servant whore?'

'This is getting tedious. You are an expectant mother now. Our child should be the focus of your attention.'

Sarah stood up to face Michael and he saw the disgust in her eyes; despite his focus shifting due to his inebriated state, he saw the glimpse of rebellion in his wife's eyes, which he took as a challenge.

'Go to bed then, my virtuous wife! To your cold, empty bed. Is it any surprise that I seek my pleasures elsewhere when all I find in our bed is your icy indifference?'

Sarah wanted to lift a hand to strike him, but when Honoria shook her head in warning she let her arm fall by her side. Michael turned away from her, and she seized her chance to flee. She fought against the tears welling in her eyes, surprised that could he still get to her and because she wanted to be strong.

Michael, rocking on his heels again, turned to his mother. 'So Honoria, are you going to regale me with your pearls of wisdom or lament my poor, tormented soul?'

Honoria sniffed. 'Tormented? No, you are just a pathetic drunk. I suggest you sit down before you fall. There is little point in me even being ashamed of you as you evidently have no sense of shame in yourself!'

Honoria pulled on the cord and within minutes Grace Metcalfe appeared.

'I am retiring for the night, Grace, if you could prepare my drink. Is the servant girl already abed?'

'Yes, ma'am, she retired in a sulk after her duties were done. I shall follow you up.'

Honoria nodded her thanks and made for the stairs before half-turning. 'You heard that, Michael? You had better go. Your lover is waiting for you, unless you intend to do the decent thing and share the bed with your wife!'

Honoria spoke in her usual withering tone as she had no doubt about which option he would choose. Michael sneered and slumped into a chair.

There was a defeated look in his eyes, as he knew that he was no match for his mother when deeply inebriated, but he did intend on spending the whole night in his lover's bed, just as he expected to wake next morning to the daunting reality that Germany had not heeded the warning of His Britannic Majesty's Government and thus a state of war would exist. He didn't dare contemplate yet what Australia's involvement might become in the days and weeks ahead, but his sense of shock wasn't cushioned by the quantity of alcohol he had consumed, because after less than forty days, a skirmish in a tiny part of Europe that he knew nothing about and cared even less had the potential now to turn everything he took as certainty upon its head and to plunge the world into a fate yet to be known.

9

October 1914

In the long, interminable weeks that followed the outbreak of war Agnes was more eager than ever to finalise her training so when the time came, she could volunteer and utilise her nursing skills to best effect at the Front. She took the news of Sarah's pregnancy with dismay, fearing that it only served to bind her sister more firmly to Michael in what she believed –based on what Sarah had divulged – was a disintegrating marriage.

Agnes would have loved to intervene but was aware of the potential danger to their parents, which, although it riled her, couldn't be ignored. Sarah was careful not to divulge the worst aspect of their marriage, his open adultery under their roof, and this reluctance was due as much to her own sense of shame as it was to the fact that *if* Agnes knew, she couldn't hold back.

'Is he planning to volunteer?' she asked Sarah one day over coffee in central Melbourne. Their meetings had become more regular and were actively encouraged by Honoria, who felt it was just the outlet she needed.

For all that Agnes believed Michael to be capable of and however much she loathed him, she didn't think he would duck his duty to King and country – and, more crucially, to his ego, missing out on the opportunity to be heroic.

Sarah nodded. 'He's biding his time until the baby arrives, which of course must be a boy…' She smiled, rolling her eyes. 'In the meantime he can indulge his favourite obsession, making money.'

Agnes pulled a face. 'Even if it does come at exploiting someone else.'

'What are your plans?' Sarah asked.

'I shall have to finish my training then I will give it my serious consideration. They will need good nursing staff, especially if the optimism that it will be over by Christmas amounts to just that. Either way I shall stay until your baby is born. You need *my* sisterly support.'

Sarah nodded. 'It has been better at home and the appointment of a housekeeper has been great. I shall try to give Charlotte the benefit of the doubt in future, having endured Yolande's laziness and frequent sulking.'

'And Honoria?'

'She is very busy with her associations like Mother, especially since the outbreak of hostilities. So I don't see much of her some days. She has become exasperated by Michael's boorish behaviour, which she attributes to his fondness for cognac. He can be very spiteful in his cups.'

Agnes nodded; having suffered Michael's spite when inebriated, she shook her head. 'I am certain whatever deal he has struck with Father was drafted in cold sobriety and was loaded in his favour with all his usual malice. Despite what you say about her being exasperated, and I am glad she is more supportive of you, I can't help thinking Honoria must shoulder some of the blame for the way Michael has turned out. I have always thought she indulged him.'

Sarah shook her head. 'Not anymore. Although he claims to be hard done by parentally speaking, I suspect most of the discipline was from his father's dictum, and I know she feels he has wasted his talents and the opportunities that the bank afforded him by bearing his father's name.'

Agnes frowned. 'Are you telling me Honoria has become an ally?'

Sarah gave her a rueful look, half-nodding. 'Nobody could be more surprised, but yes – I *am*!'

Agnes's look darkened. 'Take my advice: be on your guard.'

Agnes sniffed slightly; she wouldn't want Sarah to take Honoria's moments of kindness too seriously and so become vulnerable. On the few occasions she had been in Honoria Landseer's company she had always felt the woman was hiding something. She had also noticed the undercurrent of barely concealed contempt that Honoria had for their father.

Had she passed that on to her son, and with Michael's malicious personality he had decided to inflict as much financial pain upon the Calloways as he could for his own ends? Perhaps the images and their father's determination to be evasive were just a contributing illusion to the bare facts of what Michael wanted: their family home and any other financial rewards that he could extort from whatever weakness Jensen had succumbed to.

Agnes didn't doubt that Honoria Landseer was still the elitist snob she had always been and wondered how might Honoria have played her hand if Michael had not turned his attention to Sarah and taken her as his bride? Did she think Sarah was too easily manipulated?

Michael definitely saw Sarah as more biddable, and she came without the Women's Suffrage issue that he had so derided as the unwanted baggage he would have to burden had *he* stuck with her.

'Believe me, Agnes. Honoria is as disillusioned by some aspects of Michael's behaviour as we are, and while my eyes are open to what she is capable of, as you fear, I am grateful for her support.'

Agnes considered carefully her sister's words, hoping she might detect something between the lines of what Sarah was confiding to her that might be significant, but she decided not to probe further.

'I would still *urge* caution, Sarah. I accept Honoria is far more subtle than her son, but should it come to choosing blood will out!'

Sarah half-rose to leave as Agnes consulted her watch. The uniform of a trainee nurse suited her and she felt that her sister – fiercely held political views and a burning desire for justice aside – had finally discovered her *niche*.

Sarah pondered her sister's parting words as they embraced. Blood would win out, but through his *carnal* lust for the servant Yolande, Honoria believed her son was doomed and that the Landseer blood had been tainted by their association.

'Of course, but leave it now, Agnes, please! I have learnt to be resourceful in the months since I married Michael and I shall continue to be. I hope that he does volunteer for action once our child is born and I shall have some respite from his selfish excesses.'

Sarah blushed, knowing which excesses she was referring to; Agnes nodded. She *believed* her sister would cope with whatever challenges Michael expected her to contend with in their marriage, but she still hoped however it came that Sarah could reap – through his absence – a reprieve.

10

Michael had given serious thought to volunteering in the first weeks after war had been declared, but he had demurred for several reasons, one of which he had made public, the fact that his wife was expecting their first child, and because he knew that projecting himself as a dutiful husband and a happy, expectant father would look good at the bank, which had always attached great importance to presenting itself as a family-orientated firm, although they were keen to encourage and support any member of staff who chose to heed the calls to arms so that their patriotism was also not in doubt, and a number of junior clerks had enlisted with the directors' good wishes. When the subject was mooted at a meeting, Michael sought to reassure them that duty to King and country was important to him, but his commitments at home would come first. While Sarah remained only sceptical of his motives having anything to do with her pregnancy, Honoria was derisory, telling him bluntly that she didn't believe he had any intention of putting himself in danger, adding that her late husband's colleagues at Argate & Landseer must be utter fools to take his claims at face value.

'It's self-serving tosh. The next time they raise the subject with you, after the baby is born, I daresay there will be another excuse to delay your enlistment.'

'Luckily for me, Mother, the directors don't have as poor view of me as you evidently do.'

'A situation which I daresay would change dramatically if they knew how you went from your marital bed to that of your servant whore each night!'

Michael's face darkened, and Honoria could see the fury rising, but she stood her ground.

'I have told – sorry, asked you *not* to refer to Yolande as that!'

'I will call her for what she is and thankfully now that she is under Grace's supervision my contact with her is limited. Be thankful, Michael, that I haven't gone further than that.'

Sarah had retired earlier and although Honoria understood why her daughter-in-law chose to let peace reign within the household for the sake of her health during pregnancy, she hoped Sarah would resist slipping back into the role of a meek, obedient wife, as Michael didn't deserve to have her thus; she had no intention of going easy on him.

Michael sat in the lounge of his favourite club in central Melbourne later that evening; still aggrieved after his altercation with Honoria and with an appetite for spite in his mind, he shared his plans for destroying Jensen Calloway with his friend Aaron Crozier, the *coup de grâce* of which would be claiming the Toorak mansion as his own once the bank had foreclosed.

Aaron Crozier was astonished but not entirely surprised. He had known Michael for long enough to realise what his friend was capable of and that he didn't like to be crossed.

'It would be a double-edged sword,' Michael added gleefully. 'Give with one hand through a grandchild and then take the family roof from beneath his head.' He knew that it was standard practice in the business world and that Jensen had known the risks when he had applied for the loan.

'So what if he doesn't default on the repayments?' Aaron asked, his eyes alert, inquisitive.

'He will. I am surprised he has held out with them this long. My mother-in-law must be a very understanding and patient woman, as I am sure her legacy is what's keeping them afloat.'

'So why did he apply for the loan if they had means to avoid it?'

Michael shrugged, taking a large gulp of cognac. 'Male pride, I guess. No man likes to live off their wife, and I'm only guessing that Marguerite's money is being used, unless the Calloway brokerage is faring better than I have been led to believe. My sources are usually reliable.'

He paused, smiling lasciviously as Aaron tried to read between the lines of just why Michael found the potential downfall of his in-laws *so* appealing.

'So how is Leticia?' He didn't really care about Aaron's sister, but he asked out of politeness as Aaron usually took the bait to free himself of any sibling gripes and woes he was forced to suffer and which Michael usually found highly entertaining.

'She shocked us all the other evening by stating she was on the brink of volunteering, although in what capacity, she isn't sure. Damned nuisance, as it puts additional pressure upon me, which, of course, my father was keen to point out.'

Michael smiled weakly. He didn't see as much of Eugene Crozier, as Aaron's father had withdrawn from his parents' circle of friends some years ago and he hadn't made contact since Ernest Landseer's death.

When Michael had broached the subject with his mother, Honoria had been uncharacteristically coy, saying only that *his* father and Eugene had a disagreement over a business matter which had never been resolved, and he knew from Aaron that Eugene had tried more than once to discourage the friendship between *them*.

'Yes, the whole show is damned poor timing. I told the directors at the bank I would consider my position after Sarah has given birth, and they have accepted that, tacitly at best, but my position is hindered by the number of staff who have already stated their intention to enlist, and they will expect someone of my seniority to set the same example. Damn them!'

Aaron pulled a slightly sympathetic face and, taking a gulp of cognac, he said, 'How's Honoria?'

'As robust as an ox physically. Coldly indifferent and dismissive when she believes I merit it. She made a point of informing me that Ernest, the paragon of virtue that he was, would have heeded the calls to arms without hesitation, and while she accepts that being an expectant father is a legitimate reason for delay, I have yet to convince her that I won't seek another excuse to avoid enlisting once the child is born.'

He grimaced and Aaron leaned forward to flick ash from his cigar.

'Will you?'

'If Jensen has defaulted by then probably, but time will tell, Aaron, time will tell.'

Michael leaned back into the soft leather of his armchair and sipped gently at his third or fourth cognac – he had lost count, musing on the fact that he resisted any urge to unburden himself about another motive for delaying his need to do his duty, namely Yolande. It alarmed him on occasions just how strong his feelings for her were becoming and how potentially dangerous it could be for him to become too dependent on them. *Lust* in its purest form was acceptable to him, but to become enslaved to it, as Honoria felt he already had, was damning and on that point he had to concede that his mother *was* right. Nor did he have any intention of sharing with Aaron, as his best friend, like many of his casual acquaintances, wouldn't understand the nature of his desire for Yolande, or that he would willingly admit that was all it amounted to – although he feared it went much deeper – and that alarmed him.

At home Yolande was like a drug to him that he couldn't do without, more potent than his liking for good cognac, but outside she was merely staff, and if he ever had cause to refer to her, it would have to be as such. Although she occasionally riled against that imperative, she was sufficiently astute to accept it, however much the arrival of Grace Metcalfe had upset their relationship dynamic, which made sex between them so hypnotic and *so* undeniably essential to him. He had to concede he was powerless to bend to her wish to see the housekeeper dismissed, his mother would never hear of it, and so he was trapped by the force of his desire – his weakness, as Honoria preferred to call it. To ensure he continued to enjoy the pleasures of Yolande's caramel-skinned beauty, she had to suffer Grace Metcalfe's authority, while he hoped that whatever she felt for him was enough to make her stay.

Agnes was determined to complete her nursing training, to the extent that she allowed no other issue to distract her in the final weeks, so when Sister Freda Lomax summoned Agnes to her office at Melbourne's Alfred Hospital, the significance of the moment rendered her unusually nervous, as the importance to her of qualifying first time could not have been greater. She was forced, as she made her way through a labyrinth of corridors, to think back to the night last December when the life that she had thought she was destined to lead had altered in the course of an evening when Michael had rejected her. Nursing had afforded her the opportunity to reset her life and to strive for something more fulfilling than a dutiful marriage, and quietly confident as she was, that ambition coalesced into this moment, and her sense of calling couldn't have been greater since the outbreak of war. Australia needed nurses of calibre and she believed she had it.

Sister Freda Lomax studied Agnes's file as she waited for her to arrive, with slightly knitted brows. There was, according to her teachers, a lot to commend Nurse Calloway for, but she was headstrong and would need discipline. The sister smiled, recalling that much the same had been said about her when she'd completed her training. She answered the knock at the door with a curt, 'Come,' and she instructed Agnes to sit down while she finished reading.

Agnes was suddenly struck by the horror that she might have failed and would have to continue training. She had been forewarned about Sister Lomax and her legendary demeanour, that she didn't suffer fools and time wasters but that she also resented those who mistook their self-confidence for knowledge that only came through experience, so Agnes had marshalled herself to remain contained throughout the interview. Her palms began to perspire as she placed them in her lap. When she had first considered nursing as a career path it was a bid for independence, something she could claim as her own and that she would achieve without any assistance. It could afford her a life that she couldn't have hoped to attain through marriage. Sarah's plight in such a marriage still concerned her greatly, but for the time being she was going to allow herself a degree of selfishness.

Sister Lomax closed the file and looked directly at Agnes. She prided herself on being a good judge of character, for knowing instinctively a nurse with potential when confronted with one, and she believed in Agnes Calloway. She always presented a stern demeanour, because some trainees merited it, and often the chaff realised that it wasn't the career for them and abandoned it swiftly, before *it* abandoned them, but she had been informed that Nurse Calloway had taken everything that her tutors had thrown at her and had come back for more.

'Congratulations, Nurse Calloway. You have done extremely well. I see from your file that you are very capable, but you are not the finished article yet.' The sister paused, a slight smile curving at her mouth as she tapped the file with her pen.

'I am determined, however, to see that you become the best you can be. I see a lot of self-confidence, but I warn against letting that drift into arrogance. Pride comes before a fall, Calloway, and I have seen a great many fall from a height because they either don't take the profession seriously enough or they think it will be a breeze. I have come across trainees who astonishingly see it as a shortcut to landing an eligible doctor as a husband. You have shown that you are not suspect to either weakness or vanity, and I urge you to continue thus.'

Agnes took a deep breath and smiled. 'I believe I have the talent and determination to succeed, Sister.'

Sister Lomax nodded, the smile lighting her eyes.

Agnes relaxed slightly and the, Sister said, 'I believe I know your mother – Marguerite, isn't it?'

Agnes nodded, biting her bottom lip, fearing her mother's presence on so many charitable committees could as easily be a troubling influence as a benign one.

'I see some of her determination in you, which is a positive; however, she has, I believe, a tendency to share robust views which are often misinterpreted as outspokenness. I hope that isn't a trait you have acquired?'

Agnes shook her head, slightly relieved, as she recalled many family dinners during which her mother had vented her frustrations that some of her suggestions and advice to various committees, which sometimes appeared impractical or involved exorbitant costs, were not considered as she believed they should be, and not for the first time, Agnes had encountered someone who had bravely resisted the impossible force that was Marguerite Calloway.

'Good.' Sister Lomax tapped the file with Agnes's name on it against the desk and stood to place it in her filing cabinet. Agnes couldn't help wondering what some of her fellow student nurses, who she had seen lacked the self-discipline necessary to succeed in nursing, had written in their files, and she waited patiently for the sister to turn back and dismiss her.

'You can go, Nurse Calloway, and prove that my confidence in your abilities isn't misplaced.'

Agnes half-rose, feeling slightly flushed and not entirely sure whether Sister Lomax had set her a challenge she expected *her* to fall short of or if she was inspiring her to rise to greater heights. Agnes believed the best test of her nursing skills would come at the Front and that was the challenge she yearned to meet. She wanted to know how long she would have to bide her time on home soil, when she would be of more use where the action was. Because war was a reality Australians were having to come to terms with, even though the first shot had been fired in some unpronounceable town in the underbelly of Europe.

When the men began volunteering in greater numbers – as she was sure they would – she wanted to go with them to tend their wounds, but with all that Sister Lomax had said she was nervous about being over-confident regarding the value of her nursing skills and yet to appear keen.

Sister Lomax raised an eyebrow at Agnes as she reached the door. 'Yes?'

'When will they be calling for nursing skills to be deployed at the Front? Some of our men have already enlisted, and isn't that where valuable nursing skills will be most needed?'

Sister Lomax smiled. 'Be patient, Calloway, your time will come.'

Agnes smiled and took her leave. As she made her way back through empty corridors, she couldn't help wondering what Sister Lomax was thinking about her parting query. Had she already incurred the sister's *wrath* by ignoring her advice against over-confidence? Or was she simply stating the obvious point that about the urgent need for good nursing skills at the Front? Wasn't it also understandable that Australian volunteers would prefer to be treated by their own? The sister was urging her to bide her time and it was good advice; however, the months of sweat and toil that she had put into passing shouldn't be wasted dragging her feet in the safety of Melbourne and she was determined to earn her place among the nursing staff where her skills were needed most.

She was still very conscious of her parents' potential plight at the hands of Michael, while the threat of defaulting remained so real, but that was a situation of their making and she had tried without success to urge caution upon them, so she had to become the mistress of her own destiny, the direction of which was still within her hands to decide.

11

Melbourne 1915

Agnes had all but confirmed her decision to volunteer for nursing duties at the Front by the turn of the year, but she was keen to bide her time until after Sarah had given birth. Her parents said this wasn't necessary, as Sarah had other people around to call upon for support, but as Agnes suspected they included Michael in this, she insisted as firmly as she *dared* that her decision stood. She would wait until after the birth.

On the few occasions she had seen Sarah during the final trimester, she could see that her sister was experiencing a difficult pregnancy, and although Sarah didn't confirm it when pushed, Agnes believed Michael was offering as little in the way of support as he could get away with.

Her father was also quietly reticent on the subject of Michael and he swiftly changed the subject whenever Agnes mentioned his name, but she could see the strain it was having on him. Jensen looked exhausted, and although he was keeping the brokerage afloat, business was declining and Agnes suspected Michael might have a hand in that, as in her worst fears, it suited Michael for their father to default on the loan, and he would subtly do whatever he had to, and claim the prize she knew in her gut that he most coveted: the Calloway mansion.

If she boldly enquired about how the business was doing, Jensen would raise an eyebrow and casually sweep her concerns aside with a neutral comment which told her nothing, while her mother remained tight-lipped. So in early January, two weeks before Sarah's due date, Agnes requested a meeting with Sister Lomax and asked to be considered for duties at the Front at the earliest opportunity. She hadn't expected the sister to acquiesce immediately, and her quiet reservation to acceding to her request was a little galling.

'I want this, Sister!' She paused, fearing she had put her case too strongly. She took a long, deep breath, adding, 'As an opportunity to prove myself in a situation where it will come to mean the most, as many more of our brave young men are going to discover very soon... Unless you consider me too young and inexperienced for the task, Sister?'

Sister Lomax smiled. Shaking her head slightly, she said, 'No, I consider you very capable, and I have seen that you're no wallflower, but I don't want to lose you... That sounds terribly selfish, I know, but recently qualified nurses of your calibre are a rare find. I want you to do this for the right reasons, for *you* personally at this stage in your career. Not *because* you think it's a noble gesture or that it's expected of you. I've heard some of the stories from the Front and it's hell out there. The conditions in which all medical staff are having to work are gruelling, supplies are sparse and the environmental conditions are alien compared to what we are used to.'

'Forgive me, Sister Lomax, but isn't that exactly the noble gesture the military high command are asking of our men, some of whom are mere boys, younger than me?'

The sister smiled, but only slightly; she should have known not to have presented a moral argument against going to Nurse Calloway, and not because she was Marguerite's eldest but for the qualities she had seen for herself these last few weeks.

'Very well. I shall set the wheels in motion. I have no reservations about your skills, Calloway. You have demonstrated admirably your qualities of leadership and your dedication, but nursing in a theatre of war will test all of them. So I hope you are emotionally equipped to cope with some of the horrors you're likely to see.'

The sister inclined her head slightly, her eyebrows raised, and Agnes took it as the sobering warning the sister had intended, as it was an aspect of what she was undertaking that hitherto she hadn't given the due respect it deserved.

Agnes nodded. 'Thank you, Sister. I want to *do* this.'

'Very well, I can see you are *very* determined. You will need to call upon that determination and so much more before this mess is over with and we have come through the other side.'

Agnes looked at the sister and she heard her tone matched the gravity of her expression. Agnes wondered if Sister Lomax had already lost someone to the carnage, but as she wasn't the type to share details about such a personal matter, Agnes smiled and, with a curt nod, she left, realising later that the meeting had left her feeling strangely bereft when she had expected to feel at least inspired by the challenge she had taken on, discovering later that three other nurses of varying degrees of experience had also gone to Sister Lomax and tendered their request to volunteer the same day.

Michael Landseer leaned back in his bathtub and lit a cigar.

The water was going cold, and although the fire was banked and it was unusually mild for summer, he didn't feel uncomfortable, but morally he was in a quandary. The directors were growing concerned that senior bank staff weren't taking the issue of enlisting sufficiently seriously, and because he was one of the most senior staff of fighting age, the focus was falling unfairly upon him and, quite bluntly, he *resented* it. It didn't help, of course, that Sarah was overdue in going into labour, and when one of the directors, whom he wouldn't describe as an ally, pointedly reminded him that as his family name was on the letterhead, he should set a better example, Michael had responded angrily, saying, 'Which I would have hoped would cut me some slack, especially as I'm an expectant father.'

The tone had forced his colleague to leave swiftly and the discussion was ceased, but Michael, cursing, knew it would be revisited and once he announced that his child had been born, the clamour for a decision would become louder.

He was growing impatient, waiting for Yolande to come and tend him, and he felt no compulsion to retire to the marital bed. Sarah had grown increasingly sullen in the latter stages of pregnancy, withdrawing further from him, and it had surprised him initially how easily accustomed he had grown to this distance.

The bathroom door opened slightly and Yolande came in. She looked tired and he guessed she had been run ragged with additional chores by Grace Metcalfe, who, it appeared, took his mother's instructions to the most extreme degree, working Yolande like a skivvy. He had been forced to plead with her several times recently not to quit but realised he was asking a lot from his lover when he offered no assurances that he could improve her situation. He had tried a different tactic when he feared his pleading was falling upon deaf ears, challenging Yolande to stay because she wouldn't want to give her mistress the satisfaction of seeing her leave. This appeared to work, but only until the next evening.

Exhaling heavily on his cigar, he beckoned Yolande further into the room and watched with bulging eyes and a smile that could only be described as gluttonous while she undid two buttons and slipped out of her dull grey uniform. Her caramel-skinned beauty appeared luminous in the candlelight and he smiled as she took the sponge he offered her and squeezed foamy lather on her breasts and stomach. In a moment, she was in the bathtub with him, and he felt the urgent thrust of arousal.

Every time they made love, he was forced to confront the reality that he just couldn't give her up. The relationship would invite scorn from all who knew him should it ever become public and he knew that the hold Yolande had over him wasn't just about sex; it was the threat that she could make it known they were lovers. That was the Sword of Damocles that she held over his head and sometimes he wondered if Sarah also realised the damage that she could do should she ever let a careless word slip. If Yolande Smith were a drug then he would be an addict, and a willing one at that, and although he *knew* the danger that he lay himself open to by not showing restraint, he was ensnared by the hypnotic musk of the desire that only she had the power to unleash within him.

When the moment of orgasm had passed, his ragged breathing eased, but he remained aroused. Spitting out his cigar, he claimed her mouth in a bruising kiss; their tongues meshed and then he pulled back, but she held him still, her wet palm against his chest. He could hear his heartbeat quickening and, in a ragged breath, she said, 'I want to be with child!'

Michael cursed. This was a bombshell revelation that he hadn't been expecting. 'What?!'

'I want what you have given your insipid little wife. A child.'

'No! I never wanted fatherhood this early in marriage anyway. Hell, I never anticipated remaining bound to her for this long. My plan for Sarah changed – had to change when she discovered the truth about us. It was designed to keep her mind occupied.'

Yolande shook her head; standing up, she looked down at him. Her eyes were fiercely intent and Michael watched as rivulets of foamy water sluiced down, giving her body a luminous quality in the muted candlelight.

Yes, he still wanted *her*. So much, but this was a demand too high, a step too far into certain social ruin, and however compulsive his *lust* might be, he could never submit to giving her this.

'Think of it. If the insipid little wife bears you a girl, you will still need an heir!' Yolande's eyes grew intense. Her belief in what she wanted being in his interests was startling in its naiveté and yet he could see that she was serious and he feared wouldn't be swayed.

'Yes, maybe, should the marriage survive for that long, which I doubt, but it would be a legitimate *heir*, one that I could acknowledge. I could never do that with any child you bore!'

Yolande looked down at him as he reached for her hand, still in a sitting position, but she pulled it away and, feeling she had the advantage, he stood up, reaching for a towel, but she slapped it aside.

He looked at her and he could see her eyes had grown intense and there were tears. He had never seen her weep before.

'Very well. A child – *our* child is the one thing I ask of you and yet you refuse me when you created one willingly with her, for whom you claim you care next to nothing!' Yolande clicked her fingers to exemplify her point.

'Because she *is* my wife! I thought you understood that was how it had to be between us.' He could hear the pleading tone in his voice and he was slightly embarrassed at how desperate it made him sound, but he wouldn't surrender to her without a fight, even though acquiescing to her request to fulfil a maternal *need* was *impossible*!

'Yes, she is your wife, even though you say that you despise her and I am the one that you lust after, but you can say it as your mother usually does. I am *just* your servant whore!'

'No!'

Yolande nodded, smiling gently, then, pulling her hand away from his grasp, she stepped out of the tub and, fetching up her sodden uniform, she left.

Michael lay in the cooling water for a while after Yolande had left him, thinking. He had retrieved his cigar, re-lit it from the flickering candle and leaned back. The dynamic had shifted because Yolande had demanded the one thing that he couldn't accede to: the child that would expose their relationship to society and likely render him socially as a pariah. The directors at the bank had also secured a victory this night, because now his decision about volunteering was inevitable once the baby was born. The only way to resist Yolande was to put some distance between them and to heed the call to arms. His *lust* for her had become his *weakness* and she had turned it into a weapon with the power to destroy him. He didn't doubt that she would continue demanding and he feared his *lust* might win. He still had to force the downfall of Jensen before he volunteered, but he would have to keep Yolande at arm's length and reveal nothing to his mother. With one simple request, answering an instinctive need common to most females, she had turned *his* world on its axis and nothing could be the same again.

12

Michael was not in the least surprised by the smug satisfaction with which the directors at Argate & Landseer reacted to his decision to volunteer for action within weeks of becoming a father, but he didn't care. Their low opinion of him had long ceased to matter. The same evening he informed his mother and wife of his decision during dinner, and while Sarah feigned relief, questioning whether it would be too soon after the birth, her concerns were casually waved aside as an over-reaction. Neither had any clue to why he had suddenly become more inclined to do his duty, but Yolande's demand that she should become pregnant by him had forced his hand, and while he still *ached* to be in her bed, as long as she persisted with the foolish notion he would stay away. It hadn't compelled him back to the bed he shared with Sarah, as she looked less appealing to him as the weeks to her due date progressed, but while domestic issues could be managed he was slightly shocked when one director queried the loan arrangement with Jensen and he knew it was overdue for him to pay his father-in-law a visit and to exert some pressure.

He sent Jensen Calloway a telegram with the intention of making it appear as casual a visit as possible; however, he suggested it should happen at home in Toorak – albeit during normal business hours, and he waited discreetly in a taxi-cab until he saw Marguerite leaving for one of her charity committees and then made his way at the appointed hour.

He was intrigued to know what state of mind he would find Jensen in, as the need to push home his advantage was becoming more urgent.

He still couldn't understand how he was still meeting the repayments and he wanted to make foreclosure a stark reality before he was called up.

The maid opened the door and Jensen stood behind her, dismissing the girl and leading Michael into his study. His father-in-law looked pale and drawn, and Michael smiled. So the emotional strain was telling, but why not the financial?

'You're looking tired, Jensen. I am guessing the strain of holding it all together is taking its toll, but I realise the charade of Calloway honour is increasingly fragile and you will do everything to preserve it for as long as you can. You wouldn't want to precipitate the fall of this house of cards!'

Jensen frowned and, opening the box on his desk, he offered Michael a cigar. 'It would be becoming of you to conduct yourself like a gentleman, Michael, or is such subtlety beyond you?'

'I was sufficiently a gentleman when you decided to offer me your daughter's hand in marriage and now that she is almost due to give birth, we will be bound by blood.'

'A significant event, I agree, and one which you intend to mark by taking the roof from beneath our heads should the repayments on my loan falter.'

Jensen kept his voice level, arching a querying eyebrow, but Michael remained calm and smiled as he helped himself to three cigars.

'The terms of your loan arrangement don't differ much from what you would have been offered by any other respectable financial institution and I don't need to remind you, Jensen, that you chose to accept our offer and not one from elsewhere.'

'I was trying to be discreet.'

'And keep your indiscretions in the whorehouse a secret.'

Jensen closed his eyes as he clenched and unclenched his fists at his side. The man was insufferable. 'Is there any limit to your vulgarity?'

Michael lit his cigar and shook his head. He couldn't help wondering what Jensen would make of his liaisons with Yolande, but of course he never would as he suspected Sarah would be too embarrassed to share her husband's indiscretions.

'Despite your clumsy threats I still have some valuable contacts in this city, and I have been reliably informed that you personally dealt with the drafting of my loan application and so the exorbitant interest rates and the default clause are all your own work.'

'Yet as I repeat, they *are* standard.'

'I also know, given your instinct to over-indulge in cognac which causes you to speak indiscreetly sometimes, that you had expected the default to have happened before now, yet I keep making the repayments on time. Aren't you worried that the directors might take another look at the contract and discover something you might not want them to see?'

Michael's smile disappeared. He did have a tendency to talk too freely at the club sometimes, but he had never anticipated that word would get back to Jensen, and he was always careful not to say anything at home that Sarah was likely to overhear.

'I am quietly confident that I can be trusted to look after your account with the bank without input from directors for as long as it's necessary to tip you over the edge and then take this magnificent mansion from under you.'

Jensen moved towards him, a nervous twitch working in his face as his anger increased.

He felt his palms sweating as he clenched his fist again; however tempted he was, he wouldn't give Landseer the satisfaction of being a victim of his temper.

Michael looked around his study as if he already owned it. 'That's your father, isn't it?'

'Yes,' Jensen said tersely, caught off-guard by the sudden change of subject. Michael's tone had softened, but he wasn't fooled by the change in tactic.

'Cyrus, isn't it? I have heard a lot of stories about him, although legends are generally embellished.'

'What has my father got to do with anything? As far as I am aware Ernest never knew him; although Cyrus is from Victoria, he spent much of his early adulthood in Queensland.'

'Prospecting gold, I believe?'

'Yes.'

'The foundation of the Calloway fortune! You see, I am reliably informed. I do my research, Jensen, perhaps you should have as well and maybe then you might have found a more favourable loan deal elsewhere.'

'I took your word that Argate & Landseer would be the best. As I understand it the loan has four more repayment months to go yet, so why the urgency for you to come round now? Unless it is just to *goad* me.'

Michael smiled as he stood. 'That is something I derive great pleasure from.' He shrugged before adding, 'You might as well know, I'm volunteering for action. Soon after your grandchild is born. So I just wanted you to know that very soon your loan application will be in someone else's hands and they won't have family ties to consider.'

'If you think I take any comfort from the fact you are my son-in-law in all this then you are deluded.'

Michael went to the door. 'That's all I wanted to hear, Jensen. You might be clinging on to this fine old home of yours by your fingertips, but don't rest on your laurels – I may have a trick up my sleeve to force you to the brink yet.'

'I am surprised that you are volunteering. I have seen how much you value the finer pleasures in life. A good cognac, the best cigars which you help yourself to most gratuitously when they are mine. A good healthy meal each evening. Have you read what the soldiers in the trenches are having to survive on? Do you really have it in you to survive on meagre rations to – how shall I put this – slum it?'

Michael half-turned, pointing his finger at Jensen, and, smiling gleefully, said, 'You make a good point. I shall have to be more resourceful, but if not I will survive. But will you? We all have to make sacrifices, Jensen. You sacrificed your daughter Sarah to me in exchange for your reputation and you may live to *rue* that day yet.'

Michael opened the door and his expression grew ashen as his way was blocked by Agnes filling the doorway.

'So what exactly has he got on you?'

'Agnes, this doesn't concern you!' Jensen tried to keep his tone firm but neutral, but he knew it was too late.

'I should heed your father's words if you want to preserve what's left of your family name, but then you have always presented a weakness for the over-dramatic, haven't you, Agnes?'

'Shut up! I knew my sister had been sacrificed for some sordid little deal between you and him, and I have heard enough to know my worst fears have been confirmed. This house is at risk if you default, isn't it?'

Michael half-turned to Jensen, pointing again. 'She's very astute, your eldest – you must be a very proud father.'

'Isn't it obvious she knows enough to weaken your leverage?'

Michael shrugged. 'Only if she has the courage to use it, which I doubt because of the cost to you if she does.'

'Unless I have other leverage of my own. Something that I know about you that would make us equal.'

Michael paled suddenly. Could Sarah have unburdened herself to her sister about him and Yolande? He always regretted his wife having discovered him in Yolande's bed and he had been maddened by just how relaxed Yolande had been regarding that discovery.

'Don't try to bluff me, Agnes. You're not very good at it,' Michael warned as he tried in vain to move past her.

'The paleness of your expression tells me you have something to hide.'

'What are you doing here, Agnes?' Jensen sounded exasperated.

'I came to inform you that my request to put my nursing skills to good use by volunteering for the Front has been tentatively accepted and it looks like I have timed my visit perfectly.'

'Say you have got or that you know something that I would prefer to keep private. What is it worth?'

'Whatever you have on my father is returned for him to destroy?'

Michael looked from Agnes to Jensen and then back at Agnes. 'If I should agree – and I repeat, *if* – it would still leave the loan application with the default clause intact.'

Agnes nodded.

'Agnes, will you *please* stay out of this!'

'Are you ever going to develop a backbone when it comes to dealing with him or won't you be satisfied until he's humiliated us all?'

Michael looked at Jensen for his reaction and then he turned to Agnes. 'However strong-willed your father chooses to appear, I hold all the cards, Agnes, and my instinct tells me you're bluffing. So, fascinating as it is to watch the dynamic between the two of you, I will leave you to it.' Agnes had stepped aside and he walked out into the hall.

Agnes shrugged. 'Sarah has always enjoyed a good gossip!'

Michael tapped her on the shoulder and made for the front door.

'Thanks, but I will take my chances.'

Michael left and Agnes stepped into the study. Jensen had flopped wearily into his chair.

'He knew you were bluffing. You achieved nothing with your bluster. I just wish you would heed my call for you to stay out of this.'

'This is my family. Our home is at stake! I cannot stand aside and watch as you let him ruin us!'

Jensen sighed heavily. 'Why are you here? Aside from telling me that you're volunteering as you are virtually a stranger with your frequent absences and yet you chose this morning to visit.'

'I wanted to share my news. The military desperately need trained nursing staff as much as they need medics and it's my chance now that I have finished my training to put my skills to best use.'

'Well, good for you! I *mean* that. At least one member of the Calloway family is doing something worthwhile.'

Agnes laughed. 'I wouldn't be saying that in front of Mother.'

Jensen laughed mirthlessly, shaking his head. 'No. Indeed.'

Agnes turned to look at Jensen and she took his hand. 'Will you tell me how you came to be blackmailed?'

Jensen sighed heavily. Agnes was so very much like him, the product of the upbringing that he had instilled, and yet there were times like now when her adherence to that upbringing and the values which underpinned it drove him to exasperation.

'I'm not being blackmailed in the strictest definition. It's just that Michael has come by some facts which could lead him to discover something that I am *determined* not to have in the public domain. I admit to visiting a brothel on numerous occasions, when you were a child, after your sister was born. Your mother suffered during and after that pregnancy and then she withdrew from me physically for a time. Quite by chance I was made aware of the predicament of a woman who had become the victim of one patron's ruthless determination to protect his good name whatever the cost to her by endeavouring to get rid of the result of his indiscretion. She had been given the opportunity and the financial means of dealing with the mistake, but I offered her a safer alternative, urging her through a third party to go to the country and start her life anew. I was very discreet. After a while I ceased going to that place and felt myself cleansed by abstinence; however, I don't know whether she decided upon the course of action she had originally been *coerced* into taking or the safer option my intervention afforded her. I wasn't ever prepared to risk being exposed for attempting to facilitate an illegal termination. When I told your mother, she was incensed that I had even got involved, so when the first communication arrived accusing me of having a predilection for visiting brothels, I feared it might be related to that gesture of kindness from two decades ago, even though I was scrupulously discreet at the time that maybe it was from the woman herself. The letter coming so suddenly had me scared and I was determined to mitigate the risk. As the brokerage was going through a bad time a loan application seemed like the best option in the short term and sadly for me, given our family's long association with Michael, Argate & Landseer appeared a viable option. I evidently underestimated him and the extent of *his* avarice.'

Agnes put a reassuring hand on her father's arm. She smiled, but it was a weak smile and there was still much that she didn't understand, but she knew it would have taken a lot for her father to have shared that with her and she wasn't prepared now to judge him or to press further.

'You think Michael knows about your gesture?'

Jensen shook his head. 'He couldn't possibly. He knows I frequented the brothel – in fact, he is quite bold about referring to my vices – but he knows I would prefer my clients not to have known that. Although I saw a number of my oldest clients there many times and I daresay there were clients of his bank who aren't adverse to enjoying the delights of a brothel at some stage.' Jensen paused, looking up at the portrait of his father before adding, 'I had already hinted to Michael that business was slow, but off the record... Evidently client discretion doesn't count for a lot with him when he sees an opportunity to exploit weakness... He made an oblique reference to your grandfather Cyrus which I didn't take much notice of at first, but now it's intriguing me.'

'You're not aware of any connection between him and Ernest personally, are you, or with the bank?'

'Cyrus didn't trust banks. Besides, the additional mining rights came to him when he married my mother. They were part of their wedding present, and he told me once that it was that section that proved most lucrative. Besides which, I told Michael that although Cyrus hailed from Melbourne he spent a large chunk of his time in Queensland.'

'It's such a mess,' Agnes said with a long sigh.

'Yes, but it's largely my mess and I shall have to overcome it. I did trust Michael, although that has turned out to be a huge error, because I believed him to be an honourable man, like Ernest, whom I *did* know professionally.'

Agnes stood and smiled. 'I will let you know when I have been accepted and my passage has been booked.'

'Please do, Agnes, and although I didn't want you embroiled in my mess and I have shown my frustration at your persistence, I am very proud. You are going to make an excellent nurse.'

Agnes went to the study door; the sunlight shining through the window caught her hair and it looked as if she wore a halo. Jensen smiled and when Agnes turned to him he gently inclined his head, and when he looked again she had gone.

13

Sarah Landseer reacted in slightly different ways, firstly to the news that her sister was awaiting confirmation that she had been accepted as a volunteer nurse for duties at the Front and then to the bombshell that Michael planned to enlist. It riled her that a child that *he* had wanted so soon into their marriage could potentially be denied its father within weeks of being born.

'How soon are you talking about?' she asked, hearing her voice sounding high in timbre and brittle with emotion. Feeling uncomfortable in the eighth month of pregnancy, she now wished it were over.

'Within a month to six weeks after the birth, but obviously once I have volunteered, the timing of posting will be out of my hands.'

'So I'm to deliver you a child and within weeks face the prospect of widowhood and our son or daughter being rendered an orphan, and you didn't think this was a subject for discussion?'

Michael looked rueful; biting his bottom lip, he kept his eyes on Sarah, albeit conscious that his mother was scrutinising him intently. 'I realise it's not an ideal situation, but several members of staff much junior to me have already committed themselves to action and it looks bad that I should be seen to be avoiding it.'

'I appreciate that, Michael, but the fact remains there's no conscription bill going through Parliament as far as I am aware, so you are doing this of your free will, not by compulsion, and you are expecting me to understand it's so you can escape censure at work?'

'I *have* to be seen to be willing to volunteer, that I'm not shirking my duty.'

'What about your duty to me and *our* child, which you were impatient for me to conceive, despite my wanting to wait, so that you could exert your manhood when and wherever you can and have a legitimate heir!'

Michael winced as he suspected Sarah was referring to his infidelity with Yolande which he was committing under her nose, and that Honoria was encouraging in her silence, because like Sarah his mother felt he was rushing into fatherhood as a crude attempt to present himself as a devoted, loving husband who couldn't wait to start a family. It was a charade which should have embarrassed him, but he knew his mother considered him lacking any sense of shame.

Sarah sneered. 'Do as you wish. You will anyway. Now help me up. I'm going to bed.'

He pulled her gently onto her feet and saw her upstairs. She didn't bother to enquire whether he was going to The Club or if he would be joining her later, as she had long since ceased caring whether Michael came to the marital bed or not.

He returned to his mother and helped himself to a cognac; half-turning, he offered her the decanter. 'Your support would have been welcome. You couldn't wait to point out that volunteering, doing his duty is the decision that Father would have taken.'

Honoria snorted derisorily. 'Your hypocrisy is staggering!! Suddenly you want to be judged in the same light as your father! A little late, isn't it? Your father would never have left my bed to share one with a servant whore!'

Michael stilled, his anger rising. 'Not this again!' He slammed the brandy snifter against the wall and turned on Honoria. 'I told you I wouldn't have her described thus again.'

'I told you I didn't *care*. Your wife is right: there's no conscription yet, nobody is compelling you into action. You don't get to sully your father's name because suddenly following his example suits your ends. You're volunteering because it suits *you* to do it now. Nobody else!'

'As usual, Honoria, I can rely upon your candour when it suits, but let me remind you that your beloved husband's associates at Argate & Landseer have been very unequivocal about what they expect of me regarding this war. They have let a number of staff who want to volunteer go with their blessing and they expect me to lead by example…'

At that moment Grace Metcalfe appeared, having heard the sound of broken, glass and she moved swiftly to retrieve the scattered shards, but Michael laid a hand on her shoulder. 'Leave it!'

Grace shrugged free of his hand and she looked at Honoria, who gently shook her head, so with a slight curtsey, Grace took her leave.

Michael laughed mockingly. 'The ever-diligent Metcalfe. What an asset she has become!'

'Your sarcasm regarding Grace goes over my head, Michael, so save your breath. You have made your position clear and you *will* do whatever suits you. In war as in peace, the whims of Michael Landseer will be observed!'

Michael had poured himself another cognac and he laughed mirthlessly.

'Would you have preferred I kept postponing my enlistment and they start thinking me a coward or a conscientious objector? Another means for you to draw unfavourable comparisons with Ernest?'

Honoria rose and pulled the cord. Michael half-turned to face her.

'Any lingering hopes I had that you would meet the standards of behaviour your father set have long since passed, Michael. Your conduct since you married that poor girl have convinced me of that.'

'My God! The piety of Honoria Landseer is incredible! If you had really disapproved so strongly of me and the way I conduct myself you could have demanded I leave your home years ago, long before I ever brought Sarah Calloway into it as my wife! So tell me, how is the view from your moral high ground, Mother?'

Michael drained his glass in a single gulp as Grace Metcalfe appeared to attend to Honoria and he treated them to a look of sneering contempt.

In that moment they all heard a huge thump and moments later, he found Sarah lying at the foot of the stairs.

As Grace and Honoria rushed to his side, Michael was transfixed by the sight of his pregnant wife in her nightdress lying at his feet. He didn't know what had compelled the instinct in him to look up, but he had, and fear gripped him as the realisation hit that Sarah must have slipped – and he couldn't understand why she had left her bed as she had been so eager to retire. But if she hadn't then she had been pushed and there was only one member of the household who could have committed such a *heinous* act and that was a reality he didn't want to confront. The other immediate thought which entered his mind was that he couldn't lose their child.

He paced the hospital corridor for what seemed like an eternity.

Just as it seemed like an eternity in getting her to hospital. Sarah had pleaded with him to call Agnes, and when she suspected reluctance on his part, Honoria had insisted on it. For himself he called Aaron Crozier, but his friend was too inebriated to come, so Michael was forced to spend long hours alone in the corridor while they endeavoured to safely deliver his premature child.

Agnes arrived at the maternity wing of the Alfred Hospital as soon as she could and her expression was ashen. Michael had told her Sarah had fallen but nothing more; however, the looks on the faces of the midwifery team didn't inspire confidence that the child would survive. Sarah had been bleeding. There was, however, one certainty Agnes was fixed upon and that was that she blamed Michael for all of this. Their parents were culpable for encouraging Sarah into this sham of a marriage, but there was only one person responsible for the misery, that Agnes knew her sister had *endured* and she wouldn't be swayed in that conviction as she glared at him now.

Michael looked ashen-white but that could just be guilt, Agnes thought as she approached her brother-in-law. She had no respect for him now, but that didn't matter, because if Sarah didn't survive this, she would never forgive him.

'How is she?'

'Fighting to deliver our baby, fighting to survive and become the mother I know she has it within her to be!'

Agnes curled her lip. 'Don't bother with platitudes. I know what my sister is capable of. She will be a superb mother should the child survive. It's a pity you have failed her as a husband, Michael, just as you will probably fail as a father as well!'

Michael bowed his head. At any other time, he would have relished a verbal duel with his sister-in-law, but not now. He was humbled by the enormity of what they now faced as a couple, but it was his fear of what the true scenario was that scared him most, as he could never have believed his lover capable of that. He had seen a glimpse of someone on the landing and it could only have been Yolande, but there was no way he would offer her up as scapegoat without having confronted her first. Agnes could reach whatever conclusions she wanted as he was already damned in her eyes. If the child was too weak to survive he saw no way back for himself and Sarah, and so his anger at Yolande, *if* she had a hand in this, would be *so* all-consuming that there could be no future for them. How ironic then that what she had demanded of him, what he couldn't possibly accede to, would, if she were responsible for this, be what tore them apart, but while there was hope, he would cling to it and let the future take care of itself.

14

The child that Sarah Landseer gave birth to in the early hours of the morning after twenty-eight weeks didn't survive beyond the first fifty hours. Agnes noticed how Michael's interest diminished after being informed Sarah had given birth to a girl. He was a father and yet there was no evidence of joy for him in having a daughter and although he didn't give voice to it, Agnes saw later the expression of relief which passed briefly over his face when the midwife told him the baby hadn't survived the first crucial hours following delivery. Agnes didn't bother to challenge him for the obvious lack of compassion – what would be the point? She only hoped that he would show some remorse for their loss when he went into see Sarah, regardless of how much he had to fake it.

Sarah felt *numb*. It was as if her new-born's mortality had no impact upon her at all and when the midwife consulted Agnes, describing in detail the struggle the child had been up against to survive having been delivered prematurely, it barely registered with Sarah. There were no racking tears of anguish or resentment. Nothing. Had her sister railed against the injustice of it, Agnes would have understood. When she offered to take the trip to Toorak to break the news to their parents Sarah had nodded her acquiescence and Agnes knew that by offering she was lifting a weight from her sister's shoulders.

There was stoic acceptance from them both, although Agnes knew her mother's grief, albeit deftly concealed, was real, but any tears she had would be shed privately. Jensen closed his eyes for what seemed to Agnes like an eternity and then he nodded. He looked at her, eyebrows raised. 'Is your sister coping?'

'She's numb. She's going needs us now. All of us'

Agnes knew there was an irony to her words, as it was only a matter of days now before she could expect to receive her enlistment papers.

Nor she did care whether her father was speculating whether she included Michael in the "us" she had referred to – because she *wasn't*. She had seen for herself that his daughter's death had been a line in the sand for Michael, a pivotal moment in his marriage to Sarah. Although she would continue to bear the name Landseer, as Agnes didn't believe Michael had any desire to make life simple for his wife by setting her free by decree of divorce, Agnes was drawn to the certainty that it would fall upon the Calloways to look after her now.

Michael wasted no time in formally volunteering for action once the funeral was over. His papers arrived swiftly and he would set sail in early May, heading to the Straits of Gallipoli, to which so many Australian volunteers had been deployed since the previous November. Sarah, still feeling emotionally fragile, accepted the news with a weary, dismissive wave and then asked to be excused. He had told his mother that although his actions appeared rushed, he thought it was for the best.

The atmosphere within the household was suffocating for all of them and would be improved by his absence. He didn't expect her to agree but was prepared for her censure.

'You have proved to be a true friend to her, Mother – despite your initial misgivings about our compatibility – and a valuable *ally*. I am sure she values your support.'

'She would have no need of an ally had you the capacity to

be a better husband! She was pushed downstairs, you know. She believes it and I am convinced that your servant whore caused your daughter's death.'

Michael's expression darkened as he poured himself a cognac. Half-turning from Honoria, he marshalled his temper, as he didn't want the atmosphere to deteriorate further through another pointless quarrel with his mother about Yolande. He had his suspicions, but he would keep them to himself.

'You have proof of that?'

'No, but my instincts are usually right when it comes to her. She was jealous. Maybe she felt threatened by the baby. That it would bring you and Sarah closer together, thus driving a wedge between you and *her*. Yolande is a fool in many ways, of course, but she has cunning! An instinct for survival, for protecting her best interests. I believe her capable of such a wicked act, and if you looked beyond her obvious attributes and the primal *urges* they unleash within you, I daresay you would also think her capable!'

'There is little point in my attempting to defend her, as you will always think the worst of Yolande Smith, even if there was no doubting her innocence!'

'Which there isn't!' Honoria stated calmly.

Michael half-turned. He feared that once he had been deployed – probably before he had left Melbourne – Honoria would dismiss Yolande and she would be lost to him forever.

He had seen the look Agnes gave him in the hospital corridor and she had known that his desire to see his child survive the crucial hours after its premature birth had been dependent upon it being a boy. Although she had kept her silence, his sister-in-law had doubtless condemned him to hell once again. If his *lust* or love – however it should be described – for Yolande condemned him to hell, then he could accept that fate willingly, as he realised the prospect of losing her forever left him feeling raw inside.

15

The first surprise Agnes was confronted with on reporting for duty on the first day of her transfer from Alfred Hospital was that Sister Freda Lomax had decided, after much reflection, to follow her example in volunteering for nursing at the Front. Her years of experience would be invaluable and although the board at the Alfred were sorry to see her go, they applauded her commitment to the cause and for wanting to utilise her skills where they were needed most. Agnes was a little perturbed as she never knew what to make of Sister Lomax. Stern and impenetrable sometimes but also quietly encouraging. The news that she was also going to be promoted to matron for the term of her service didn't come as a surprise, adding authority which Agnes knew the sister took in her stride. With a rueful smile, she knew this would present a challenge to some nurses whose commitment to the vocation Sister Lomax had reason to doubt. The sight of another colleague reporting for duty cheered Agnes considerably more and she embraced Nurse Laryssa Nicoledes warmly. She was of Greek descent, darkly attractive with jet black hair and eyes that were expressive brown pools. Agnes suspected Laryssa was going to capture many a soldier's heart. She had a sweet, engaging smile but was quiet by nature, so it had taken time during their training for Agnes to earn her trust. She didn't doubt Laryssa had the temperament to cope with the horrors they had been advised to expect and she hoped they might be deployed together.

Nurse Elizabeth Whitman, by contrast, was skittish and overly obsessed by men. She had exasperated the senior staff during training and Sister Lomax had struggled to retain her mask of inscrutability when she learnt that Nurse Whitman had volunteered, urging her staff to watch her like a hawk. Agnes didn't believe that she had much in common with Nurse Whitman and saw no reason to develop any bond of friendship with her.

She would remain polite and friendly to Whitman, even though she found her incessant chatter about which medic would emerge as the most potential suitor irritatingly juvenile. When she noticed Nurse Whitman scrutinising her on numerous occasions during their first day, Agnes was curious as to why she was the target, wondering if she was being sized up as competition. Sensing trouble, she determined to distance herself from Nurse Whitman's circle of influence as much as possible.

They were billeted in a central Melbourne hotel the night before departure for Port Albany, and typically Nurse Whitman was groaning about the imposed curfew which prevented her from spending the night with her latest *beau*, whom many of her new colleagues suspected would be dropped should a better prospect from the medical corps catch her eye.

Agnes was keen to see her sister prior to departure and had sent a telegram to arrange a farewell. Sarah was still feeling emotionally fragile, and Michael's decision to formalise his enlistment so soon after their daughter's funeral hadn't helped. She received a reply acceding to her plan and Sarah hoped Agnes wouldn't mind Honoria coming with her.

Smiling ruefully, Agnes felt a little uneasy as she read Sarah's reply when Sister Lomax led her aside.

'I am relying on you with some of the younger recruits, Calloway. I see you have formed an attachment to Nurse Nicoledes, which is encouraging, as I am not sure about how emotionally robust she is...' Sister looked around the large dining room and continued, 'As for the ubiquitous Nurse Whitman I am despairing already, sadly. I can only hope that the physical realities of what she is likely to witness will somehow soften her demeanour.'

'I agree she has developed an unrealistic perception of what she is likely to experience.'

Sister Lomax nodded. 'That is *an* understatement. So far, based on what I have seen and heard is that she views it all as a potential husband-hunting market, and that *she* considers herself as the prize catch they are all seeking to secure.'

Agnes smiled, although she felt slightly awkward at being singled out by the sister, whose promotion she had been informed would be officially announced on board the ship as they left Port Albany, and she knew that she should take it as a compliment that her opinion was valued.

'So I can rely on you, Nurse Calloway? To be a steadying influence on some of our younger volunteers?'

Agnes half-nodded. She wondered sometimes if Sister Lomax looked at her as having an old head on young shoulders and whether that was to her advantage. She also knew however that Sister Lomax was sparing in her praise, so she must have earned her confidence.

'I cannot guarantee that we shall be deployed together, Calloway, but I will use whatever influence I have to see that we are.'

Agnes looked across at Nurse Whitman, wondering how she might react to taking orders from her, and it amused her. Turning back to Sister Lomax, she nodded. 'Of course.'

Sister Lomax nodded and, patting Agnes's arm, she took her leave.

Agnes looked back at Nurse Whitman; she could hear her bitching about something in the background. There had to be some benefits to being singled out and winning the sister's confidence and if keeping Nurse Whitman in close scrutiny was one of them, she smiled at the realisation of how much satisfaction that gave her.

The Officers' Bar, Melbourne Barracks – Same Evening

Captain Tyson Mallory had been watching Second Lieutenant Michael Landseer all evening and he had decided that he didn't much like what he saw. What irked him more was that he could hear Landseer above the din. Mallory had discovered from a steward that another officer had signed Michael in; however, Mallory's view was that Landseer saw this gesture as his right rather than as a privilege and that he wouldn't have gained admittance had it been up to him. His perception of men like Lieutenant Landseer was not favourable and he was the type that he struggled to engage with.

'That Landseer chap has a very high opinion of himself. He *is* talking as if he is going to trounce the enemy all by himself. What do you know about him?'

Lieutenant Nichols, who had known Mallory for years, smiled. Leaning in, he said, 'I believe he is from the banking world. His father, Ernest Landseer – now deceased – was a partner who helped establish the Melbourne-based bank. He was acquainted with a friend of mine.'

'Who was that?'

'Eugene Crozier. I haven't seen much of him in recent years. His son, who has also volunteered, and Landseer are close friends; however, I am not sure who signed them in Tyson, but we will have to discourage whoever it was from repeating the error…'

Mallory smiled, shaking his head as he summoned the steward to order another round.

They received instructions that they would leave for Port Albany the following morning, from where the hospital ship would take them on the first leg of their journey across the Indian Ocean to Durban, South Africa. Agnes was hoping that Sarah and Honoria would arrive before she had to leave Melbourne and thankfully they did, as she didn't want to leave Australian soil without seeing that her sister was at least showing signs of physical recovery, although Agnes knew the emotional scars relating to her loss would take longer. She received news they were waiting for her in the lobby and Agnes saw that although Sarah still looked perilously thin, her complexion was not as pale as it had been the last time they met. When Sarah spoke it was in a neutral tone and she was acutely aware of the awkward look that Agnes exchanged with Honoria.

They exchanged pleasant conversation for a few minutes and Agnes was conscious of the effort she was making to avoid mentioning her brother-in-law but was surprised that Honoria showed no inclination to mention him even in the most casual way. The conversation had a jaded edge to it which Agnes knew instinctively was making them feel uncomfortable, so she embraced Sarah, kissing her on both cheeks before offering her hand to Honoria.

'Look after her!' she said with more firmness than she imagined she might ever have used in talking to Honoria, and she received a curt nod.

She knew from Sarah that Honoria had felt ashamed by Michael's treatment of her and although that didn't absolve her in Agnes's eyes, she was grateful that Sarah could rely on her mother-in-law as an ally in the weeks ahead, especially while their parents seemed so absorbed in the evolving issue of the loan from Argate & Landseer. She treated Sarah to a vibrant smile which was meant to speak volumes for how much she meant to her, but Sarah's smile was weak, evidently a reflection of what she felt inside. Agnes wondered in that moment whether Sarah had given any thought to the enormity of what *she* was taking on by volunteering and what the worst possible outcome could mean. Their parents knew, because Agnes had seen it in her father's eyes at least. However, it had remained unspoken, but Sarah was still too overwhelmed by her sense of grief to give much thought to the reality of what might befall *her*.

She watched them take their leave, feeling the weight of anxiety wash over her as myriad thoughts flooded through her about how much more anguish Sarah would have to *endure* before she got to see her on home soil again. So there was a new sadness as she headed to ride the lift back to her room.

Standing at the guard rail of the hospital ship as they moved slowly out of Port Albany, Agnes was struck by the impact her last meeting with Sarah had on her. Matron Lomax had kept her busy the previous evening after she had shared the news of her promotion from sister with all the nursing staff assembled earlier than previously planned, and Agnes had also endeavoured to placate Laryssa Nicoledes when she was struck by a late surge of homesickness which had helped Agnes in forcing her own eleventh-hour doubts aside. She was diverted from her thoughts suddenly by the pleasant male voice of the young man whom she had seen edging his way through to stand beside her and who was now offering her his hand. There was something vaguely familiar about him, and he possessed a natural charm.

'It's Ashworth. Dr Lennox Ashworth, to be precise.'

'Hi, I am Agnes – Nurse Calloway.'

'I know, although the vague looks that you are giving me confirm you don't remember me, which is excruciatingly embarrassing – although not surprising, as I only allowed myself to be bullied into accompanying my mother to three, maybe four of your parents' annual pre-Christmas soirees, and on those occasions your attentions were directed elsewhere. I only agreed to attend to please my mother, as my father *loathed* such occasions and she liked to ingratiate herself as a means to getting better acquainted with those that she considered to be in a position to assist her ambitions, volunteering for good causes. *Your* mother provided the inspiration to mine.'

Agnes laughed slightly, realising it was she that should be embarrassed as she had no recollection of him at any of her parents' soirees, and the fact that her attention was probably being wasted on Michael Landseer made her feel worse.

'I am sorry. So you eventually found reasons not to attend?'

Lennox Ashworth nodded. 'Yes, very valid ones. My medical studies. I think my mother reasoned that having a son who was training to be a doctor gave her sufficient *kudos* in Melbourne society. Although she continued to attend every year.'

'I must have known her. My mother was always very keen for me to meet the guests she considered to have the most worth.'

'Constance Ashworth,' he supplied, and Agnes smiled politely.

'I know. No more to be said.' He offered his hand again, this time more forcibly, and Agnes took it just as the ship lurched slightly as it cleared the harbour and they left Australian soil behind to embark on their noble cause – definitely – but *still* a journey into an *uncertain* future.

16

Troop Ship to Gallipoli – May 1915

Captain Tyson Mallory always took pride in the fact that he had the respect of the men who served under his command but that he did so with a gruff demeanour which had served him well over many years. He had, however, developed an almost instant dislike of Second Lieutenant Michael Landseer. He couldn't explain or rationalise the fact that his dislike had swiftly turned to a strong antipathy as the sea voyage across the Indian Ocean progressed. He had no reason to cast doubt on the banker's abilities as a soldier as they had not yet been tested, but he resented the fact that Landseer was such a poor loser at cards, and he recalled his arrogant boasting in the officers' lounge in Melbourne prior to sailing. Mallory was of the view that as Second Lieutenant Landseer wasn't very good at cards he should cut his losses, as his friend Aaron Crozier was urging him to do, but as it was the idea of losing which irritated Landseer more he kept on, signing chits as IOUs, while remaining convinced that with a couple of decent hands, he might recoup some of his losses.

Mallory was considerably more skilful as a poker player and Aaron saw his friend's anger rising most evenings as his losses mounted. Michael confessed to Aaron privately that Honoria had been incandescent when he wired her for funds to be released upon his arrival in Durban to settle his debt to Mallory.

'I did *urge* you to go careful when your losses were moderate and *still* manageable, but alas, you wouldn't take heed,' Aaron pointed out as subtly as he could.

Michael Landseer banged his fist on the table and said, 'I'm not playing to manage my losses. I want to take Mallory.'

'Well, that is unlikely to happen. He's a better card player than you and I'm guessing you need to hide your thoughts better. He can read you when you have a half-decent hand which is how you enjoy some wins but ultimately you end up losing more.'

Michael's expression darkened. 'Are you prepared to lend me some stake money for tonight?'

Aaron hesitated, so Michael put a hand on his friend's shoulder. 'No?' He gave Aaron a questioning eyebrow, his expression darkening when Aaron hesitated. 'In which case you can keep your advice.'

Aaron looked around him, feeling slightly embarrassed, but he knew from whispers he had overheard that Michael wasn't winning many new friends and most of the men probably didn't know why he *still* bothered, and that was a sentiment he was coming to share, even though they had been friends for many years. He knew all too well that Michael could be his own worst enemy when he chose to, and growing up as an only child hadn't helped. Michael had been over-indulged. He wasn't particularly clubbable, and it didn't surprise Aaron that when the men gathered around the card table in the saloon to watch Mallory taking on Michael at poker, it was the captain they were cheering on.

When another second lieutenant pulled Crozier aside, urging him to advise Michael to quit, Aaron threw up his arms in surrender. 'I have tried. It's getting personal with him now and all the support there is for Captain Mallory just makes him more determined. I fear he is prepared to lose even more to *prove* his point.'

The second lieutenant shook his head sadly as he walked away, and Aaron stopped a steward to order a drink, unaware that Lieutenant Nichols was standing behind him.

By the time the ship reached Durban, Michael's losses were excessive and his request for additional funds were met with mounting disdain by Honoria, but she had little choice but to accede. She pointed out that he had a wife to support who was still grieving the loss of their child, but when Michael read this he screwed the telegram into a ball and tossed it aside. Aaron was still prepared to share a drink with his friend despite Michael's sullen looks and his short temper, but he had given up on attempting to caution him about his losses. It was as if the moment the troop ship had left Port Albany Michael Landseer had reverted to being a carefree bachelor again.

Hospital Ship

Agnes Calloway was, in contrast to her brother-in-law, winning friends and admirers on board, and as they left Durban, her burgeoning friendship with Dr Lennox Ashworth was attracting attention and some green-eyed envy from Nurse Elizabeth Whitman. Matron Lomax had reiterated several times that Agnes was a nurse that she had confidence she could rely upon in a crisis and she was keen to *stress* to all the volunteer nurses of varying experiences that they would experience numerous crises once they were deployed to the Front. A long-time colleague and friend of Matron Lomax of Irish descent named Sister Bryan began taking notice of her, and Agnes confessed that she found the scrutiny *unnerving* as it was unwarranted. Sister Bryan had no reason to feel threatened by or jealous of her, nor did she believe she was actively courting Matron Lomax's praise, but when she saw Nurse Whitman having a quiet word with Sister Bryan, she immediately sensed trouble.

Although she welcomed Dr Ashworth's attention and discovered she had the skills and inclination for some casual flirting, she was careful to be discreet. She was content to let Nurse Whitman continue being the most adept at drawing attention to herself, and while she was prepared to encourage Dr Ashworth's interest it wouldn't be to the detriment of her career.

He joined her at the guard rail one evening as the sun was beginning to dip below the horizon, a bright red orb. The breeze had caught her hair and it looked different in the fading of the sun. He lit a cigarette, offering one to her. Agnes shook her head and, looking past him, she saw Elizabeth Whitman throwing her a cold look. Lennox half-turned and smiled as Whitman disappeared from view.

'I think she is another of your admirers and that gives her another motive to despise me.'

Lennox shrugged his shoulders. 'I met many nurses like Whitman during my training and invariably they earn the disdain of the matron and sister they are reporting to. I suspect her greatest talent is for drawing attention to herself and that rarely works in their favour.'

'She makes no secret of the fact that her main ambition is to bag herself a husband, so you had better be careful around her.'

'I will. Although my lack of interest will speak volumes.'

'So what qualities will you be seeking in a potential wife when you consider the time is right?' Agnes feared that she was being too forward and suddenly she went quiet.

Lennox sensed the change of mood and reached for her hand, which she swiftly withdrew from the rail.

'What is it?'

'I didn't mean to ask you that, I thought you would think me intrusive.'

Lennox smiled and it reached his eyes. She had come to love his smile and that realisation caused her to blush.

'Not at all. We were discussing Nurse Whitman's eagerness to find herself a husband, so it wasn't entirely inappropriate. To be honest, it's not a subject I have given a lot of thought. My mother, whom I told you about *en route* from Albany, was flushed with pride about me training to become a doctor and she insisted I focus upon that *until* I had passed. Girls, or young women, were definitely off the agenda. I frankly dread to think how far her efforts would go in the matching stakes should she ever put her mind to it.'

'So none of those nurses you met during training ever caught your eye?'

Lennox exhaled heavily on his cigarette before flicking the butt over the rail. He turned fully to gaze at Agnes and she felt the force of his scrutiny.

'That would be telling, Nurse Calloway, but I can say with some confidence that there are none that I can remember *so* vividly as the girl that I *so* wanted to approach – and doubtless would have, but for my nerves – at her parents' soirees in Toorak, and who is as attractive now as I remember her then.'

Agnes blushed again, only more deeply. To have doubted the sincerity of his words would have been disingenuous. She believed them very strongly and the depth with which they had been spoken scared her.

She put the back of her hand against her mouth to stifle a sob and she could see his expression darkening for fear that he had offended her, but to the contrary: he had excited her in ways she had never experienced before, and in that respect, she feared herself more than she could fear him. Gazing out to sea, she wondered if he was going to kiss her, and she hoped for and feared the gesture all at once. Lennox was nervous as well, because he feared he had said too much in one evening and that some of it couldn't be taken back without over-complicating the ease they had found with each other. The truth was, he didn't know her much at all. She was a face from his past, and it shocked him how suddenly he so wanted her to become a part of his future – at least in the short term – as they were both steering into a venture the fate of which was unknown.

He took her hand, held it gently and gazed once more into the depth of her eyes. 'Goodnight, Nurse Calloway.'

Agnes smiled at the formality. 'Dr Ashworth.' She pulled her hand free, turning from the intensity of his gaze. He had decided against a kiss when for a moment it had seemed to her inevitable that he would. They had shared a moment tonight which had been mutually understood without words, but Agnes was unsure of how she wanted to proceed. She knew that she liked him, but she had known ever since Michael Landseer had rejected her for Sarah that she didn't need a man to help define her, and she regretted ever having set so much import to her marriage prospects.

Liking Lennox Ashworth in that way was *so* easy, but it held dangers, as they could be separated by their deployment when they docked in Alexandria. Matron Lomax had made it clear she wanted *her* to work close to wherever she was going to be deployed and that could mean separation from Lennox for the duration of the war. To place so much faith in a relationship as yet untested – which fate could yet conspire to hamper – would be a serious error of judgement. She had vowed to herself in her bedroom suite in Toorak one December night seventeen months ago that she would never put so much faith in such a future again.

17

Although Matron Freda Lomax was slightly intrigued by the swiftness with which the attraction between Nurse Calloway and Dr Ashworth became apparent, she was not unduly concerned by it. She definitely gave no heed to Nurse Whitman's attempt at gossip which was designed to cause trouble for Agnes, as she knew instinctively that Nurse Whitman was motivated by jealousy alone. Her friend and confidante Sister Bryan confessed to being less impressed by the developing relationship; however, the matron advised her that placing too much faith in anything that Nurse Whitman might impart to her would be an error of judgement for someone with her years of experience. Sister Bryan acceded to her friend's judgement. Matron Lomax did agree to speak to Agnes at the sister's urging but only because she wanted Agnes to be aware that a colleague was seeking to cause conflict where she believed none existed.

'It has come to our attention, Nurse Calloway, that you appear very friendly with Dr Lennox Ashworth. I can only guess that given the strength of your friendship that you knew him previously?'

Agnes smiled. 'Yes. He remembers me from some social gatherings my parents hosted prior to him commencing his medical studies. Alas my memory of him from that time isn't as strong.'

'Well, no matter. You appear to have renewed your acquaintance with each other on board. I know I have no need to doubt your professionalism, Nurse Calloway, but I feel obliged to advise discretion *and* some caution. There are some among us who require little motivation to court conflict where none exists.'

Agnes smiled and Matron Lomax nodded. 'You can go, Nurse Calloway.'

Agnes nodded to the matron and Sister Bryan as she took her leave, and Matron Lomax stood to replace her files. Sister Bryan stood beside her with pursed lips.

'What's the matter? I spoke to her as you urged that I should. So I hope your confidence in my judgement hasn't been dimmed. I understand your reservations because you don't know Agnes Calloway as well as I do and you want to reserve judgement about her competence as a nurse until you have seen her in action, but if my years of experience count for anything your trust will be rewarded in her case. Alas, I cannot have the same confidence in the person whom I suspect brought the relationship to your attention. It was Elizabeth Whitman?

Sister Bryan nodded. She admitted to not having taken to Agnes and she couldn't explain why as yet she didn't share Freda Lomax's confidence, but she knew her friend's instincts were very sound from the many years they had worked together. As for Nurse Whitman, she was unlikely to trust her again.

'So you are convinced my source was motivated by jealousy?'

'Definitely. I speak from experience in her case. I realise this has been a long voyage and the nurses under our charge are bound to have become restless by the tedium. So I hope now, Kathryn, that the matter is at rest.'

Sister Bryan nodded.

'I have been informed we shall be docking at Alexandria in a couple of days and soon after the deployment of nursing and medical staff will begin. I have mentioned to Nurse Calloway that I would like to have her in my team, wherever it is that I am to be working, and as I will obviously use what little influence I have to canvass for you to be there with me, I trust that should my efforts to secure Nurse Calloway services be successful it won't present a problem?'

Matron gave her friend a quizzical eyebrow and Sister Bryan bowed her head. 'No.'

'Good. Because we are going to face many challenges at the Front, which will test our nursing skills to the limit and in an environment they have never been tested before. I have no endurance and less time for petty rivalries that serve neither us nor the patients any advantage. This is *not* the place for egos.'

Sister Bryan nodded as she took her leave, feeling slightly chastened.

Had it been Nurse Whitman alone who had given her reason to question Nurse Calloway, she would have given it less consideration, but she had heard word in Durban from one of the lieutenants that Agnes Calloway could, when it suited her, be emotionally demonstrative, highly combative to authority and even sly. She wasn't sure if her source knew this for a fact or they were speaking from experience or perhaps they had only heard it second-hand, but the lieutenant had pointed her out in a crowd on the dockside at Durban and she had taken him at his word.

When Dr Lennox Ashworth was invited by a senior medical officer to explain the nature of his developing relationship with Nurse Calloway, he was less sanguine about it, as he resented the intrusion into his private business and was tempted to tell the MO to mind his own business. However, mindful that he was hoping for the best possible deployment upon arrival in Alexandria, he held his tongue. He had reconciled himself to the probability that he and Agnes would be deployed in different locations, however much he hoped they might be working together, and thus he saw no purpose in antagonising his medical superiors unduly. He also placed the blame for them being the subject of idle gossip on Nurse Whitman.

When he met Agnes at the guard rail the evening of his meeting, he was still mad and indicated as much as he lit them both a cigarette.

Agnes laughed. 'Perhaps we are courting further gossip being together now?'

Lennox nodded as he handed her the cigarette. 'Admittedly. I don't care, so I hope you don't…?' On her shake of her head, he added, 'A damned cheek, that dressing-down, because that is what it amounted to. Never mind this "clarification of the nature of our relationship" nonsense. It's prying. I told them we had a friendship and I *stressed* the word. It's a strong friendship born out of previous association but I had to remind him that I am totally professional and so are you. It's that damned Nurse Whitman and her jealousy we have to thank for this… *humiliation!*'

Agnes nodded as she exhaled on her cigarette. As she could see how furious Lennox was, she felt reluctant to admit that she hadn't come out of her meeting feeling so chastised, but like Lennox she believed that Elizabeth Whitman had crossed a line with her juvenile jealousy and she wasn't inclined to forget that.

Lennox turned from her and, resting his arms on the rail he looked out to sea. 'I guess we were always likely to be deployed separately, but this nonsense will make that certain.'

Agnes smiled. 'Matron Lomax told me before we left Australia that she hoped I would be working under her supervision. I think that's why she felt obliged to heed Sister Bryan's concerns. I have seen Whitman trying to take the sister into her confidence, after seeing us together'

Lennox shrugged. Gripping the rail, he allowed his frustration to dissipate then flicked the cigarette butt into the sea.

'As far as she is concerned, I am monopolising your time, which you could be devoting to her so that she can regale you with her qualities as a potential wife. Nurse Whitman isn't so much a husband hunter as a ruthless bird of prey.'

Lennox Ashworth laughed. 'I shall consider myself warned. Although I could make it clear that she is wasting her time.'

Agnes shook her head. 'Sadly, I don't think she would see it that way, and it's likely to antagonise her, thus motivating her to bring *us* – you – even more trouble.'

Lennox looked at her keenly, wondering why she had rushed to correct herself. Surely he hadn't read her wrong? That she was as keen as he to see where and how far their relationship could go?

'I see your point.' He nodded and, half-turning, he gazed out to sea.

'Are you sure she holds no appeal for you? I can see her appeal to the male species, even though she is *too* obvious. There's no challenge for a man in pursuing her. She reminds me of someone I knew in Melbourne who made baiting me at social gatherings a kind of occupation. She may have had you in her sights at one of my parents' soirees that you attended with your mother.'

Lennox turned and leaned his back against the rail, exhaling on his cigarette. He sighed heavily. 'I think we have wasted enough time this evening on Nurse Whitman.'

Agnes smiled as he leaned closer and for a moment in the diminishing light of the setting sun, she thought he was going to kiss her, which she thought would be viewed as a gesture of provocation by those who chose to attach too much importance to a relationship that she was as yet uncertain about, added to which, she couldn't claim to know how she might feel about him kissing her.

A kiss that appeared like an act of possession of branding her as his went against her instinct and she knew Lennox felt sufficiently angry with today's events to be riled into such a gesture that she was not yet ready for.

He pulled away and the moment was lost. She felt relieved. She wanted his kiss when the time was right, not for it to be motivated by his anger.

'If the venture we have embarked upon as medical professionals has taught me anything, Agnes, it's that we cannot wait for tomorrow. Because for some of the poor souls we are likely to treat at the Front, there will be no tomorrow!'

Agnes gulped. She couldn't deny the veracity of his words nor have any doubts about the intent with which he had said them, and yet she still felt he was moving faster than her instinct told her to go; it was scary to think she may risk losing him by holding back. He looked at her again, his hand under her chin as the last glow of the sun caught her hair, the breeze whipping it up. He brushed it aside with his free hand and Agnes glimpsed the intensity within him. There was no doubt that Lennox Ashworth had known what he wanted in life for many years.

He had the self-confidence to make it happen. Professionally he had achieved, yet until recently she'd had no idea of any career path she had wanted to pursue. Now it appeared that he *wanted* her and that he was ready to lay his cards upon the table and gamble on making his claim. She felt she should say something, but when his brows pleated in confusion, she glimpsed a flash of... what? Impatience or perhaps anger? He leaned in and kissed her gently on the forehead instead of the devouring, passionate kiss he had wanted to give her, and when she remained silent in response to his questioning look, he cursed gently under his breath and walked away.

18

Captain Tyson Mallory sat on the hotel terrace as the sun was setting, a bright crimson orb, and regaled the company, which usually gathered around him in the evening – a mixture of fellow officers and nursing staff. The conversation invariably revolved around his life prior to military service, as the son of a Queensland stockman. He revelled in being the centre of attention and although Matron Lomax thought him an affable chap and acceptable company for the last hour of the day before retiring, she didn't take much of what he said at face value.

Agnes, who had been invited as the matron's guest along with Dr Lennox Ashworth, sat apart from Mallory and his group; however, both were keen to be included in plans to visit the historic landmarks of Cairo before they were deployed elsewhere.

Agnes had heard rumours, second-hand, that she might be sent to the tented hospital on the island of Lemnos, which most nursing recruits dreaded as the conditions there were rumoured to be the most basic, but Matron Lomax had tried to reassure her that she was doing as much as her authority allowed to keep her in Alexandria.

Agnes couldn't help wondering if there were other forces at work determined to thwart Matron Lomax in her efforts. For tonight, however, she had resolved not to fret about something that ultimately she couldn't control. She had expressed some concern regarding deployment to Dr Ashworth but found him lacking in offering her a positive vibe, added to which she had found his distance towards her since they left the ship at Alexandria irksome, so when he announced that he was accepting the challenge of a frame or two of snooker, she gladly saw him go, remaining at the balustrade but away from Captain Mallory's attentive group of admirers.

The teeming sounds of the city at night were fascinating to her and she stood at the balustrade alone for what seemed like an eternity. When she heard footsteps behind her, she half-turned, hoping it would be Dr Ashworth, but was startled to find Captain Mallory standing behind her, his cigar mingling with the aromas of the city. She looked at him and smiled. He was good-looking in a rakish manner; his jaw was firm, although his moustache looked as if it could do with a trim, but his eyes – although they twinkled as he returned her smile, she was certain they could contain more than a hint of menace when the occasion demanded it. She didn't know why she was making so many mental notes about his appearance but attributed it to feeling nervous at his sudden proximity and wishing that either Lennox or maybe the matron would come swiftly to her rescue.

Nor did she doubt Captain Mallory had female admirers and he would likely meet more during the war, but Agnes was certain he did nothing for her romantically speaking and wished that he could respectfully keep his distance. She was ambivalent to his charms, and although she acknowledged that to some men reticence represented a challenge, she was determined to remain so.

'Could I get you a drink?' he offered, in a voice that was slightly gruff.

Agnes shook her head as he offered his hand for her to shake.

'Captain Mallory.'

'I know. You have been pointed out to me.'

'So my reputation precedes me *again*.'

Agnes smiled, suspecting it was a reputation that he was more than content to bask in.

'I don't merit an introduction, Nurse Calloway?'

Agnes turned to him with a saccharine sweet smile. 'The fact that you made a point of knowing who I was prior to coming over negates the need for, one Captain Mallory.'

Tyson rocked on his heels, smiling. He liked a woman with spirit and he could see that Nurse Calloway had some.

'Touché.' He took a long gulp of Scotch and, moving closer, he placed the glass on the stone balustrade. Agnes could feel his breath in her ear and she longed for a means of escape, which it appeared his move had denied her. She didn't know how many glasses he'd downed this evening, but it was evident how he imbued too many, and *she* expected better from a man of his rank.

He exhaled heavily on his cigar, and the blue-grey smoke drifted into the inky blackness of the sky as Agnes turned, seeking another route of departure, as he moved closer, his arm snaking out to her lower back.

'I have heard rumour, Nurse Calloway, that Second Lieutenant Landseer is your brother-in-law?'

Agnes blushed; she wasn't certain quite how he had come by the information, but she saw no point in denying it.

'Well, we all have our crosses to bear, Captain Mallory.'

Tyson Mallory laughed. 'Indeed, Nurse Calloway, and unfortunately for me, my particular cross to bear with Lieutenant Landseer comes in the shape of a wallet full of IOUs.'

Agnes smiled uneasily. She could tell by the derisory curl of his lip that Michael had made a similarly poor impression on Captain Mallory, but that was their problem; all she wanted was for the captain to move aside and let her pass. Instead, she found his left hand resting on her hip as he pulled her to him. Although she writhed against his hold, she felt trapped as her chest met the bulk of his. She struggled again but was trapped between him and the balustrade as he held her tight.

'You are a feisty little *minx*, aren't you? I imagine your sister must have been very alluring if Landseer was prepared to let you slip.'

As Agnes continued to struggle against his hold, she hadn't seen Lennox's return to the terrace or that Matron Lomax and Sister Bryan had also been alerted by the sound of voices.

'I assure you that Lieutenant Landseer was not worthy of having my sister as his wife any more than he would have been having me. I also think that you have neglected your manners, Captain Mallory, in your conduct towards me.' She pushed against him then as Captain Mallory struggled to retain his balance.

'Let her go, Mallory!'

They turned to look in Lennox's direction as he crossed the terrace in a couple of angry strides. Captain Mallory retrieved his glass of Scotch from the balustrade and turned to Lennox, his laughter mocking.

'Here comes Dr Ashworth! Your "*Sir Galahad*" in khaki! I think she is definitely worthy of your gallantry, medic!'

At this moment Captain Mallory saw his good friend Lieutenant Horace Nichols – or "*Horatio*", as he invariably referred to him – emerge from the shadows, shaking his head slowly. Captain Mallory turned angrily back to Agnes. He was not inclined to lose face among his men. Agnes took a long, deep, steadying breath, trying to rationalise whether Lennox's intervention made matters better or worse for her; she knew only that it went against her instinct for independence and she couldn't easily forgive that.

'It isn't necessary for you to involve yourself, Dr Ashworth. There was a misunderstanding, but I was handling it!'

Lennox was beyond being angry with her. 'Handling it? From where I stood, he was *mauling* you!'

Agnes blushed deeply and Matron Lomax looked at Captain Mallory with her own sense of dismay, but her instinct told her it was Dr Ashworth who was struggling, evidently conflicted by his feelings for Agnes Calloway.

'It looks like your gallant knight routine has backfired on you, doesn't it, medic? But I suspect that Nurse Calloway might forgive your *faux pas* before she forgives me mine!'

Agnes saw her opportunity to flee, feeling wretched that so many had witnessed the scene that Captain Mallory's conduct had caused, including Matron Lomax and Sister Bryan, which only served to compound her humiliation. She was thankful that Nurse Whitman hadn't been present to see it; however, Lennox's determination to prolong the agony by confronting Captain Mallory was the *finale* she least wanted.

As she reached the edge of the terrace, she felt all eyes were still focused on her as Lennox appeared at her side, grabbing her hand. 'I didn't like the way he was treating you. I think that given our relationship you owe me an explanation for what has taken place tonight. I can see that he is *drunk* and boorish—'

Agnes glared at him angrily. 'Our relationship is what exactly? I don't begin to guess what you believe you are *entitled* to be told, Dr Ashworth – unless you believe that a past acquaintance rekindled on the ship out here is the basis for anything. I don't think I *owe* you anything!'

Lennox let his grip of her hand slip and he leaned closer. 'Did you think I could stand by and not act?'

Agnes could feel the tears, but she refused to shed them. 'Yes,' she hissed. 'That is exactly what I expected, because I am not your *responsibility*!'

Lennox's expression darkened at her words as he took two steps backwards and said, 'In that case I know exactly where I stand, Nurse Calloway, and I bid you goodnight.'

He turned away from her so that she wouldn't see the depth of his hurt, while Agnes, feeling as stunned by the evening's events as by her reaction to them, strode with head bowed into the hotel.

Captain Mallory returned to his table alongside Lieutenant Nichols, who was still shaking his head. He summoned the steward to order another round of drinks, gloating at Lennox's retreating back.

Nurse Calloway's reaction to her self-appointed knight was very intriguing, because he hadn't been deterred by her reaction to his overture. He meant to have her in his bed and he believed that when the opportunity came, she would go to him willingly.

Sister Kathryn Bryan had watched the scene with a mounting sense of dismay, reminding her as it did of the comments made to her about Nurse Calloway on the dockside in Durban which now confirmed her instincts that Nurse Agnes Calloway was not the asset that Freda Lomax believed her to be: she was a magnet for conflict. Shaking her head sadly and basing her argument solely on the evening's events, she had no choice but to risk her friend's censure by warning her that striving to have Nurse Calloway remain alongside them in Alexandria could turn out to be the gravest error of Matron Lomax's distinguished career.

Given Tyson Mallory's rank Dr Lennox Ashworth agonised over whether he should report him to his CO based on what he had witnessed between Mallory and Agnes. He knew he could be risking any chance of repairing his friendship with Agnes and that motivated him not to act rashly more than any fear of falling foul of the military top brass. It was likely Mallory's colleagues would close ranks behind him, and given Agnes's very public rebuttal of *his* intervention, he could appear the troublemaker. He refused to give Mallory the satisfaction.

That fact aside, he couldn't decide which infuriated him more: Mallory's obvious sense of entitlement or Agnes's obsession with female emancipation at all costs, and that in her determination to exert that principle, she had been prepared to refute all that he believed they meant to each other. How could he have read her so wrong?

He still hoped she might open up to him the following evening; however, this opportunity was to be denied him as he was informed she had declared herself sick that day by Sister Bryan, who he could tell by her expression was deeply sceptical of the authenticity of Agnes's claim, although Matron Lomax was satisfied, and he knew enough of the dynamic in their working relationship to know that Sister Bryan wouldn't second-guess the decision.

He knew how eager Agnes was to be included on the trip to see the Sphinx, so when he heard she had offered her place to someone else, he was *so* infuriated that he confronted Captain Mallory.

'Making a nuisance of yourself on Nurse Calloway's behalf again, are you, medic? I thought you would have learnt your lesson after last night's little scene. She didn't appear to appreciate your intervention then, so what makes you think she would welcome it now?'

Mallory smiled; exhaling heavily on his cigar, he blew smoke into Dr Ashworth's face, and while some among the uniformed group guffawed, which Lieutenant Nichols knew instinctively Mallory would construe as encouragement to inflame a situation, he was keen to diffuse it he instructed them to hush.

Dr Ashworth, knowing he was being provoked, stood firm. 'Your conduct towards Nurse Calloway last night was intolerable, as you well know, and I have a mind to report the incident to your CO.'

Mallory shrugged, giving him a rueful look. He paused reflectively as he sipped his Scotch and aggressively jabbed his finger at Ashworth's chest. 'That would be a brave, but foolish step on your part, medic, given our respective ranks, and that what occurred between myself and Nurse Calloway was a misunderstanding. Based on how she reacted to your misplaced sense of valour, I would wager you may have already ruined any chance you may have with her.'

'Rubbish! There was no misunderstanding. You had your filthy paws all over her and she was struggling to get away.'

Mallory's expression darkened as he took a step nearer to Ashworth and he said, 'You have a nasty tongue, Dr Ashworth, and I would advise you to be careful about who you subject it to. We have come out here for a few quiet drinks and as we have no wish to enjoy your company than you have ours, I suggest you take your leave.' Mallory jerked his head in the direction of the bar and Ashworth smiled as the steward brought the tray of drinks. He snatched Mallory's glass of Scotch, and as the uniformed men looked aghast at Dr Ashworth, fearing what he might do, he raised it to Mallory.

'Cheers,' he said, and he took it with him into the lounge bar as Nichols approached Mallory.

'So what was all that about?'

'I think the medic has it really bad for Nurse Calloway and he's not prepared to give her up regardless of how many times she may decline his overtures. Apparently I am to blame for the fact that she is no longer joining us on the trip to see the Sphinx, which I think is a great pity!'

Lieutenant Nichols, shaking his head, said, 'I don't know why you have to bait him so mercilessly, Tyson! Although Dr Ashworth is a subordinate, you may well have to rely upon him to save your life once we are in the field.'

Tyson Mallory shrugged as he resumed his seat, taking another huge lungful of his cigar. 'Well, I hope you are wrong, Horatio, because based on his fury tonight, I fear I might be doomed!'

Lieutenant Horace Nichols had known Tyson Mallory long enough to realise he could be anybody's worst enemy, and he felt no disloyalty in wanting to warn Ashworth of the fact. Prior to their call-up, Mallory had been experiencing major problems in *his* marriage, which he didn't think could survive whatever Mallory's fate in the field of battle. While he despaired sometimes of his friend's methods of letting off steam – last night's confrontation with Nurse Calloway being a good example – he wasn't prepared to condemn his friend, but Nichols was deeply concerned as they sat on the moonlit terrace that the bad blood which existed now between Mallory and Dr Ashworth was a situation that could only get worse and that it didn't bode well for either.

19

The trip to see the Sphinx by moonlight went ahead the following evening as planned, but it wasn't the enjoyable experience that Dr Ashworth had hoped it would be and for him it was due to Agnes Calloway's absence.

He tried once more to persuade her to attend, but she remained resolute in refusing. He saw through the crack in the door, which she'd only opened ajar, that she was already packed for her deployment, confirming that despite Matron Lomax's efforts to keep her in Alexandria, she was to be sent to the tented hospital on the island of Lemnos.

He reluctantly accepted her decision as final and left with a renewed determination to secure his deployment to Lemnos so they could work alongside each other. He knew there would be little Agnes could do by way of objection should that be the outcome and he was convinced their constant proximity would be the only way of mending their relationship, accepting, albeit with some reluctance, that his conduct was the reason behind the fracture.

The taxis were waiting as he reached the entrance of Shepherd's Hotel, and his expression immediately darkened at the sight of Captain Mallory sharing with Matron Lomax,

141

while Lieutenant Nichols joined with Sister Bryan, and junior ranks of military and medical personnel were left to team up as best they could. Ashworth felt he was being punished, finding himself in a taxi alongside Nurse Whitman, whose incessant chatter and eagerness to please him spoiled the trip to see the fabled Egyptian monument. He vowed he would have to see it again sometime with only Nurse Calloway for company.

He discovered the antipathy between Agnes and Elizabeth Whitman was mutual and it ran deep with each of them, as his companion wasted no time in making her feelings known.

'I don't how you can bear to spend so much time with her. She is so aloof!'

Lennox lit a cigarette, obligated to offer one to his companion, which he lit and then saw the glint of mischief in her eyes as she leaned closer to him.

'Not from what I have seen she isn't and her colleagues hold Nurse Calloway in high regard – although I realise not in your case – I know Matron Lomax speaks highly of her abilities.'

He could see her eyes blazing with fury. 'Well, Matron would because she confides in Calloway to be her eyes and ears with the newest volunteers.'

He could tell from the venom in her tone there was no hope in attempting to resolve the hostility between her and Agnes, so he decided to try another tack.

'Is it possible that you have a problem with discipline and *adhering* to authority from whomever it comes, or is your dislike of Nurse Calloway more personal than that?'

He exhaled heavily on his cigarette, watching for her reaction. Her body language betrayed a slight bristle of indignation, but her silence spoke for itself and he hoped she might be awed into silence by the splendour of the Sphinx.

Captain Mallory sat morosely in the taxi alongside the matron. He wasn't smoking his customary cheroot as she had asked him to refrain in the confined space of the taxi, albeit in a gentle tone which brooked no refusal. He did take several discreet sips from a hip flask of Scotch when her attention was diverted, but he was convinced he had a poor choice of companion; however, a rueful glance in Ashworth's direction as they had set off told him he wasn't alone. He had a deep respect for Freda Lomax's nursing and administration skills, but he preferred the company of younger women. His personal life was a mess. His wife Jeanette had never been an easy woman and had it not been for the outbreak of war, he was sure she would have begun divorce proceedings before now. Only Lieutenant "*Horatio*" Nichols knew the truth of his tortured home life and that was why he cut him so much slack, but he had seen how "*Horatio*" had reacted to the imbroglio with the medic Ashworth, and while he could always rely on Nichols's loyal friendship, he knew not to push it too far.

'I hold my nursing staff in high regard, Captain Mallory, and I have been much impressed by Nurse Calloway – to the extent that I fought very hard to keep her working alongside me. Sadly that hasn't been possible, and while I didn't see the whole incident between you and her the other evening on the hotel terrace, I am satisfied by her version of events that it probably was an unfortunate misunderstanding, which corroborates what you have told me. Nurse Calloway asserts very strongly that she didn't encourage your overtures, nor did she welcome them. It *is* an error of judgement that should never *occur* again. Nor will I be *so* tolerant, should you similarly *err* for a second time. Understood?' Matron Lomax raised her eyebrow at him as the Sphinx came stunningly into their line of vision.

Captain Mallory half-nodded, but his expression was solemn. It was all the affirmation she required.

One of the first and most enduring friendships that Agnes made among her fellow nurses during training at the Alfred

Hospital was with Nurse Laryssa Nicoledes, who also hailed from Melbourne. She was of Greek descent and Agnes was struck the first time they met by how very beautiful Laryssa was, with expressive brown eyes and dark raven hair, which seemed to her like it shone as smooth as silk. Laryssa had been born in Australia, after her parents and infant brother had left to make a new life in Australia. So for Laryssa, the prospect of her deployment on Lemnos would be especially poignant, just as her brother Theo serving with the Australian Expeditionary Force on Greek soil was ironic.

'I do hope you will be deployed on Lemnos, Laryssa, so we can work alongside each other, although I understand why that will be hugely significant for you!'

Agnes smiled as she spoke, taking Laryssa's hands in hers. She felt a greater sense of kinship with Laryssa than she had enjoyed with any fellow trainee, and although different, it was closest to the one that she could recall having enjoyed with her sister.

The distance that she had put between herself and Lennox was of her choosing, because she didn't yet feel obliged to forgive him, and that was one of the reasons she had opted to remain at the hotel, watching from the window in her room as the caravan of taxis set off and wondering, despite her desire to remain aloof, whom Lennox had paired off with, knowing that as Nurse Whitman was going – she would view *her* absence as an opportunity.

Laryssa shook her head, smiling as she tightened her grip on the hand Agnes had offered her. She had confessed to feeling homesick as she had never left Australian soil prior to them leaving Port Albany.

'That would be very strange. As I am an Australian by birth, but… we remain Greek in culture.'

Agnes smiled. 'I was hoping to avoid the tented hospital on Lemnos, because of the rumours regarding the conditions there. Now that it has been confirmed, I have accepted it as my fate.'

Laryssa nodded, her brown eyes expressive as she said, 'I am sure you are hoping that Dr Ashworth might also be sent there?'

Agnes found Laryssa's coquettish giggle engaging, but it was a subject she would rather avoid. She had told Lennox along with Matron Lomax that for her, the whole incident on the terrace had been very embarrassing. From Captain Mallory's clumsy pass at her – which she had rebuffed instantly, it being no doubt inspired by the several double Scotches he had consumed – through to Lennox's impulsive intervention, which she still found a hugely patrician gesture, she also had another strong motive for not taking her place on the trip to see the Sphinx.

She had heard some rumours to the effect that her brother-in-law Second Lieutenant Landseer was also planning to go, and confronting Michael was a risk she definitely wasn't prepared to take. In truth it was a trio of male company she could happily do without. She looked away slightly as the stewards, clad in their red tunics and matching fezzes, came out onto the terrace to light the lamps lining the balustrade. Agnes was *so* tired of men who felt they had a claim upon her. No matter how basic the conditions on Lemnos might be, she was going to prove herself, and if she committed herself now, with all that had occurred between them, to a future with Dr Lennox Ashworth – or any man – they would know that *she* would do so *on* her terms or not at all.

20

The Tented Hospital, Lemnos – August 1915

The conditions on Lemnos were as dauntingly basic as Agnes had been warned they could be, and she arrived on the island determined to meet the challenges she was presented with head-on. She was relieved to have her friend Nurse Nicoledes working alongside her, and while Sister Challoner didn't inspire the unswerving loyalty that Matron Lomax could claim, she was approachable and sympathetic to the concerns raised among the nursing staff and orderlies about the conditions in which they were having to work. What surprised Agnes even more was Dr Lennox Ashworth striding into the main ward three weeks after her arrival. She hadn't dared to hope that he might be deployed there and was ambiguous regarding her feelings about him, until she had to confront them again.

It had taken all his powers of persuasion to convince the MOs that he should come to work on Lemnos, as the instinct was to deploy a man of his abilities at the number one Australian hospital in Alexandria, but without *stressing* the personal motive, he argued that as negative rumours regarding the conditions on Lemnos had been circulating for some time, having a doctor volunteering for deployment there might be to their advantage. He eventually told Agnes that he wasn't sure if any outside influence had been exercised to convince them to accede to the deployment he wanted, but she had her doubts given that Matron's efforts to keep her in Alexandria had failed. They had been convinced by his argument and here he was. Her first sight of him in the tented ward provoked mixed emotions within her, but she had not time to dwell on them as his timing coincided with another arrival of wounded men from the Front via the hospital ships and he swiftly got his first taste of triage in a makeshift tented ward, where the sand on Lemnos beach was as much an enemy to sound nursing practice as guns of the Ottoman forces were to the men they had to treat. He looked at Agnes and smiled as she moved swiftly into action, averting her gaze. The patient in front of her was writhing in pain and there was a gaping hole in his left leg, the effects of an enemy bullet, which would have to be removed. She looked at his face, seeing that he looked no more than a boy. She froze momentarily and could barely hear the sound of Dr Ashworth's voice until he jolted her.

'Nurse Calloway?'

She looked up, took a steadying breath and begun to detail the patient's injuries, angry at herself for her reaction. It wasn't as if he were the first fresh-faced adolescent volunteer to be brought into the tented ward and she refused to let herself be swayed by Dr Ashworth's arrival.

At the end of that long shift, which, like many, lasted for ten hours, Agnes was exhausted but relieved they had been able to save so many of the latest intake from the Front, including the adolescent volunteer whose effect on her composure had been so troubling. She had learnt swiftly the imperative of some emotional distancing as a protective armour, as there was so much else to distract them from their focus on the matter at hand; the conditions notwithstanding there was also the problem of medical supplies being sparse at best, which she knew Sister Challoner was fighting an endless struggle against.

She came out onto the beach, which was bathed in moonlight, and within minutes Dr Ashworth was beside her, offering a cigarette.

She took one, gazing intently as he lit it, and then she sighed. 'So why did you *want* to come here?'

'Because I was needed.' Off her look, he nodded, adding, 'And yes, I wanted to be close to you. I am not ready to give up on you, Agnes. I don't know if there will be an *us* – or if there was ever going to be. That is as much your choice as it ever will be mine. For what it's worth now that I have seen your nursing skills in action, I can understand why the matron was so keen to retain your services alongside her, and I know she regretted not having succeeded in that respect. I am sure she wanted you to know that, and she sends her regards.'

Agnes smiled, wondering how much of what he had said were actually the matron's words, but she didn't press him. She was conscious also that she could have extinguished any prospect of a future for *them*, which would have made his determination to work here redundant, but she had not and was aware that he could cling to that fact as some hope, as the silence between them seemed endless.

'I think we all did well today. Has it been like this since you arrived?'

Agnes nodded; she took the last draw on the cigarette and then tossed it onto the sand.

'Some days it's slightly better, but not by much, and the casualties keep on coming and the conditions are against us. Keeping the wards free of infection and the sand out is a constant problem. So with all that I have told you are you still glad that you swapped the fan-cooled wards of Cairo for this?'

He looked at her without speaking and she saw a brief nod in the encroaching darkness. They both knew why he had come to this makeshift tented hospital on a godforsaken stretch of

Greek beach close to the Front, and it had nothing to do with wanting to test himself in the harshest conditions.

'We hear snippets from the wounded as they come in and the offensive isn't going the Allies' way. The Ottoman troops are more resilient than we had expected them to be, and they are as determined to defend the port of Constantinople as we are to take it.'

He ground the butt of his cigarette into the sand and looked at Agnes once more. 'So are some rumours I have heard that some injuries you are called upon to treat are self-inflicted or is that another casualty of war?'

'The truth being the first, you mean?'

'Exactly.'

Agnes shook her head. 'I haven't seen any evidence of self-inflicted wounds, and given the agony I see many of them come to us with, it would be a very drastic act. I am sure the hierarchy would take a dim view if such a case could be proved. Fact is, war is hell, Dr Ashworth, wherever and however it is waged.'

He nodded. 'However, sometimes it is necessary.'

The look that he gave her was laden with intent and she smiled as she bade him, 'Goodnight.' Agnes walked away.

Undressing for bed in the dormitory, Agnes took time to absorb what he had said, along with the subtext of what had been left to hang in the silences between, which had felt so awkward to her and, she was sure, equally for him. There was no doubt his seniors had wanted to deploy him at hospitals in either Cairo or Alexandria and yet, faced with those options, he had fought to be sent to the more primitive conditions on Lemnos, disregarding all the information about how bad it was. Because of *her*. She couldn't deny that was his motive, that he wasn't prepared to give up on the girl that he remembered that he was too hesitant to approach at those formal soirees at her parents' home in Melbourne, but who chance – in the most extraordinary of circumstances in a theatre of war – had brought back to him, if only she would offer him a chink of hope that his efforts and the sacrifice were not in vain. Agnes slept that night with a heavier heart, knowing that although he would give her time, ultimately she would have to trust her instinct that despite all that her experience with Michael Landseer had taught her, this was a chance at happiness that was worth the taking.

21

In the weeks that followed the fighting grew more intense. The Ottoman forces proved as determined as the Allies, who were focused on their mission to defeat them at Gallipoli and then seize the crucial port of Constantinople. The tented hospital on Lemnos was still barely equipped to meet the demands of the wounded men who were brought the sixty kilometres from the front. The quality of nursing care they were able to offer was barely adequate. Fresh water was a luxury and the nurses finished each shift mentally and physically exhausted. While Dr Ashworth had urged Agnes to take her time in responding to him, telling her how strongly he felt, along with the suggestion they should consider letting a formal relationship develop naturally, he began to fret that the longer she waited the less likely it would be that she would give him the acquiescence he sought.

Sister Margaret Challoner was under considerable pressure and it showed. She had come to rely heavily upon her experienced nurses, like Agnes, who could see the level of stress the sister was working under and she feared there would come a moment when she could barely keep her head above water and she would buckle under the strain, leaving them without the leadership they required. Agnes feared she might have overstepped the mark one morning when the strain of doing a night shift and returning to duty on just a few hours' sleep was etched upon the sister's face, the shadows under her eyes being another sign.

'We need a matron here!' She spoke in a more forceful tone than she had intended and Sister Challoner looked at her sharply.

'Why do you say that, Nurse Calloway?'

'Forgive me, Sister, but you are doing the work of two and frankly, you look exhausted. You are doing your best for us *and* supporting the patients, but where is your support?'

Sister Challoner softened her expression, laying a hand on Agnes's arm. 'I know what you mean, Nurse, and I *am* exhausted, but I have no choice. I need my most experienced nurses here during the day when the demand is greatest. I have done every night shift since I was deployed here and try to catch up on sleep sporadically whenever I can. It's not enough, I agree with you.'

Agnes nodded. 'I will do the night shift – no arguments – and you can get a full night's sleep. I will start again tomorrow afternoon. There's no other option, Sister Challoner. Anyone would give way under the strain eventually and then we would be stuck.'

'I can't let you do that, Calloway. You are one of my best nurses. I will cope.'

Agnes shook her head. 'You won't have to. Nurse Nicoledes isn't on duty yet. I know her and we work well together. May I suggest you reassign her to the night shift alongside me? I can coach her while it's quiet and when we have a group of nurses who competently cover the night shift as well as you have been, there will be no need for you to shoulder so many.'

Sister Challoner smiled, as impressed by Agnes's boldness as she was by the suggestion. She nodded. 'OK, I will. Thank you, Nurse Calloway...'

Agnes hadn't noticed Dr Ashworth's appearance at the

end of the ward, and as Sister Challoner made her way in his direction, he smiled. 'Magnificent, isn't she?'

Sister Challoner laughed slightly, but she gave nothing away. 'Nurse Calloway? Yes, she is one of my best, Dr Ashworth, and I intend on keeping her, so don't you act so rashly that you scare her away.'

She pushed the flap of the marquee, pausing to raise a quizzical eyebrow at him, which could also have served as a warning should he choose to see it as such.

Agnes didn't relish the prospect of a night shift but felt that she had no choice. It would be better than an offer of sudden promotion, that she didn't feel ready for, should the sister have fallen sick. She looked down the ward, sensing Lennox's arrival, and she smiled, thinking how dashing he looked with a stethoscope around his neck, in his white coat. She couldn't help wondering how he was coping as one of the junior doctors who had been assigned the night shift on numerous occasions without complaint. He seemed to be coping, though, and based on the morning's evidence, Sister Challoner wasn't.

The Trenches, Gallipoli

Captain Tyson Mallory sat in his dug-out writing letters of condolence to families back home. It was a huge task, with which he struggled constantly to find the right words for each comrade who had fallen without sounding trite. He would gladly delegate it if he could, but that would be abdicating his responsibilities and it didn't sit right with him.

He had felt his confidence with routine matters waning of late and he knew Lieutenant Nichols had noticed because he had been 'nagging' him about it – in a way that only "*Horatio*" could – and know that he would get away with it. He paused and lit another cigarette, which were a poor substitute for his usual

153

cheroots, which he had run out of until his next consignment arrived from Cairo.

He read the last paragraph again in the waning light offered by the paraffin lamp at his side. Making a face, he shook his head and, screwing the sheet into a ball, he tossed it aside. His personal letter home to Jeanette had been an ordeal to write, but he had expected that, given the state of their marriage. There were many things Jeanette believed she needed; his compassion wasn't one of them, but the grieving families of his fallen men did. The Allied losses had been especially heavy in recent days and not just among Australians but New Zealanders and the Canadian volunteers as well. He thumped the small folding table and it wobbled. Damn it! The enemy weren't proving to be a pushover as they had been led to believe, with their sub-standard ammunition gifted them by the Germans. Defending the Straits of Gallipoli and the route to Constantinople was as much an issue of pride for the Turkish forces as it was a military objective to the Allies and thus it would be a fight to see which side could *endure* the most to achieve their objective. Mallory just hoped that for all the losses he had seen, a victory at Gallipoli and the capture of the jewel that is Constantinople would be worth the cost in human life.

He cursed under his breath. What was *wrong* with him? A letter home to a grieving family had sadly become routine, so another one shouldn't get to him like this. He wasn't a man given to introspection, let alone self-pity, even though letters to Jeanette invariably put him in a foul mood. He knew there wasn't anything left to build on with Jeanette now even if either still *wanted* to. He knew that he *didn't*. His priority now was to survive this mess for his own sake, so he could lead his men to some kind of conclusion they could be proud of.

Suddenly, unbidden, his thoughts turned to Nurse Agnes Calloway and he wondered if he might get the chance to apologise, because he recognised he owed her, having behaved quite badly in that respect.

He hoped they wouldn't meet again in a professional capacity and the irony of having the medic Ashworth tend to him was too much.

His trusted grapevine from Cairo told him they had been deployed alongside each other on Lemnos, and that Ashworth had fought to be sent there. Mallory chuckled. Boy! That Ashworth had it bad! He would like to have sampled Nurse Calloway's luscious curves, but he doubted he would have surrendered a relatively 'cushy' deployment in Cairo for the hell that he had been told Lemnos was. He whistled joyfully.

What it must be like to feel that strongly for a woman he had no idea.

Nor had he been tempted to sample the seedy brothels of Cairo and Alexandria, as he had no more appetite for them here than he had in Melbourne, but then, he was no romantic either.

He lit another cigarette and, cursing softly that they weren't his favourite smoke and then reaching for his swagger stick in the dwindling light of the dug-out, he made his way out into the glaring hellfire of the trench.

The Tented Hospital, Lemnos – Late September

As the weeks passed swiftly by summer on Lemnos gave way to autumn, but there was no lull in the intensity of the fighting, nor any sign of a significant breakthrough on either side. Yet casualties remained heavy. Fresh water was still deemed a luxury, and each shift was viewed as something to *endure*. Agnes finished many – both night and day, feeling almost dead on her feet, sometimes so weary she was functioning on instinct. The change in shift pattern had benefited Sister Challoner immensely, but now, she was growing concerned about her staff – Nurse Calloway especially, but when the hospital ship docked with the latest wounded, some only minor, but so many with major, potentially life-changing injuries, the sense of being overwhelmed by the enormity of it confronted them again and *morale*, which always seemed low at best, seemed like it had dipped again.

Agnes didn't know how Dr Ashworth coped with the magnitude and complexity of some of the cases he had to deal with. Amputations were becoming routine, and subtlety and diplomacy were additional skills that nursing staff were expected to have at their disposal. Many of the wounded remained defiant against having their limbs removed until the threat of gangrene was spelt out to them in the harshest of terms.

Late one evening Agnes was ordered to take a break, having worked through her previous two when a new intake of patients was expected, and stepping out of the putrid-smelling tented ward into the fresh breeze which whipped at her hair on the beach, she was startled by the sight of Dr Ashworth also taking a much-needed break. He offered her a cigarette, but she shook her head as he approached. It had been a test of his curiosity up until now not to enquire whether she had yet reached a decision about how she saw her future and whether he had any place in it. Although the endless pressure of work had provided him with a distraction, he still feared that if pushed *too* hard she would turn him down. They stood close to each other listening to the lapping of the waves and trying to ignore the anguished cries from within the marquee.

The moonlight and what little was offered by the paraffin lamps hanging from the tent poles was sufficient for him to see her face, how exhausted she looked, as he reached out, pushing random strands of hair from her eyes.

'You're OK?' he asked, and was thankful that in the darkness, she probably couldn't see him grimace, because he knew how inane his question was, although typical of the choreography they did around the subject. They needed more time to discuss it properly but were conscious always to be seen doing their duty. Forfeiting scheduled breaks had become normal to meet the demands of the incoming wounded from the hospital ships, which were relentless. She smiled awkwardly. He was trying – perhaps too hard – to be diplomatic, and she respected him for that. He stubbed out his cigarette and looked out to sea.

It was a rare moment of tranquillity for them amid the madness of the tented ward and he wasn't going to spoil it by pressing her for an answer – at least not tonight – but soon he would have to find the courage to ask again and accept whatever decision she made, because the weight upon him wanting her as much as he did was becoming too great to bear.

So the pattern continued for the next few days, with each shift demanding more from them than what the previous day had taken as the toll of casualties mounted. Some nurses, who felt unclean and were conscious of the shortage of fresh water, started cutting their hair very short for practicality's sake, and Agnes saw the sense in that, although taking scissors to her mousy-brown locks felt a like an act of sacrilege.

When she suggested it to her friend Nurse Nicoledes, however, it was met with a look of sheer horror and a vigorous shake of her head. She combed her fingers down her raven hair and smiled. 'No, Agnes, I cannot do that! Theo would expect me to have my hair long!'

Agnes smiled; she had known for a long time how close Laryssa was to her brother, Theo, and how great an influence he was upon her actions and the decisions she took. She had told many colleagues that growing up in Australia, Theo had been more than an older brother. He had been her protector and when he had volunteered to fight for his adopted country, she had felt compelled to volunteer with only basic training to follow his example.

'It is the Greek custom to look up to the boys in the family. I am sure my parents wouldn't have been disappointed to have had a second son. Theo is like a hero to us all in our family, regardless of how he might be acknowledged by his CO. All we really *want* is for him to come home safely.'

Laryssa had bowed her head. Agnes had remained silent for a moment.

She could never imagine being prepared to defer to a male sibling in the way that Laryssa did. It was clear Theo was such a very precious son and beloved brother. Agnes was curious to hear more about Laryssa's family, but she was reluctant to appear intrusive. Better that Laryssa revealed the facts about her family in her own time. Agnes came away from their conversation, however, with one fervently held hope, that Theo Nicoledes survived this offensive, because she feared that for her friend Laryssa, the burden of his loss would just be too great.

22

Honoria Landseer was growing accustomed to the changes that had occurred in her household since Michael left on the troop ship to Gallipoli. The first unexpected change came about two weeks after Michael's departure, when Yolande disappeared overnight, her absence discovered by Grace Metcalfe. No specific incident prompted her decision to leave, but she left a barely legible note, typifying her poor grammar, in which she stated that she knew her presence within the household would be *intolerable* without the master's support and she wasn't going to endure the torment that she expected to come her way.

Grace presented the note to Honoria shortly after breakfast in Sarah's presence and Honoria had sneered with derision at Yolande's inference that she was the *victim*. Sarah was trying to conceal her delight as Honoria read the rambling note aloud. Honoria finished, handing it back to Grace Metcalfe with a dismissive shrug, and said, 'Fairly typical of the wretched girl's ingratitude. Well, she has saved me the task of dismissing her now, as she rightly anticipated I might!'

'Only might?' Sarah asked.

Honoria shrugged. 'I daresay she would have presented us with ample opportunity. Through her insolence or laziness...'

She looked at her housekeeper with a nod that she could leave and then turned her attention to Sarah.

'Do you think Michael knows that she has gone?' Sarah asked.

Honoria half-nodded, keen to move the conversation on from Yolande and on to more important matters. She feared Sarah was in danger of settling into an unhealthy rut and she was keen to help her avoid it.

'No doubt they discussed it before he left for Port Albany. Just as I have no doubt Michael will pretend to know nothing of her plans and blame me for the girl's decision. Although she may yet come to regret her rashness, as she will need to find a new position and no household will hire her without a reference, and as her only employer… she *will* have to rely upon me.'

Sarah smiled broadly at what she saw as the poetic justice of her mother-in-law's words.

'So do you have a commencement date for your nurse's training yet?'

Sarah shook her head, nervously biting her bottom lip. 'I haven't plucked up the courage to enrol as yet.'

'Don't worry. You have my full support, whenever the time is right!'

Sarah half-smiled. While she no longer believed that she and Michael could have any future together, especially after the trauma of losing their child, his sudden departure, regardless of her own needs, had demonstrated his selfish nature at its very worst, although she realised since that it had come at the right time. She had still been grieving her loss when he sailed, but she couldn't be sure how much Michael was grieving, or that he even cared. She would, however, miss Honoria's moral support, if the time came when she could no longer rely on it.

Which was ironic, as *she* was once the *last* person Sarah could have imagined as an *ally*.

Sarah had been writing to Agnes regularly since they had said farewell to each other in Melbourne and she had received a reply at least one a week until the hospital ship docked in Alexandria, although since Agnes's deployment on Lemnos her letters had become fewer and the time span between each was longer. Her letters to Michael were much less frequent, and from him she had received only a few. Honoria had sniffed with indignation at this and said, 'Too busy losing money at cards, I suspect...'

The prospect of starting her nurse's training scared her a little, although she believed it was a good career move for her, although even at this stage she realised she probably wouldn't attain the sense of vocation that Agnes had achieved.

The Tented Hospital, Lemnos

Agnes had struggled for days about how she saw her future after the war – although thinking that far ahead was dangerously tempting fate – and more importantly whether Lennox Ashworth would be part of it. She couldn't yet admit to being in love with him, but she felt secure at the prospect of perhaps one day becoming Mrs Ashworth.

She didn't believe she was being presumptuous thinking of that as a likely outcome, because instinct told her that feelings ran that deep on Lennox's behalf. She was surprised more by her initial response to considering it, because after Michael's rejection in Sarah's favour, she had seriously contemplated never committing herself to a man, or suspecting that she might inspire interest, but as Lennox had been swift in confiding an interest of many years standing on the ship out from Australia, she had dared to hope that despite her fiercely independent nature, a second chance at marital happiness could be hers after all.

The only person to whom she had confided the news of Lennox's suggestion was Laryssa Nicoledes, who had been ecstatically happy at the prospect of them becoming a couple, especially for Agnes, whom she kissed on both cheeks, delighted that she was the only colleague to be trusted to keep it secret. Her overall reaction was hopelessly romantic, which Agnes knew was at odds to how she viewed such matters.

When she later confided in Laryssa that she was going to make her commitment to Lennox, Laryssa had embraced her, saying, 'That is fantastic news, Agnes. The boost we all need. So when are you going to tell him?'

'Whenever I can. Our next spell of leave together would be good, should we ever manage to get them to coincide... Until then, though, it's lips sealed...'

Laryssa had nodded silently, delighted to be part of her joint conspiracy.

Agnes was, however, prevented from telling Lennox her decision by a major offensive in early October which resulted in some of the heaviest Allied casualties they had dealt with on Lemnos. She was deeply shocked by the sight of several men brought in on stretchers from the hospital ship to the beach adjacent to the tented ward.

Especially when she recognised one patient, with a badly injured leg and facial lesions, as her brother-in-law Second Lieutenant Michael Landseer. Whatever she had previously thought of him, even in their darkest moments, he didn't deserve this. For a moment she was frozen in shock at the sight of him, and she thought of Sarah. Dr Ashworth stood in front of her, amid the chaos around them, and shouted her name to force her out of the inertia.

'Nurse Calloway?' She stood looking at Michael; her complexion had gone very pale and she slowly shook her head, so Lennox spoke again, only louder. 'Agnes, what's wrong?' He looked at Sister Challoner for inspiration but, feeling confused, she shrugged her shoulders, as Agnes was usually the calmest in the chaotic moments before a new intake of casualties. Sister Challoner gently laid a hand on Agnes's shoulder, moving her aside.

'Nurse Calloway, is there a problem for you assisting Dr Ashworth in treating this patient?'

Agnes half-turned and stared at her, as if she were in a trance, and then she nodded. 'What? I'm sorry, Sister. Yes, I think *I should* be excused from treating this patient and attend to one of the others.'

'May I ask why?'

Agnes looked at her again and said, 'Because his name is Michael Landseer, and he's my sister's husband.'

Sister Challoner looked across at Dr Ashworth, who silently nodded, and then she instructed another nurse to take Agnes, despite her protests for a short break, while she went to assist Dr Ashworth.

'I think you should keep an eye on Agnes – sorry, Nurse Calloway. I have never seen her freeze like that. She is usually the coolest among us.'

Sister Challoner kept her expression neutral as she set to work, inspecting the poorly applied tourniquet which had stemmed some of the blood loss, but evidently not all, as she ripped his blood-soaked khaki trousers. She looked grimly at Dr Ashworth. The facial lesions would heel in time, but it would be a fight to save his leg.

The Allied Trenches – Earlier

Second Lieutenant Landseer and Second Lieutenant Crozier had been as inseparable in the trenches as they had been around the private clubs and the public bars back home in Melbourne, and each knew that the other had their back. Theirs was a friendship that had *endured* so much, and it was as strong in this hell that was war. The action in the Allied lines had grown increasingly fierce in recent days, and they stood on the parapet waiting for the whistle to signal they should advance over the top. The resilience of the Turkish troops continued to confound the hierarchy, and although they hadn't given up on the objective, they knew that while the mission to take the Straits of Gallipoli, disable the enemy's fighting capability and then advance on to the jewel of the Ottoman Empire – their crucial port at Constantinople – could still be achieved, it would mean heavier casualties than had been suffered thus far, and was that a price worth paying?

The conditions in the trenches were as merciless as the enemy and as winter set in the elements threatened to test their *endurance* further.

First Lieutenant Nichols was in charge of the battalion, but there was no sign of Captain Mallory, which Michael was relieved about, as he had felt Mallory's residual anger at the losses he had suffered at cards on board the troop ship more than once, as some of the debt hadn't yet been settled, largely due to Honoria's stubbornness.

It had been raining steadily all morning, but it was cold rain and the men felt miserably wet and increasingly disillusioned. Nichols had tried to rouse them and he urged his second lieutenants and Sergeant Clancy to do the same, but it was largely futile.

'So I guess this is it, Aaron! The big push?'

Aaron Crozier nodded silently. He felt his finger against the cold trigger of his revolver, and Michael said, 'I will see you on the other side. You will have my back?'

Aaron smiled uneasily, because for him the question didn't have to be asked, but given that he had seen the extent to which Michael had failed to win friends among their comrades – in fact, he barely made any effort after the first few weeks, without having achieved success. So he guessed Michael had to rely on him more in battle than he ever had at home.

Lieutenant Nichols nodded encouragement at the men as Sergeant Clancy approached. Nichols was tentative, wondering why Mallory hadn't yet emerged from the dug-out, ready to give the command to go over the top. When Mallory emerged from the dug-out Michael bowed his head, determined to avoid his gaze. It amused Mallory that Landseer looked embarrassed now in the minutes before orders were issued to begin the latest offensive, when he had showed no respect to his rank when amassing his losses en route from Australia. But what did it matter when both their fates could be sealed by what took place once the attack had commenced?

Mallory stood on the parapet and looked at Nichols beside him. "*Horatio*" was a man he would trust to save him if the occasion arose. Could he have the same faith in some of his volunteers? Somehow he doubted it and he couldn't help including Second Lieutenant Landseer in that assessment of character.

'You're ready, Ty?' Nichols asked him, and Mallory smiled, prepared to overlook the moment of informality from his first lieutenant. He nodded.

They waited for the whistle and when it came, their line went over into the mist of smoke and a fierce hail of fire from the Ottoman troops.

Nichols took a forward position and he ran swiftly into battle; he had Landseer to his left and Crozier was next to him. The sub-standard guns they had heard so much about, which had been a gift from the Kaiser to the Ottoman troops, were proving more than adequate at keeping the Allied forces at bay, and Landseer was one of the first to fall from a direct hit to the leg. He fell to the ground in agony and he was prepared to remain there to meet his fate head-on until Aaron offered him his hand, pulling him from harm's way while firing randomly at the enemy line. He continued to pull Michael further back to the trench, but there was chaos all around them. The pain in Michael's leg was excruciating and he fell to the ground once more as Crozier shouted at him to make the effort.

'It's no good, Aaron! Just leave me, save yourself!'

'You asked me to have your back, and that's what I'm doing, so get the hell on your bloody feet, man!' Aaron offered Michael his hand and kept nodding, but Michael's vision was blurred and in that moment he heard a shot and for a moment he thought that he had been hit again, until the hand of salvation wasn't there anymore and nor was Aaron towering over him, ordering him to get to his feet. Because one of the Ottoman forces had fired a direct hit at Aaron's temple and he had fallen onto his knees, the blood oozing from his head. Leaning over, Michael didn't have to see if his friend was breathing, because he *just* knew.

He could see that Aaron Crozier had perished in the heat of battle attempting to save him. Michael started to scream louder in anguish.

He felt pain in his leg and the immediacy of his grief at losing Aaron in the way that he had. His best friend, who had never asked him to have *his* back but had promised in the moments before the order came that he would have *his*.

The next thing Michael could remember was being back in the trench.

Blood oozed from the gash in his leg as two comrades attempted to stem the flow with a swiftly applied tourniquet, but he knew he had lost a lot of blood and even for Aaron's brave sacrifice, he may yet succumb to the fate he had been willing to submit to, which Aaron had paid the ultimate price for in his determination to avert.

Nichols looked at Landseer, trying to keep his expression neutral. 'What happened to Crozier?'

'The brave stupid fool caught a sniper's bullet trying to save me when I told him to look after himself.'

Nichols shook his head slowly. 'I saw some of his courage up there, and yours as well, Landseer.'

Michael reached down, putting a hand on the tourniquet, and felt the agony seep through. Gritting his teeth, he looked up at Lieutenant Nichols towering like a giant over him and said, 'Well, if anyone is to be commended for their bravery today, it's Second Lieutenant Aaron Crozier! The best bloody friend a man can have and the best man I have ever known!'

Nichols pleated his brow. He had known Landseer and Crozier had been friends back in civvies, but he hadn't known to what extent or how deep their friendship went, although he did now. It was the first time Landseer hadn't been *so* self-absorbed or obnoxious. He had seen enough in battle to know that it wasn't just the physical scars that Landseer would have to bear from today's action.

'Why didn't he just save himself, Lieutenant Nichols? Like I *urged* him to. Why?'

'I guess it's because that is the kind of man he was, Landseer. He chose to save you because he believed he could, that it wouldn't come at the cost of his own. That's the fifty-fifty gamble you take in the thick of the action sometimes. It's instinctive. So you will have to prove that his sacrifice was worth it by getting fit! Surviving!'

'So that I can come back and fight another day?'

Lieutenant Nichols gazed down at Michael's leg, with the blood-stained khaki trousers and the tourniquet which hadn't quite been applied correctly, but someone had done their best. Landseer would live, but he wouldn't see another day's fighting. This was probably it for him and it could be quite a feat in the hospital to save his leg, but Landseer didn't need to hear that now, not from him.

He lit a cigarette and put it between Landseer's lips. 'It's not one of those cigars you like, but it will have to *do*…' He shook his head, laughing. 'What is it with you and Mallory and all the fuss about what you smoke? Perhaps you are more alike than you think.'

Michael smiled. 'I wouldn't let Captain Mallory hear you make that comparison, Lieutenant!'

Two stretcher bearers had come for Michael, placing him gently onto the stretcher ready for transfer to the hospital ship. Nichols knew that Landseer hadn't tried very hard to endear himself to his comrades since leaving Port Albany. There was an arrogance about his demeanour which military authority hadn't managed to quash, but he felt many would acknowledge his bravery in facing the enemy and try to sympathise with his loss.

Nichols nodded at Michael. 'Good luck, Second Lieutenant.' Then he nodded at the stretcher bearers as they carried him away.

23

The Tented Hospital, Lemnos – September 1915

For Agnes too much had occurred between their families, with too much ill will directed at her personally – aside from what Sarah had *endured* at his hand during their marriage – to allow her to forget all of his misdeeds, but she would set them aside and be the professional she knew herself to be. Because he was, above all things, a patient who needed medical care, but she made the effort to tend the needs of other patients where she could, trying subtly to avoid too much contact with Michael in the days following his admittance. He was in a bad way, that much was evident, and the physical injuries aside, it was his mental state that caused much concern. He had been rambling incoherently aboard the hospital ship, which the orderlies had put down to him possibly developing a fever. Agnes believed it went deeper than that, and reading between the lines of his rambling in the tented ward, she had deduced that Aaron Crozier hadn't made it.

So for him, his parents and for his sister, her one-time *nemesis* Leticia, she felt a deep sadness. Michael had been in denial, insisting they treat Crozier first as a priority, and when the nurses expressed confusion at his rambling he became aggressive. An orderly had to restrain him when he grabbed

Nurse Nicoledes' arm, continuing to shout while she struggled to break free of his hold. Agnes's patience snapped and she rushed to her colleague's side.

'Lieutenant Landseer. You need to let us treat your wounds… Michael. Listen to me. Aaron isn't here. They didn't bring him because he died from his injuries at the Front. From what I have been told, he was very brave…'

Michael pulled back from her, his eyes widening suspiciously. 'You're lying! It's a trick. She's tricking me with her lies. I know what she is like. This is her opportunity to get her own back for all the ills that she accuses me of inflicting upon *her*!'

When she finally managed to restrain Michael, after a while, he grew calmer. Agnes left him to the care of colleagues including a new recruit to the tented hospital, a very eager young man called Simon Rowlett about whom Lennox was very impressed, although Agnes imagined he might just have been relieved to have another doctor to help share an ever-increasing burden, as the latest offensive had resulted in many more casualties. She felt it had been typical of Michael that he would choose to cast doubt on her professionalism by attempting to force a personal angle where none needed to exist, when all she had been trying to do was settle him and protect her colleague. Remaining totally professional meant she had to rise above the provocation and accept that despite all his sins, Second Lieutenant Landseer deserved to survive so Honoria would have no need to grieve.

She had been led to believe from Sarah's letters that her sister felt the marriage had no mileage left. Sarah had hinted at asking Michael for a divorce. Agnes could only hope that she would stay true to that course. The night shift was coming on duty and she would be back on in a matter of hours. For now she needed her bed; as makeshift and uncomfortable as it was, she guessed she would sleep soundly tonight.

Agnes woke the next morning after a fitful night, during which she had dreamt a lot, but she had also come to a decision regarding her future which would include Lennox Ashworth. She wanted to give him her answer and believed that she had found a man with whom she could trust her future. She shared so many of his ambitions, especially about establishing a rural hospital, which she had known was his long-term aim since they were on the ship from Port Albany. He had said he wanted to start work on the fundraising as soon as possible after the war. It was a noble pursuit and she wanted to be a part of all that such an establishment could achieve. She had no fear that he had changed his mind; he had acted honourably in never having pressed her.

Although the increasing burden of work had proved a distraction, she realised she had prevaricated for perhaps too long. Now, however, that patient diligence of his would get its reward and she could claim the future that had always been hers for the taking.

Having made her decision, Agnes wanted to confide in Laryssa Nicoledes, but her bed was empty so she called out to her as she dressed in the drab grey uniform. She found Laryssa at the water's edge as she made her way to the tented ward and she could see that she had been crying. Agnes felt her heart sink. 'Not Theo! Please don't let it be Theo. I cannot take on that grief today!'

While she knew how selfish that sounded, she couldn't help it.

She wanted to share her good news with the person who had most encouraged her to accept Lennox's proposal. Laryssa looked at her and Agnes could see from the tears on her eyelashes that she must have been crying for a while; now her bottom lip quivered.

'Tell me, please!'

'He's listed as missing, believed killed!'

Agnes's instinct was to embrace her, but Laryssa held her at arm's length, shaking her head 'I can't, Agnes, not yet! If I give in to that, I am accepting it's over, that all hope has vanished, and I won't do that… Not until it's beyond all doubt.'

Agnes reached out for the photograph creased into Laryssa's fist, and she smoothed the creases out and smiled, choking back her own tears because Laryssa needed her to be as strong. 'The first time you showed me this on the ship out from Australia, all I recalled from that first sighting was his smile. It lights his eyes. He is such a good-looking young man, your brother… I believe he will be found. He will come back to you!'

Laryssa smiled through her tears, and in a voice choked with emotion, she nodded. 'You can't know that for sure, Agnes, but I bless you for saying it anyway, but I do believe in him, in his courage and determination.'

She took a long, deep breath as Agnes squeezed one hand and placed the creased photograph of Theo, face up, into the palm of Laryssa's other hand. Stray tears began to roll gently down her cheeks as she took one more look at her brother's smiling image before closing her fist around it and slowly walking away.

Agnes's heart clenched in a vice as anguish for her friend swamped her.

It was late afternoon before Agnes got to speak to Lennox and he looked worn out. So many back-to-back shifts had taken their toll while they waited for additional medical personnel, and although Dr Rowlett's arrival had been welcome, it swiftly lost its impact as the list of casualties grew.

Lennox leant back against the marquee pole and lit a cigarette, offering one to Agnes. He could see she was pensive, and as word of Theo Nicoledes being listed as missing and Laryssa having been excused from duty on compassionate grounds spread, he understood why.

'I've made a decision about the future, Lennox… Our future.'

'I see. Well, you know how to keep a guy waiting and *hoping*. I will concede that to you, Agnes Calloway.'

She could tell by the lightness of his tone that he wasn't showing his impatience at the wait.

'I know, and I'm sorry, but I had to be sure of the idea of us as a couple… of having a future together, and now I *am*. I hope you haven't changed your mind and turned your attention to someone else.'

'Such as who?' He stubbed out his cigarette and laid both hands on Agnes's shoulder. 'I was sure years ago, when there seemed to be no hope, when you barely noticed me at your parents' soirees. I love you, Agnes. As long as you were in my sights every day, even here in this wretched hell, there couldn't possibly be anyone else.'

Agnes stifled a gasp, putting one hand across her mouth, and she willed any tears – albeit happy ones – to remain unshed. She looked at him with intent in her eyes.

He took her into his arms and said, 'I promise you won't ever have reason to regret this decision, Agnes, or to doubt my commitment to you – us – and I'm not in possession of a ring; besides which, it's hardly the time or place for proposals…' He paused to look around him, adding, 'I am *not* getting down on bended knee in the sand. I think I was certain of how I felt about you on the ship out, Agnes, and your answer has convinced me that I was right to be patient.'

Agnes smiled as he kissed her hard on the mouth. It was an all-consuming kiss which he intended to seal the decision of their future, and it left her in no doubt that he loved her. That was one certainty that she could rely upon. Because none of them knew what the next twenty-four hours could bring them in this hell, but she was convinced that she had done the best she could for her future by saying yes, and that she had earned the love of a man who wouldn't let her down.

In the days that followed there was precious little time for Agnes to draw breath and absorb the enormity of what she had committed to, but she knew she was happy and there was no disguising that. She would exchange rueful looks with Lennox across the ward whenever they were on duty together. Her mood was tempered, however, by other realities unfolding around her. No news came of Private Theo Nicoledes for days. Waiting… and hoping, but when it did, it was as tragic as Laryssa had secretly feared it could be. She had vowed never to give up hope for her brother until the reality of his loss was confirmed, and only then did she succumb to the deep well of her grief.

Sister Challoner had the difficult task of telling Agnes the grim news about Theo Nicoledes, and although she gently advised her to give Laryssa some space, she knew that it went against Agnes's instinct and Agnes found her friend in the dormitory, face down on her bunk. The worn sepia image of Theo was crumpled beside her and when she raised her head in response to the gentle touch of Agnes's hand on her shoulder, it was evident she had cried until there were no tears left.

Laryssa shrugged off her hand and Agnes's heart sank. She knew there was nothing she could do, nothing that she could say.

'Please go, Agnes. Leave me alone!'

'I can't!'

'You must!'

'I want to be here for you. To support you in your grief.'

'But you are happy! In love and that is how it should be… but I cannot bear that now and I don't want to drag *you* down. You are a good friend, Agnes, but I need my solitude to accept this…' Her voice faltered slightly as the tears began to roll down her cheeks, and she added, '…To accept that Theo has gone.'

Agnes laid a gentle, calming hand on Laryssa's back and then she rose. There were times, she recalled, after the shock of Michael's rejection, when she had sought solitude, if only to lick her wounds, but that had been about wounded pride, not grief. Theo had been everything to Laryssa. A brother that she had worshipped as a hero. His death brought home the wretched futility of this war and Agnes knew that for her friend the coming days would feel more like an eternity as she came to terms with her loss. As she stood for a moment at the dormitory door, she feared that the friendly, engaging, laughing Laryssa Nicoledes that she had taken to from the very first day and had come to love like another sibling may have vanished forever.

While Laryssa Nicoledes was left to grieve, there was work to be done in the tented wards, and the burden of casualties arriving from the hospital ships was relentless. Second Lieutenant Landseer continued to be a challenging patient. They were determined to save his leg if they could, but not at the expense of losing him. He was morose, and from the little Agnes saw of him, he appeared to lack the *will* to survive.

For a man who had once rejoiced in his excesses, regardless of the impact on those around him, he had become a pale shadow of the man she knew and had come to resent so bitterly for all the misery he had inflicted on Sarah.

The risk of gangrene had become much higher than it had been when he was first admitted, and both Dr Rowlett and then Dr Ashworth had outlined the options should his condition worsen. Amputation was starkly spelt out to him, but he rejected it robustly, shouting at them in a manner she knew so well, which was a truer reflection of the man he was, to leave him alone.

On reflection Agnes wasn't surprised that Michael was in denial about the extent of his injuries. Although he was entitled to grieve for Aaron Crozier for as long as he chose, his arrogant refusal to confront the realities of his own predicament were in her view a by-product of having enjoyed an over-indulged childhood. Dr Rowlett was calm but persistent in urging him to reconcile himself to the possibility that amputation might become a necessity to save his life, but in stark, unapologetic language he refused to accept that he might, in his words, end up a "cripple", managing to make the word sound like an expletive. His manner was cruelly dismissive to patients around him already having to make the consideration themselves and, from what Agnes had witnessed, managing the enormity of their decision with more maturity than Michael was in his typical self-pitying way. Eventually Dr Rowlett threw his hands in the air in frustration, walking away. Sister Challoner, who had witnessed the scene, felt compelled to admonish him, but Dr Ashworth laid a gentle hand on her arm.

'Allow me, Sister. Dr Rowlett may have been ill-judged, but Second Lieutenant Landseer is an obstinate patient when it suits him and he finds it difficult to accept that we *are* advising on what is in *his* best interests. He may well have given up to some extent and I accept that he is grieving, but our job is to save his life and his attitude makes that harder.'

'That may be the case, Dr Ashworth, but outbursts like what I have just seen are not acceptable and I won't tolerate them.'

Dr Ashworth inclined his head as Sister Challoner took her leave.

It was widely believed – although yet to be officially announced – that she had been promoted to the role of matron. So he guessed she had to demonstrate that her promotion had been justly earned by asserting her authority more robustly. He would speak to Rowlett, because his behaviour had been unprofessional and so out of character.

Agnes was told that she was to become a sister, but the impact of this news was less significant than it should have been to her, coming after her decision to commit to Lennox and the pall of despondency which had assailed her on hearing of Theo Nicoledes' death. Her efforts to support Laryssa in her grief were having mixed results, and she was resigned now to losing her friend who had been given compassionate leave to visit her family after a short burial service, in which Laryssa, with Agnes at her side, holding her hand, saw her beloved brother committed to the earth of Lemnos. It was a symbolic end to a life that had begun and ended on Greek soil, which was ironic for a young man who had sworn his allegiance to Australia.

It was in this mood of defiance, having been given the morning off to attend Theo's service, that Agnes bent her rule of keeping as much distance as she could from her brother-in-law. As Sister Challoner approached his bed, determined that he should *heed* the medical advice that his gangrene was getting worse and he should now consider amputation of his left leg as the best chance of survival, Agnes held her arm and said, 'Allow me…'

'But you said in the circumstances…?'

Agnes nodded. Squaring her shoulders, she took a long, steadying breath and approached Michael's bed. 'Are you *so* determined to die? To make Aaron Crozier's gesture worthless?'

Michael turned to her and she saw a glimmer of a smile, but knowing him as she did, it could easily have been a sneer.

'I would have thought that my demise, if it were as likely as your colleagues claim, would be a cause for rejoicing for *you*… And, I daresay, my wife!'

'Don't be so childishly self-indulgent! Don't the Croziers deserve better than this self-pity? They are grieving a loss and here you lie with a chance of survival – yes, albeit minus part of your leg and some re-adjustment. Either way, your war is over. You get the chance to go home. Only this morning I attended the burial service for the brother of a nursing colleague. You may remember Nurse Nicoledes? Whose arm you grabbed so aggressively when you were first admitted with fever, demanding to know why we weren't attending to Aaron first? Well, she is grieving now for her brother as Leticia Crozier is grieving. At least your going home will offer them some solace that his sacrifice wasn't wasted!'

Michael bowed his head and for a moment Agnes thought she had got through to him, although she was probably the last person he would have wanted to hear that from.

'What do you care for the Croziers? Aside from Leticia, you barely knew them and you had a mutual loathing of her. You thrived on exchanging barbs and sometimes physical blows with her. Aaron was *my* best friend. He stood beside me as I exchanged wedding vows to Sarah. He should still be here and he isn't because of *me*. I asked him if he would have my back when we went over the top. He never asked me, but I had to be sure of him, and when I fell he put himself in the line of fire to save me at his expense. So do you still think mine is a life worth saving?'

Agnes bowed her head. She had never imagined seeing Michael Landseer thus. Yes, there was still the self-pity, but it was mixed with a raw and unyielding sense of grief at Aaron's loss – for which he blamed himself – and if nothing else an acknowledgement that Aaron Crozier was the better man.

Agnes looked at him and calmly said, 'Yes. Because that is what we do here. We save lives…The doctors have the chance to save yours. Only you can give them consent. Only you know whether you deserve that chance—'

'Go away, Nurse Calloway! I am sick of the sight of you and your home-spun wisdom.'

Agnes took a deep breath and walked away. Sister Challoner looked at her with a questioning eyebrow as she approached and Agnes shook her head.

'At least you tried.'

'What good it did me… or him. Let him wallow. He will change his mind, but by then it might be too late.'

In the days that followed Michael's condition worsened. The gangrene had spread and it swiftly turned into a desperate fight to save his life.

Dr Rowlett said they should take the decision to perform the amputation, and despite his earlier reluctance to go ahead without consent, Dr Ashworth agreed. Agnes steadfastly refused to participate in the procedure and although this annoyed Dr

Ashworth, Matron Challoner, as she officially was now, offered to assist. The decision to amputate just above the left knee was approved by the major-surgeon, who had been kept informed about Lieutenant Landseer's worsening condition along with his ongoing reluctance to consent. His final words were a terse, 'Do it!' to Dr Ashworth, but his expression was grim and he hoped that it wasn't already too late because of the patient's delaying tactic and that they wouldn't unnecessarily lose a patient.

It struck Agnes with irony that on the day the decision was made to amputate Michael's gangrene-affected leg she received a letter from Sarah, who had commenced initial nurse's training and that it was progressing better than she could have hoped. She asked about Michael, as Agnes had told her he was at the tented hospital, as she guessed he would have written and she didn't want her sister thinking she was being evasive. She thought briefly about writing and telling Sarah about the amputation to prepare her for the shock, but she *demurred*. It was *his* decision to share it with whoever and this time the burden could fall upon him. As Sarah was staying with Honoria, Agnes knew she would hear the news via her mother-in-law should Michael bother to write to her. The troop ship home to Australia was the best option Michael could hope for now and for Honoria's sake Agnes hoped that through his stubborn reluctance to consent he hadn't left it too late for that to be his reality.

24

The weeks passed with an agonising slowness. The shifts were still too long and exhausting, with new casualties brought into the tented hospital faster than they could be adequately assessed. There was an all-too-brief respite for news of Dr Ashworth's engagement to Sister Calloway to be shared among the staff and congratulations offered before returning to duty. Agnes was still growing accustomed to now being addressed as Sister, although Matron Challoner, who found the change in her job title easier to adjust to, told Agnes her promotion had been well deserved.

Second Lieutenant Landseer was still being belligerent, refusing to accept that without the amputation he probably wouldn't still be alive, but despite being told Agnes had played no part in the procedure, she was still the source of his *ire*. He didn't believe anyone who told him Agnes had withdrawn herself from his operation, until the major-surgeon bluntly told him that *he* had made the final decision to proceed and that he was luckier than those who hadn't had the luxury of taking their time. This intervention succeeded in silencing Michael for a while, but Agnes, who witnessed the exchange from a distance, doubted the major-surgeon's words would have an impact for very long, because she was convinced now that her brother-in-law was determined to wallow.

For her, his discharge papers couldn't come soon enough. She was attending to a patient in the adjoining bed, along with a new volunteer nurse, when Michael leaned over and said, 'I hear congratulations are due. For your engagement.'

Agnes tried to marshal her surprise and, without looking at him, she mumbled her thanks. 'I didn't expect them from you. Aside from knowing what opinion you hold of me, given that my fiancé is the man that you hold responsible for the amputation, I didn't expect you would want to congratulate Dr Ashworth either.'

'I *still* do hold him responsible! However, I obviously did you a favour two years ago, as Dr Ashworth is evidently more your equal.'

'You didn't do Sarah a favour by turning your attention to *her*, given how much she has suffered – the loss of your child being the most traumatic. Thanks to the spiteful actions of your maid! I *might* have escaped the torment of becoming Mrs Michael Landseer, but… Sarah hasn't faired so well!'

Michael sneered and Agnes looked around her, realising that she had been provoked.

'You don't wish us well at all, do you? Well, I guess that is my fault for believing even for a moment that you might yet have a shred of humility in you!' Agnes could tell from several pairs of eyes staring at her now that her tone had been raised.

Matron Challoner approached and dismissed the volunteer. 'Is there a problem, Sister Calloway?'

Agnes took a long, steadying breath; glancing swiftly across at Michael, she could see he was sneering at her. 'No problem, Matron. I evidently made the error of believing that Second Lieutenant Landseer was being sincere when extending his congratulations on my engagement. Given how well I know him, I should have realised that such a kind gesture is beyond his characteristics!'

Matron Challoner bowed her head to suppress a smile. Agnes finished taking the temperature of the patient in the adjacent bed and then walked away.

Michael's sneering ceased as Matron gave him a scathing look as she took her leave and then he felt several pairs of eyes on him. He had never been popular with the lower ranks in the trenches because of his patrician attitude, similar to the one he had displayed with junior clerks at the bank, and he swiftly realised he would also struggle to find favour with fellow patients in the tented ward.

Agnes and Lennox had been granted five days' leave together for their wedding ceremony, for which they would travel by hospital ship to Egypt. This pleased Agnes enormously, as it meant she could have Laryssa Nicoledes as her bridesmaid, which for her was the next best thing to having Sarah alongside her, as she exchanged vows. Laryssa had been redeployed at Number Two Australian Hospital following her compassionate leave, which, given the circumstances, Agnes understood, although it didn't stop her from missing her friend. They had corresponded regularly and in her letters Laryssa had rediscovered the joy she had once shared with Agnes about her relationship with Lennox before the trauma of grief had assailed her.

When Nurse Elizabeth Whitman, also serving at Number Two Australian Hospital, heard that Dr Lennox Ashworth had proposed to her rival Agnes Calloway and had been accepted, she was philosophical but still dismayed that he hadn't chosen her. She was oblivious to the fact that her charms had no greater effect on Lennox than they did on many other men who caught her eye, soldiers and medics alike. Agnes couldn't help smiling when she read in one of Laryssa's letters that Elizabeth Whitman had earned a reputation as a troublemaker and that her failure to keep a man interested for more than a few dates was becoming notorious, along with the fact that she lacked tact in her dealings with some of the most wounded patients and that she could be neglectful in the most basic nursing duties, especially when her attention lay elsewhere.

So she was becoming a constant source of exasperation to the senior nursing staff. When Agnes showed that particular passage to Lennox on the ship from Lemnos, he smiled, raising an eyebrow, remembering the *torment* he had suffered sharing a taxi with her to see the Sphinx.

Agnes smiled, knowing that Matron Lomax would have been relieved not to have to put with Whitman in Alexandria.

As the month's end approached, patience with the ongoing strategy in Gallipoli was wearing thin. The losses suffered by the Allies were considered too heavy against too little gain. The Ottoman forces knew the terrain and it showed in their resilience to the elements. The rain and mud throughout the autumn months had been as much an enemy to the Allied cause as the Ottoman troops determination to defend the Straits of Gallipoli, thus blocking access to the ultimate Allied target: the port of Constantinople.

As Agnes and Lennox boarded the ship for Egypt, the decision to evacuate Gallipoli and cut their losses was already being mooted in London.

Agnes wasn't sorry to be leaving Lemnos, even for a short while. Never could she have imagined a worse place in which to put her hard-earned nursing skills to good use than in the tented ward on that desolate stretch of beach, where the elements of sand and mud were as much against them as enemy fire inflicting the wounds that they were called upon to treat.

The Shepherd's Hotel, Cairo – Late November 1915

The marriage ceremony was to take place on 2nd December on the terrace of the Shepherd's Hotel, which gave them two whole days to prepare. Agnes was delighted to be reunited with Laryssa Nicoledes, and later with Matron Lomax. Laryssa was filled with joy to be her bridesmaid, but Agnes wasn't fooled by her friend's effort to appear upbeat. She knew she felt Theo's loss very keenly and deciding to come back to Egypt and continue her nursing duties couldn't have been easy.

She was surprised to see Captain Tyson Mallory on the hotel terrace that evening, standing at the balustrade. She touched Lennox gently on the arm to alert him to the fact and he smiled, taking her hand.

'Have no fear. I got the answer I wanted from the woman that *I wanted*… Apologies if that sounds too possessive to you, but he cannot rile me now. Go and talk to him if you wish.' Lennox gave her an encouraging nod and she squared her shoulders, took a deep breath and approached Mallory, who turned to her on a nudge from Nichols.

He wore the scars of battle. His left arm and shoulder were in a sling and he had a gash on his cheek. He took a long drag on his cheroot and laid it aside, smiling uneasily. He had lost out with her, partly due to his boorishness, but truth be told, he never stood a chance alongside the ever-so-self-serving medic.

'This is just a scratch. I will be back in the action in due course… I just want to say that I made a grave error of judgement on this terrace that night – to be brutally frank, I made a great fool of myself and you had to suffer me at my worst. I will always regret that…' He paused, took a long gulp of whisky and then a deep breath. He added, 'I wish you every happiness for your nuptials. I hope it brings you the happiness you deserve. Dr Ashworth is a very lucky man. I hope he knows how much…'

Agnes smiled, nodding her head. 'We are as lucky as each other, Captain Mallory, but thank you, that is very gracious…'

Tyson Mallory exhaled heavily on his cheroot, grateful for the cloud of smoke he had created as a shield between him and

Agnes. The fez-wearing stewards came out onto the terrace to complete the nightly ritual of lighting the lamps along the balustrade as the sounds of the city at dusk that were unique to Cairo began to be heard in the chill of a winter eve.

She returned to Lennox's side, linking arms with him, and he nodded in Mallory's direction. 'I guess if the swagger has gone, that's a good thing.'

He kissed his fiancée on the lips with more fervour than usual, and if Captain Mallory caught a glimpse of that, then so be it. It was at that moment Matron Freda Lomax appeared on the terrace and came to embrace the happy couple. What Agnes and Lennox hadn't seen was Tyson Mallory's sneer as he glanced in their direction. He guessed he would never find any common ground with Ashworth, so he wouldn't try. He had acknowledged *his* error of judgement and cut his losses where she was concerned by offering her his best wishes, but Mallory still couldn't help thinking that Sister Calloway could have betrothed herself to a better man.

The Shepherd's Hotel, Cairo – 2nd December 1915

Agnes hadn't considered how she might feel on the morning of her wedding until she woke and knew that she felt different – albeit in a good way. Sadly relations between herself and Sarah had been slightly strained on her wedding day, so she never had the chance to ask her sister what had been going through her mind as she prepared to exchange vows with Michael Landseer. Agnes took a deep breath. She could feel the butterflies fluttering in her stomach, but there was so much about this that *just* felt right. She had won for herself a decent, caring man and she had seen his capacity for caring with the patients they were called upon to treat.

Lennox Ashworth was a man worth building a future with, of that she was certain. She sighed, attracting Laryssa's attention, because if anyone had good reason to suffer a moment or two of melancholy, it was Laryssa Nicoledes. Yet she could see her bridesmaid looked content that she was here, sharing this moment with *her* best friend, which somehow compensated her for the fact that Sarah couldn't be here standing by her side, as they had always imagined they would for each other growing up, on occasions such as these.

She had chosen a simple white lace dress with no frills and Laryssa had artistically woven yellow flowers into her hair, which was still short but which had benefited from the most care and attention that she had given it in weeks. Yet still the faint aroma of Lemnos lingered, along with a reminder that the stark reality of the war awaited their return after this all-too-brief honeymoon away from the Front. Agnes shrugged such thoughts aside, determined to enjoy her day.

'What is it, Agnes? Are you nervous…? Have you changed your mind?'

The look of horror on Laryssa's face made Agnes laugh. She shook her head and said, 'About marrying Lennox? No! That is one certainty I have in this crazy world…' She bit her bottom lip, thinking of how Laryssa must be feeling with her grief over Theo still *so* raw.

'I'm sorry, Laryssa… I *am* being selfish. Please forgive me.'

Laryssa shook her head, taking Agnes's hands in hers. 'Don't worry. Not a day passes when I don't think of my brother, and I *mourn* for him still. Theo is in my heart, but this day is yours in which to be happy… and to banish all other thoughts until tomorrow…' Laryssa nodded at her encouragingly, smiling gently.

Agnes nodded, took a steadying breath and accepted her wedding bouquet.

The padre married them in a simple ceremony on the terrace of the Shepherd's Hotel and Agnes thought when she saw Lennox that he looked more handsome than she had ever imagined him. Her heart did a somersault again and she felt a rush of tears assail her, but she was determined to keep them at bay. So she said her vows in a firm, confident voice, thinking of how were it not for the wretched war, which had swept the world into its vortex of misery, she might never have met him *again*, this brilliant young doctor, who had been gently *coerced* by his mother into attending several of her parents pre-Christmas soirees in the hope that she might notice him among the throng of guests, but she rarely ever had. Now on a chilly December afternoon in Cairo, she was committing herself to him for the rest of their lives, and as the padre pronounced them husband and wife, she knew she couldn't imagine ever being as happy again.

The attending soldiers raised their swords, forming a guard of honour as they made their way into the hotel for the reception.

They were raucously cheered by all their guests and Agnes spotted Captain Tyson Mallory and Lieutenant Nichols raising their glasses in salute.

Matron Lomax came over to them first, looking slightly glum that a last-minute change in the roster meant she was on duty later and would have to make her exit earlier than she wished.

'Couldn't you pull rank now that you are matron?' Lennox asked lightly.

Matron Lomax pulled a face and then smiled. 'If I thought it would work I would do it, for an occasion like this, but sadly with rank also there comes responsibility... I was glad to be here for the important part. There were times I feared you two wouldn't make it, and that would have been unimaginable. Had you both been working alongside me, as I had hoped, I think I would have given you each a not-so-gentle nudge in the right direction.' Matron Lomax gave them a look they both knew so well and then, after shaking hands, she moved away.

Lennox stood slightly to the side of Agnes with his hands on her shoulders. It was the kind of a possessive gesture that she generally resisted, but for today she felt content to be seen as *his*. In the months and years to come, she would assert her authority and they would enjoy a union of equals. She admired his ambitious plan to establish a hospital in rural Victoria and she would share in the endeavour to make that happen. It would, she was sure, be their biggest challenge after the war was over.

He kissed her cheek. 'Happy?'

'Supremely,' Agnes said.

Lennox smiled. Looking around, he nodded his approval. For him, the long wait to win the heart of this woman had been worth it.

25

Agnes and Lennox spent their wedding night in a suite at the Shepherd's Hotel. The French doors onto their balcony remained open until late, when the chill air became too much and they had heard enough of the sounds of the city, which were a welcome change from the lapping of the waves on Lemnos beach that they had become accustomed to.

Agnes was fascinated by Cairo. It was a world away from what she had known growing up in Edwardian Melbourne. Like Lennox, standing at the guard rail as they sailed out of Port Albany had been the first time she had left Australia.

Lennox, who rarely drank, had poured himself a whisky, having already toasted his wife with champagne. The reception had seemed interminable when all he had wanted was for their guests to leave them. Agnes had guessed at his impatience and now they were alone, she could see the contentment in his smile.

Agnes stood at the balustrade as he came to stand alongside her.

'What are you thinking?'

'How even the smallest subtle change can make a difference. With a signature upon a register, I have become Agnes Maria Ashworth.'

Lennox half-nodded. 'Are you happy with this subtle change?'

Agnes nodded. 'How could I not be? Married to such a *talented* doctor?'

'You have a remarkable talent for praising me in such a manner that I am never sure whether you are being entirely serious.'

'I guess you shall have to learn to read between the lines, to know when and if I am *teasing* you, Dr Ashworth...' She started moving towards the suite until, laying his glass aside, Lennox captured her hand and gently brought her back and into his arms.

He kissed her firmly. It was the kind of kiss that she would have marked as possessive with anyone else, as if she were being branded, but with him she was content to accept the intent, and if she were being entirely honest with herself, she could admit to liking it.

'I have wanted to kiss you like that for years, Agnes Maria Calloway. If I only I had dared...'

She felt the warmth of him against her and it caused her heart to flutter slightly. So this was what desire felt like? She had never experienced anything approaching this even when she had believed that she had a future with Michael Landseer, and he had always been more far more demonstrative in his actions and in expressing his needs.

'Why didn't you?'

'I lacked the nerve, I guess. Or the fear of rejection, which would have sealed my fate with you forever. No second chances.'

Agnes made a moue with her mouth, her head tipped slightly sideways. She smiled as she wrapped her arms around her husband's neck, neither willing nor confirming that his fears would have been groundless.

Instead she nodded gently. 'I can see how that would have deterred you.'

'Well, I have no such fears now, Mrs Ashworth...' He clutched her at the waist, pulling her closer. Smiling with intent, he added, 'I know that I owe you a trip to see the Sphinx, but aside from that I won't be letting you out of this suite until we have to report for duty…—

Agnes put a finger against his lips. 'Ssh.'

Lennox reached for his glass, finishing his whisky in a gulp. The burn it caused in his throat made him wince, but he didn't care. Looking with intense longing into Agnes's eyes, he said, 'I have never wanted anything as much as this. You! *Us*, together…'

Agnes nodded and he pulled her into the suite, firmly closing the doors onto the balcony, shutting out the world. He undressed her with aching slowness, but Agnes willingly acceded to his pace and soon they were in bed together. When he took her, it was with an urgency, a passion that he could never have thought himself capable of, but it was if all the years had melted away and from somewhere deep in his *gut* he had found the courage to stake his claim the first time they met, when he had glimpsed her across a crowded room in a Toorak mansion when her attention was focused on someone else and she barely acknowledged his existence.

She gasped when he entered her the first time and their union was sealed. Then she wrapped her legs around his waist, enjoying the feel of his skin on hers. They lay content within each other's arms for what seemed to Agnes like hours, making slow, languorous love to each other, until she knew without looking that Lennox was asleep. She lay with her head against his chest, keeping sleep in abeyance to enjoy this moment, to sear this night into memory, and although he had unnerved her from the moment they had met again on the ship from Port Albany with the intensity of his certainty that they would be together, now she knew that whatever the fates might throw at them in the coming months of the war, she would never have cause to doubt his love.

26

Honoria Landseer received two letters on the morning the ship taking Michael back to Australia left on the first leg of its journey to Durban.

She knew from his recent letters how bitter he was at being invalided out and still resenting that the amputation had been necessary. She read the first two lines of his latest letter, suppressing a sneer, and turned to the other in the cream embossed stationery of the bank Argate & Landseer. She frowned deeply as she read the contents, requesting her presence at the bank to discuss a matter of the utmost delicacy but without giving any details as to why.

She immediately thought it had something to do with Michael, but she was prepared to have her worst fears assuaged. She had remained a director of the bank her husband had established and she would do whatever was needed to protect Ernest's reputation. Michael could, if the situation demanded it, look after himself.

She called the bank first, asking for one of the directors, but was told none of them were available and that nobody below director level was authorised to discuss the matter at hand and under no circumstances could it be dealt with over the phone.

Suspecting the secretary was overestimating the importance of her position, Honoria slammed the receiver down and scanned the letter again, reading it minutely. There was only one clue – if it could be described as such – so she decided instantly that she would pay another visit to see if she applied sufficient pressure whether she might get some answers. So, summoning Grace Metcalfe, she steeled herself for the task – for the first time in years – of approaching Jensen Calloway.

The Calloway Mansion, Toorak

It was Charlotte who opened the door the moment Honoria's taxi pulled away, and if Honoria was surprised they could afford to retain a maid, she didn't show it.

Jensen approached soon after, trying to disguise that he was surprised by a visit from Sarah's mother-in-law.

'Honoria. It has been a while. I am afraid that Marguerite is out at present. I trust Sarah is OK?'

Honoria nodded stiffly. 'Very busy with her training. You have two very talented and dedicated daughters, Jensen. You must be very proud?'

Charlotte, hovering between them, said, 'How is Mistress Sarah?'

While Jensen frowned at the interruption, Honoria smiled. 'She is doing very well. She often spoke of you when she first came to stay at my home. Charlotte, isn't it?'

Charlotte nodded, smiling. Honoria saw no purpose in saying more, but she recalled that Sarah wasn't as glowing in her praise of the Calloway maid as Agnes tended to be; however, she reminded herself that she hadn't come to exchange pleasantries, and although she knew it might be a waste of time if Jensen refused to divulge anything, she wanted to go into her meeting with the bank directors well informed.

'Shall we talk privately, Jensen?'

'Of course. Could you bring us coffee, please, Charlotte?'

He led Honoria into his study and she was startled by the portrait of his father Cyrus Calloway. She had only ever seen him in an old sepia photograph that Louise had kept for many years after his breach of promise.

'So what is it that you wish to discuss, Honoria?'

Honoria accepted his invitation to sit as Jensen took the seat behind his desk. She could see from his eyes that he was a man under enormous strain and she wondered how much of that was down to Michael.

'Your loan agreement with the bank, for one thing.'

Jensen took a deep breath, trying not to betray emotion. He knew from Marguerite, given the committees they had served upon, and from Sarah that Honoria Landseer liked to be direct, but this had to be the first time he had been subjected to her bluntness directly.

'I would have thought that would be confidential between myself and the bank directors, or through Michael. I am *sorry* to hear of his injuries in the course of duty. It will be a difficult adjustment for him.'

Honoria raised an eyebrow. Jensen's overt politeness was *jarring* because given all that Michael had inflicted on him, it couldn't possibly be genuine.

'Forget Michael. I have received a letter from the bank directors indicating an issue that has given them cause for concern, and the only reference I have is that it relates to the loan you have with them. If you are concerned about my credentials, I have remained a director through Ernest...'

'Very well. What do you need to know?'

'The contract. Could I see your copy?'

Jensen stood, his brows pleated in a deep frown. Honoria didn't want to concede too much, but she needed to show some of her hand to get anything from Jensen. Michael may have succeeded in exposing his weakness, but he was still a shrewd businessman and he was naturally suspicious.

Jensen half-turned to retrieve it from the safe, handing it to Honoria. 'What are you hoping to find?'

'Nothing that could bring shame to the Landseer name.'

Jensen folded his arms and looked at her as she read. 'I was led to believe Michael drafted the terms of that contract.'

Honoria looked at him directly and nodded. 'Exactly! That is why I *need* to know the nature of the bank's concern.'

'Have you?'

She shook her head. Whatever was concerning the bank, she wasn't going to find it within the body of Jensen's copy.

'You said there was another matter you wanted to discuss. What is that?'

Honoria looked at him directly without flinching. These were cards she could now lay upon the table. It was time, perhaps, to lay the ghosts of Louise and Cyrus Calloway to rest.

'Your father. Cyrus Calloway!'

Now he was biting! 'What about my father?'

'Did you know he was once engaged – albeit briefly – to my mother Louise?'

'No, I didn't. You have proof?'

'Only from my mother's journals and from what she told me. There is also among her papers a worn sepia photograph of Cyrus when he was approximately fifteen to twenty years younger than he was in that portrait.'

'Does that prove anything other than that they knew each other?'

'I know from documents found in my grandparents' home that they sought legal advice about suing Cyrus for breach of promise. Sadly they couldn't afford it, and the action was never served, by which time Cyrus had become engaged to your mother and he secured, I believe, crucial mining rights in Queensland as part of her dowry.' Honoria spoke quietly, without emotion, never once taking her eyes off Jensen as she watched his complexion visibly blanching before her eyes.

'So your mother was jealous, heartbroken? So what?'

'There must have been something between them. Why else become engaged? Cyrus threw my mother over because he wanted those mining concessions. Come, Jensen, you have lived on stories of what a likeable old *larrikin* Cyrus always was. Surely a breach of promise was worth the risk for a fortune in gold?'

Jensen folded his arms defensively, determined to stand his ground, but Honoria had hit a *nerve*. He knew and she knew that had got to *him*.

'I know that my father loved my mother.'

'I know that he also loved mine as well once. Enough to ask for her hand in marriage and to be accepted. The law would have been on her side. It was only a lack of funds that deterred my grandparents—'

'Supposing all this is *true*. Where do you intend on going with it? I cannot undo any sins Cyrus may have committed, any more than you can be held responsible for any of Michael's excesses.'

Honoria smiled. 'I guess I have let this fester for too many years. It ruined my mother, because she let it. I daresay Cyrus put Louise out of his mind soon after he had secured your mother's hand and her father's mining concessions. It shows, doesn't it, that the connection between our families goes back much further than the day Michael and Sarah exchanged their vows?'

Jensen's complexion paled. 'Indeed. You will inform me if your meeting with the bank's directors throws up anything I need to know about the loan?'

Honoria thought for a moment. Then she nodded and stood to take her leave.

In the hallway Charlotte was hovering with the coffee tray. Jensen shook his head wearily as Honoria smiled.

'I shall give Miss Sarah your regards, Charlotte...' She paused to offer Jensen her hand – not a gesture she had anticipated making when she had arrived. She had come looking for a clue to Michael's potential *subterfuge* and to protect the Landseer name. She was leaving having laid what had once been her trump card on the table and so begun the process of laying the past to rest.

'...Goodbye, Jensen, and good luck!'

Jensen took her hand and saw her out. He stood frowning at Charlotte and said, 'I wanted that half an hour ago.'

He waved Charlotte away and returned to the study, watching Honoria leave. 'What an extraordinary woman!' He cursed under his breath, knowing how determined she was to protect the Landseer name and fearful for what she might find.

Three days after her visit to Jensen Calloway, Honoria was invited to the impressive building in the commercial centre of Melbourne by the grandson of the man who had helped her husband establish the bank. Honoria was struck by the irony of being received by one of her godchildren, Spencer Argate, who had diligently made his way up the ranks to achieve the status of director long before Michael had even come close. He showed her into the boardroom, seating himself at the head of the long, highly polished mahogany table, with one junior member of the secretarial staff to minute the meeting.

Spencer Argate cleared his throat and Honoria understood immediately the gravity of the situation by the tone of his voice as he pushed a copy of the contract Michael had drafted between the bank and Jensen Calloway across the table to her, and she noticed very swiftly that it was a different document to one that Jensen had – albeit reluctantly – shown her.

'We are very concerned, Mrs Landseer, given your late husband's contribution in establishing this bank alongside my grandfather...'

Honoria groaned inwardly. She had known Spencer all his life and she found his prevarication irritating. She wished he would come swiftly to the point.

Her instinct told her they suspected Michael of some irregular conduct in his duties at the bank, and as their letter suggested, it related to the loan application from Jensen. She knew Spencer was nothing like how Michael liked to describe him and she could see why her son wouldn't get on with Spencer Argate, but if her worst suspicions were to be confirmed, this man had it within his power to seal Michael's fate within the bank that bore her husband's name and she knew where her protective instincts lay.

'We have been concerned for a while about the loan application that we approved for Mr Jensen Calloway, who, I understand, is also Michael's father-in-law, which adds to the delicacy of the matter.'

This was becoming painfully tedious. Honoria asked him bluntly, 'Forgive me, Spencer, but has Mr Calloway defaulted on his loan repayments or is he likely to in future?'

Spencer Argate's expression was grave as he shook his head. 'No. He isn't, Honoria. On the contrary, in fact. He has repaid the loan in full. We were going to contact him by letter to inform him the last two payments were in excess of what he owed. Mr Calloway originally asked for a higher sum than we were inclined to approve, so the contract in our files – the one that I have presented to you today – is based on the figure we approved, although Michael argued strongly that we should sanction the amount Mr Calloway applied for. So we have conducted an audit within the bank and discovered that two contracts were drafted – either by accident because Michael anticipated we may have sanctioned the amount the customer requested or for motives of his own, upon which we can throw no light. We did find a copy of another contract and that is for the original figure among Michael's papers, and I would make an educated guess that Mr Calloway holds a copy of the contract that Michael was concealing, not the official draft showing the amount we had approved.'

Honoria betrayed no emotion, but she did look ashen and Spencer instructed the secretary to bring her a glass of water. Honoria had two mouthfuls and then she looked at her godson again. 'Are you implying that Michael has been misappropriating funds due to the bank?'

'I don't know what his motives were, Honoria. Aside from the fact that he drafted a contract for a loan this bank hadn't sanctioned and offered it to a client as the agreement with the bank, which, had we not been diligent in our procedures, could have resulted in him defaulting, causing him to lose his family home to this bank.'

'Surely the Calloway mansion is stated as collateral against defaulting in this version of the contract?' Honoria jabbed her finger at the contract in front of her.

'There is no other version, Honoria. I don't know why Michael retained a copy of the contract we found among his papers, because the directors had already declined that application; however, had he not gone off to fight and Mr Calloway had subsequently defaulted, we wouldn't have prosecuted for seizure of his home... because.' He paused to reveal another contract from his leather attaché case. 'This is not signed off by the bank. It doesn't have our seal. It's voided. Mr Calloway has been making payments on a non-authorised loan, and given the years Michael has been working at this bank, we cannot understand why he would let this basic error occur.'

Honoria suddenly felt nauseous. She knew why. Of course she did.

Michael's greed was at work. He had never just wanted to punish Jensen; he had wanted to *humiliate* him, to claim the Toorak mansion for his egotistical gratification and to pretend that he was doing it in his grandmother's memory.

'May I enquire as to what you intend to do if any deliberate impropriety can be proved or Michael admits to his error?'

Spencer Argate steepled his fingers and said, 'We shall require an explanation and his future will depend upon his answer. We can refund Mr Calloway the last two payments and explain that rates of interest have fluctuated, that he was paying more than the minimum he was required to for some months, and that will save the bank any unnecessary embarrassment. This cannot, however, be overlooked.'

Honoria nodded silently.

'And Jensen – sorry, Mr Calloway – will be informed that his home is no longer at risk.' Spencer coughed slightly. 'As far as the bank was concerned that was never a likely outcome based on the loan that *we* sanctioned. However, if Mr Calloway understood something different from Michael, we cannot be responsible for that.'

Honoria still felt slightly nauseous, but she concealed it well. Spencer was impressed by her serenity and by the inner core of steel he had always known she possessed. Given that Michael may yet be in trouble should the other directors not be satisfied with his explanation, she would need that inner core more than ever. Spencer had always admired Ernest Landseer and he adored Honoria as one of his godparents, but he had always struggled to find common ground with Michael. He considered him lazy, full of a sense of his importance and an entitlement to climb the ladder within the bank rather than *earn* it. He hoped now for Honoria's sake that Michael, if pushed to explain why Jensen Calloway had a different, bogus version of a loan contract, could prove it was just an error that he had omitted to correct and was not proof of his *greed*. Because then the Landseers' fall from grace at the bank they had worked to create would be complete.

Spencer walked Honoria out to her taxi and they embraced. She wore a mask of inscrutability until she was inside the taxi and it was moving away, and then she cursed Michael. She had known that one day his greed might be his undoing, but never through lazy incompetence.

She said a silent apology to her deceased husband, because he had always resolutely resisted using the bank against the Calloways in Louise's interests and now she wished that she had listened. She had to some extent resisted but she had allowed Michael to persuade her and this may yet be the cost. The tarnishing of the Landseer name at the bank that bore its name.

Jensen Calloway never mentioned Honoria's visit to Marguerite, because he saw no point. He stood in his study, looking up at the portrait of Cyrus, and he saluted him with his glass of cognac. It tasted especially good tonight, that was certain. 'You old rogue!' He hadn't known about Honoria's mother, but it didn't change his opinion of his father either.

As far as he was concerned, Cyrus had loved his wife. The woman who bore him children, and that through her father Cyrus had secured the mining rights that helped pay for this mansion, which he had so feared losing to the bank in the event of a default.

Now the letter in front of him set that threat to rest and it appeared he had overpaid. He couldn't understand how, but he wasn't going to query it. Perhaps Michael's business acumen wasn't as astute as he believed, but set against his son-in-law's other sins, that was one to overlook. The bank may just have been correct in putting it down to interest rate fluctuations.

He didn't know what else Honoria might be aware of, but he hoped it didn't involve his visits to the brothel. He would never be ashamed that he had come to that woman's aid and probably saved her from being mutilated in some sordid back-street medical procedure almost two decades ago. He had realised at that time it had been a huge risk. Although her life should have been saved by taking his money and the advice that came with it via his intermediary to disappear to the country and begin a new life, because his financial gift had been sufficient to cover that. Marguerite had never understood why he put himself at risk out of kindness to a stranger he had only met briefly, but she had conceded that her distancing herself physically from him had been a motivating factor in his visits to the brothel.

That was over now. They had come through this recent *crisis* together.

If Sarah pursued the divorce they had urged her to seek from Michael, then they would be free of the Landseers' influence forever, and he was grateful that according to Sarah, Honoria would support her in seeking a divorce, because she deserved her freedom from Michael. Jensen sighed as he drained his glass, realising it just might in time allow him to *forgive* himself for the sin of encouraging her into it.

Honoria took to her room from the moment she returned from the bank, instructing Grace Metcalfe that she wasn't to be disturbed. Michael's fate was in the bank's hands and they would do whatever they deemed appropriate. She needed to revisit the past and that journey started with re-reading her mother's letters, along with the journals she had kept.

She had always taken Louise's version of events as gospel. That the sense of hurt Louise had relayed to her could have been down to *her* father or even her maternal grandparents. Now Honoria had to look with fresh eyes and apply some of the objectivity that Ernest had *urged* upon her.

Louise hadn't been jilted by Cyrus Calloway in the purest sense of the word, but that hadn't mitigated her sense of hurt. Nor was it *her* father's fault that Cyrus had remained Louise's great love even after she had married, because Honoria knew instinctively that Tom Chandler had been a good father to her and she remembered that he had tried being a loyal husband, but only to the extent Louise had allowed him to be! As she read on, Honoria saw the bitterness Louise had carried long after Cyrus's breach of promise – as Louise had always described it – or could it be that Cyrus Calloway simply changed his mind? Had his feelings been transferred to someone else? Honoria shook her head. No!

Because the mining concessions he had secured were too much of an incentive to be explained away by a change of heart. The letters and journals also contained a consistent theme which Honoria couldn't deny.

Her grandparents had not wanted her rushing into another engagement with Tom Chandler. They felt she could do better. Louise poured vitriol into almost every line of her letters and she shared her sense of shame at being rejected with her journals. Could Louise's poison have been passed on to her? Ernest always feared so, but she had brushed his fears aside.

Now as she read each line of every letter, she could no longer avoid the reality that Louise had carried her sense of betrayal throughout her life and that she sought retribution on Cyrus Calloway for all of it, however it may come. Honoria gasped with shock at one letter in which Louise had responded to her engagement to Ernest Landseer, to all the potential it represented for her. It was a cause for celebration. Could Louise have shared her desire for retribution against Cyrus with Ernest without her knowledge? It was possible, and it would explain why Ernest had been so resistant from the first time she ever shared her mother's story with him.

By the time Honoria came to read the last letter, there were tears in her eyes, for Louise and all the heartache her mother had carried through the years. Could her parents have enjoyed a happier marriage if Louise had been willing to let go of the past? Who knows?

Oh, Mother! Why didn't I just let your anguish go instead of letting it consume me all these years and passing the legacy on to Michael so that he could twist it to his own ends?

Honoria cursed under her breath as she briskly wiped her tears away. She rarely ever wept, sad though the letters were, but she felt she might have finally understood Louise rather than simply shared her anger and a desire for retribution. She also realised her mother didn't need to be put on a pedestal and that it was time to consign the painful legacy of her past to the ashes.

27

Sarah Landseer completed her nurse's training in Melbourne and then made herself available for duty at the Front but was advised it was unlikely she would be sent to Gallipoli, as the decision to evacuate the Dardanelles was seriously being considered as Christmas approached.

She saw nursing as a means of escape, although the irony of beginning her nursing career at the Front, as Agnes had before her, alongside so many new qualified young women was not lost on her. Australia needed its brave young women to be seen as willing to work in the most demanding arenas. The most senior strategists and many of the generals considered the Western Front to be the main theatre of the war, where most of the resources needed to be focused. The Straits of Gallipoli had become something of a sideshow, as far as many were concerned, and a costly one at that, which was viewed as crass and hugely insensitive given the heavy losses that the Allies – Australian and New Zealand forces in particular – had already suffered in what had begun as a *crucial* strategy in trying to push Turkish forces out of the war, thus creating a viable alternative option to what had become a stalemate on the Western Front.

Sarah told Agnes in one of her letters that she planned to spend Christmas with their parents in Toorak, a decision for which she had Honoria's blessing, as it was anticipated Michael could be home in time for Christmas, albeit still heavily imbued with residual bitterness over his amputation, and Honoria didn't think she should be subjected to that.

Cairo – December 1915

The visit to see the Sphinx and the pyramids was an absolute joy for Agnes, and having only Lennox to share the experience with added to her sense of joy. Although they tried to push thoughts of returning to the hell that was the tented hospital on Lemnos to the back of their minds, it loomed large, having the potential to take the shine off their happiness at being recently married. Saying farewell to Laryssa Nicoledes brought tears to Agnes's eyes as they embraced on the terrace of the Shepherd's Hotel. They had no idea of when they might see each other again, but Agnes made her best friend promise to write regularly. She also admitted to feeling low and weighed down with weariness at the prospect of returning.

The Tented Hospital, Lemnos – December 1915

On Christmas morning there was a carol service in the ward, followed by a traditional Christmas lunch. Soon the evacuation from Gallipoli would begin and Agnes knew there was little she would miss from this stretch of beach, sixty kilometres from the Front, where the carnage was taking place. The humility displayed by the Greek inhabitants towards their guests had been a boost to morale, but she would always associate the island with witnessing some of the very worst that mankind could inflict upon itself. So she felt her voice quivering slightly as she sang the carols, the irony of it not lost on her. When she looked across at Matron Challoner, Agnes saw that she shared some of her scepticism.

When Lennox saw her struggling with the carols, he came to her side. 'All right?' He held her arm and she nodded, squeezing his hand. She would be. What other choice did she have?

Melbourne, Australia – Three Weeks Earlier

Honoria kept her promise about consigning Louise's letters to the ashes, realising she had clung to the past for too long and so it had attained a toxic legacy. Reading them hadn't brought her all the answers she sought, but they had forced her to acknowledge that her father had been as responsible for Louise's continuing sense of melancholy as much as what Louise had seen as Cyrus Calloway's betrayal.

The journals in which Louise had revealed her parents' doubts about her rushing into a relationship with Tom Chandler had been very revealing, even though they cut to the core of her existence had Louise taken heed of their advice. Honoria finished reading the last letter with the conviction that Cyrus Calloway had become a convenient scapegoat for all that Louise had endured in the years after her marriage – just as Honoria acknowledged Jensen had become the source of her ire with all the toxic words Louise had spoken to her.

With the letters and journals destroyed, she turned her attention to the report the private investigation firm had sent her. She had become determined to unearth the truth behind what Michael had described as Jensen's sordid secret, which had made him so *vulnerable* to blackmail.

Because the simple act of visiting a brothel on a number of occasions shouldn't have got him so worried that he fell prey to Michael's greedy attempts to expose him, and now that the red mist of retribution against the Calloways had been cleared from her eyes, Honoria could see more clearly, and what alarmed her, if all the pieces of the jigsaw fitted together, was the small but not insignificant role that her husband Ernest had played in a tawdry tale in which she had urged he was right to play no part. Now that she had most of the facts to go with what she knew of their history, she had the opportunity, if she chose, to do some good, but it would require her to visit a woman that she was prepared not to like, if she was anything like her daughter.

Honoria emerged from the taxi and waited until the driver, who had been sceptical when she had showed him the address, drove away, as she wasn't accustomed to visiting near-derelict-looking tenements in St Kilda. All that her husband Ernest had told her, when she had come home one night and overheard an argument between him and one of their friends, was that she didn't need to know all the details, and that had been good enough for her. She had always trusted his judgement, so when Ernest had assured her that it wasn't a problem he was going to help fix, even if it cost him a friendship, she had acceded to his decision. The matter was closed and they never referred to it again, accepting with good grace the friend's decision to sever ties. Luckily, though, someone had intervened via a third party, and what her investigations had unearthed thus far suggested that Jensen Calloway had been the saviour without whom the woman she was here to visit would have been medically mutilated and could easily have died. She wasn't doing this entirely for woman she was about to meet, but in her desire to repent, she was willing to do it for a man whom she could have happily seen destroyed.

She squared her shoulders and took a deep breath, and then, suppressing an urge to sneer at the drab surroundings, she approached the front door of the woman she believed to be Yolande's mother – Zola Smith.

Jensen and Marguerite Calloway never anticipated being able to enjoy Christmas – and they certainly hadn't expected to still be living in their Toorak mansion. He hadn't been compelled to feel too sorry for Honoria's mother Louise, given all that Michael had threatened to inflict on them. It staggered him to realise the extent to which he had come to distrust his son-in-law, and there was a time when he could never have imagined Michael Landseer capable of such deceit. While the letter from the bank confirmed he had repaid the loan in full, it still confused him when he re-read his copy of the contract. At Marguerite's urging he wasn't going to dwell on it, as it was at long last time for a little rejoicing, as Sarah, newly qualified as a nurse, would be joining them for Christmas.

The Tented Hospital, Lemnos – Late December 1915

For Agnes Christmas had been an all-too-brief oasis of hope amid the ongoing misery of war. Morale remained low and Lennox was becoming deeply concerned about the effect it was now having on Agnes. Up until their wedding leave in Cairo, she had appeared to be coping so well, even in the depth of Laryssa's grief over losing Theo, Agnes had been a tower of strength for her friend, outwardly confident, but now that demeanour had vanished and she was counting down the shifts until evacuation. As far as the military top brass were concerned, the bold attempt to seize the Straits of Gallipoli was now a busted flush.

It was a failed strategy that had the effect of sapping the confidence of the troops, still fighting at the Front sixty kilometres away and causing some of the injured in the great white marquee on Lemnos beach, and those transported by hospital ship further to larger hospitals in Malta, Alexandria and Cairo, to question what their sacrifice had been for.

Lennox had his frustrating moments, usually to do with the agonising slowness with which essential medical supplies took to reach them on Lemnos. He lost his temper at times with colleagues, including Dr Rowlett, and once almost with Matron Challoner, which did bring a smile to Agnes's face to think that her husband would have the courage to incur the matron's wrath.

As 1915 passed to a New Year, they were informed officially that the evacuation from Gallipoli would begin soon and so the tented hospital on Lemnos would become obsolete. January brought freezing rain and the sand on the beach turned to beige sludge which overwhelmed the blood-stained duckboards and threatened to invade the floors inside the ward. Lennox railed at the major-surgeon that the conditions were unfit in which to treat fighting men and prepare them to face the enemy again.

While his concerns earned some sympathy, he felt he was fighting a lost cause. Agnes, who witnessed Lennox's outburst with the major-surgeon and then attempted without success to placate him afterwards, during which time he stormed off, confided in Dr Rowlett, who tried to quell her concerns.

'Be glad that he cares enough to risk the censure for speaking to a senior officer in that fashion. I wish I *had* a fraction of his courage...'

Agnes nodded. 'I see your point, although I don't doubt that he *cares*. It is his own well-being I am worried about. I don't want my husband to become a broken shell of a man, suffering nightmares, or worse, a breakdown, Dr Rowlett!'

Agnes realised how selfish her response to Dr Rowlett had sounded, but for once she just didn't *care*. Because she had seen Lennox pushing himself too far ever since they had returned from Cairo. The strain of trying to treat patients in the most basic conditions was weighing more heavily, so he had snapped. She was convinced now that their departure from Lemnos couldn't come soon enough.

28

Michael Landseer contacted his mother by telegram to inform her that the ship bringing him home would dock in Port Albany on the same day that Sarah received instructions to report for duty in Melbourne prior to beginning her trip to France. For reasons she couldn't rationalise, Sarah was a little disappointed she wouldn't have the opportunity to see Michael and inform him that she intended to file for divorce.

Honoria encouraged her not to worry, promising to make the case on her behalf, confident that Michael would have little grounds on which to resist.

Honoria's visit to Zola Smith had been as difficult as she had expected it to be. The woman's resentment for what she described as *"a rotten, arrogant, upper-class"* was palpable, and she looked on Honoria as a prime example of it. Nor did she spare the vile man who had sired her child and then encouraged her to *"get rid"*. When Honoria showed her the photograph of Jensen Calloway Zola did confirm – albeit grudgingly – that he wasn't the guilty party, but she admitted that she had received financial assistance from another man via a third party and that he could have been the man who had arranged for her to leave Melbourne and safely give birth in a quiet rural setting.

211

When Honoria asked her if she knew the father's name Zola was reluctant to say any more, but she thought that he might have been French in origin.

That comment had caused Honoria to smile and Zola bristled with anger.

'So you know this man?'

'My husband knew him casually some years ago.'

Whether Zola believed the lie or not, Honoria didn't care. Zola bore a corrosive bitterness towards those she believed had done her wrong and she made no effort to conceal it. Honoria suspected she would carry that bitterness to the grave. She believed she had enough, albeit circumstantial, evidence. This was combined with her memory of the night Eugene Crozier had stormed out of her house, incandescent that Ernest had declined to assist him in a delicate matter, and that Zola had said Jensen *wasn't* the father when she had no reason to do so, given the extent of her resentment, and protect the culprit by lying.

Honoria was confident now that Eugene Crozier had sired a child with a prostitute and that the child was her former maid and Michael's *lover*. Even thinking the word caused Honoria to sneer with contempt.

She knew Michael wasn't going to like any aspect of the story she had to tell him, but hear it he would, because without it he wouldn't get to learn of Yolande's whereabouts and that was Honoria's bargaining chip to *urge* him to agree to giving Sarah her divorce.

Although she was not given to open displays of emotion Honoria made an exception as she bid farewell to Sarah at home. Embracing her daughter-in-law, she wished her good luck. Sarah had received Agnes's latest letter, outlining her departure from Lemnos for Egypt, but much beyond that she didn't yet know. Sarah left to spend the night with other nursing volunteers in a Melbourne hotel before leaving for Port Albany the following day.

Agnes was delighted to reunited with Matron Freda Lomax, who had been informed by Matron Challoner that her support on Lemnos had been priceless. Although she blushed slightly at hearing this, Agnes felt she had done a good job under difficult circumstances and that she deserved her promotion to sister. That Sister Bryan, whose own promotion to matron was imminent, echoed her colleagues' views was gratifying, even though Agnes felt the sentiment was a little forced.

For her, however, it didn't matter where she would be deployed next, although she hoped it would be alongside Lennox. For his sake she was just glad they were off Lemnos, as he had been buckling under the strain in the final days there and he was fortunate that his uncharacteristic outburst at the major-surgeon had been overlooked.

She enquired about Laryssa Nicoledes and was informed she had been transferred to the Helipolis Hospital and Dr Rowlett would also be there, but there was no word yet on where she was going to be sent and was worried this might mean she wouldn't be close to her husband.

Agnes also saw Captain Tyson Mallory, who looked very forlorn, and she queried this with Matron Lomax.

'There are a number of issues playing on his mind. His left arm isn't healing quickly enough and he is impatient to be back in the action. Added to which I have heard his wife has started divorce proceedings, which has angered him because he wanted to get in first, and from what I know via a mutual friend, it's the captain who has greatest cause. Jeanette Mallory is a difficult woman, I am told, but it's a pride thing with him. I would tread carefully if I were you. He's very irascible...'

Agnes smiled. Not only had she made her peace with him; she also believed she had the measure of Tyson Mallory now.

In the days that followed Agnes made herself available for duty, although she was officially on leave, which Matron Lomax insisted she took advantage of, so she reacquainted herself with colleagues that she remembered on the ship from Australia who had been deployed in Cairo and Alexandria, including Nurse Whitman, who, she was informed, was making little progress in her nursing career and, much to *her* frustration – which caused Agnes to smile ruefully – not having much success with her prime objective of getting a ring on her finger.

Agnes had shaken her head sadly, as Nurse Whitman hadn't changed, and that given her lack of success with medics and soldiers alike it hadn't yet dawned on her that she wasn't the "*catch*" she had always believed herself to be.

The Shepherd's Hotel, Cairo – Evening

Captain "*Horatio*" Nichols warmly welcomed Agnes onto the terrace of the hotel that evening. He knew what a hellish experience the hospital on Lemnos must have been, while she congratulated him on his promotion. He bowed his head, saying it was of little comfort given all the good men he had lost in the trenches, including Private Nicoledes, and typically of Nichols he remembered to express his sorrow for Lieutenant Landseer, which earned him one of Agnes's smiles. When Nichols her left to join his friend Captain Mallory, Agnes was surprised to see that he had Nurse Whitman for company. She looked at Agnes, hoping for a reaction, but Agnes wasn't going to give her the satisfaction.

She found herself suddenly feeling slightly sorry for Elizabeth Whitman, who, it seemed, could only define herself through her attractiveness to men. Mallory obviously had his reasons for enjoying her company and he was lapping up her attentiveness, but Agnes understood that given what Matron Lomax had told her about his wife, the respect she had come to have for Mallory was diminished by him having set his sights so low. She noticed Elizabeth Whitman placing her hands on Mallory's shoulders and whispering something into his ear, then laughing as she looked in her direction.

'Leave Sister Ashworth alone, Ty. You are better than this,' Captain Nichols said, but Mallory waved him away.

'Don't worry, Horatio. Sister Calloway – apologies, it's Ashworth now, isn't it? – I believe we have the measure of each other now and all that misunderstanding is done with.'

Agnes approached their table. 'Well, I understood we had reached an understanding, Captain, as you spoke very graciously at my wedding. However, you appear to be behaving less gallantly this evening, so unless that is due to you having too many cognacs or to the quality of the company you are keeping, I can't decide…'

Captain Mallory grinned at Agnes as he laid down another winning card.

'I hope you are not impugning Captain Nichols's good character, Sister.'

'I was referring to the young woman hanging on to your arm like a limpet… Captain Mallory. As you well know.'

Mallory whistled and Nurse Whitman glared at Agnes. 'She has always been jealous of me, Tyson…'

Agnes raised a quizzical eyebrow, but she said nothing, as the eyes of everyone on the terrace homed in on Mallory's table. Agnes was just glad Lennox wasn't here as her husband would lay the blame on Mallory and perhaps invite more trouble on himself after his altercation with the major-surgeon, and that was something she was eager to prevent for his sake. Although Mallory's conduct was beneath a man of his rank, she blamed Nurse Whitman for having goaded him.

'Let it go, Ty!'

'Just deal the cards… please, Horatio. Would you like to join us, Sister? You are more than welcome, although I hope

215

for your sake you are a better player than that brother-in-law of yours...'

'Thank you but no, Captain Mallory. Cards have never interested me, nor do I suspect your female company would appreciate it, as she likes having the attention of men all to herself... Perhaps Miss Whitman would like to be included – that is, if she can loosen that grip she has on you!'

Captain Nichols looked at Agnes, raising an eyebrow, as Mallory whistled loudly. He whispered something in Elizabeth Whitman's ear and she laughed too loudly, earning herself several irritated looks from other patrons, and Agnes suppressed a smile as Captain Mallory slapped Elizabeth Whitman on her bottom and said, 'It's OK, Sister. I know that Miss Whitman's talents lay elsewhere...'

Agnes looked at Elizabeth, who was blushing now, and then back at Mallory as he organised his hand of cards.

'Indeed, Captain! I have heard that Miss Whitman's talents have been widely enjoyed!'

Agnes walked away at that moment and Mallory shrugged himself free of Elizabeth Whitman's hold around his neck.

'Was that really necessary, Ty?'

Mallory swore under his breath and then he took a large gulp of whisky. 'Lighten up, will you, Horatio? She loves it!'

Nichols wasn't sure which of the women Mallory was referring to with that comment, but as he glanced across at a chastened Elizabeth Whitman, he was certain *she* didn't love it at all.

Hospital Ship – Night

Sarah Landseer didn't make the acquaintance of many of her fellow nurses en route to France as Agnes had, so the long days at sea quickly became tedious for her. She did, however, attract the attention of two young men who weren't deterred by the sight of a wedding ring which she had continued to wear in the hope that it would keep unwelcome suitors at bay – even though as she far as was concerned her marriage to Michael was effectively over and she trusted Honoria to keep her word and encourage Michael to agree to setting her free.

Ryan Mitchell, who introduced himself to her first, was volunteering as an ambulance driver, as his family business was in haulage, based in Croydon, New South Wales. He looked much younger than he was, with piercing grey eyes and sandy hair. He was slightly nervous around girls, he admitted embarrassingly, confessing that some of men that she had seen him with onboard had been urging him to approach her ever since the ship left Port Albany.

Sarah blushed slightly. Over the tortuous months of her marriage to Michael, followed by the humiliation of discovering his lust for Yolande, followed by her anguish over the loss of their child, she had become numb to most human kindness, while the attention of men had ceased.

Now she was conscious of being noticed again and she didn't yet know whether she liked it. She looked down the deck to where some men were giggling and then she looked back at Ryan. 'Are they your friends? The ones being *so* dismissive?'

Ryan half-turned, nodding sheepishly. 'They have been encouraging me to approach you for days, but they suspected I would lack the courage, so they are waiting for me to bail without success…'

Sarah smiled, moving closer. 'Then we will have to convince them otherwise, won't we? Just to teach them a lesson.'

He looked at Sarah quizzically as she leaned in to kiss him gently on the cheek, taking one last look at his not-so-encouraging friends as she smiled and walked away.

Melbourne, Australia

Michael decided on the ship home from Egypt that he wasn't going to return to work at the bank. He told several of his invalided comrades that he couldn't bear the pitying looks of his colleagues as he went about his duties. As before, he struggled to engage with many of the men he had fought alongside, and although he was still resentful that the amputation had been necessary, he had lost some of the arrogance he had displayed on the outward journey, which he attributed to his guilt over the loss of Aaron. He swerved company when it suited him and preferred to wallow in too many cognacs.

Life wasn't going to be the same, however, and he would have to adjust to that. He was also surprised by his lack of reaction to the news that Sarah was leaving Australia to start her nursing duties at the Front, just as he was coming home. He hadn't given much thought to how he was going to react had she been there to see him with part of his leg missing and was glad now that he would be spared that ordeal for a while.

One of his first tasks on reaching Melbourne would be to see Aaron's parents, as he felt he owed them that. He didn't know what kind of a reception he would get, given that Eugene Crozier had severed links with his parents some years ago over a business dispute and that he had encouraged Aaron to do the same without success, so he was nervous about how they would feel having him in their home when they knew that Aaron had fallen to the sniper's bullet attempting to save *him*.

He still maintained that Aaron should have put *his* own survival above all other considerations, and he was convinced his parents and Leticia would feel the same. Nor did he doubt that the friend he had known almost all his life would have coped better if their fates had been reversed. He recalled what the doctors at the tented hospital had told him, even what his sister-in-law had said in urging him to consent to the amputation, which he had steadfastly refused. Nor did he accept that it was all self-indulgence on his part, and at least some of his comrades on the ship home who had suffered amputations themselves understood his *rationale*.

Honoria had prepared herself for his arrival and the fury that he was likely to vent once he realised Yolande wasn't there, although she suspected the wretched girl would have shared her plans with him.

She had secured an address from Zola, but that woman was as *cunning* as her daughter, so she had little faith in it being a valid address.

Resentment was in their blood and their sense of victimhood was palpable.

First of all, he would have to agree not to contest Sarah's desire for a divorce and then she would tell him the whole sorry mess involving his grandmother and the truth of the Calloway's role in Louise's past, so much of which she had accepted without question.

Then there was the issue involving Zola Smith and her connection to the Croziers. All of it, the whole sordid mess, and she was prepared to include herself in that, to lay her own lack of humility on the line and to accept she had much to repent, and that she expected him to do likewise.

When the knock came at the door, Honoria squared her shoulders and took a long, steadying breath, but when Grace Metcalfe appeared at her side, she realised it wasn't Michael arriving by taxi-cab, as the housekeeper handed her the telegram Michael had sent, telling her that he was staying at his club for a few days, adding that he was aware that Yolande had taken her leave and they would discuss the matter on his return.

Honoria, who had prepared herself for telling him all that she had unravelled, felt slightly peeved at being let down and she sneered with derision.

'Damn him!' she said, dismissing the housekeeper with an indolent wave of her hand.

Michael's meeting with the Croziers proved to be as difficult as he had feared it would be. Leticia was overwhelmed by her grief again just at the sight of him, while Eugene remained stiffly polite, which caused Michael to wonder whether he was still overcome by grief or if his cool demeanour was influenced by other issues which should have been reconciled in his mind years ago. His father Ernest had never fully explained why Eugene Crozier had severed ties with them and Aaron had never been sure why Eugene had been *so* eager for him to let their friendship drift. Now, however, fate had conspired to make Aaron his saviour despite Michael's urging to the contrary, and Aaron had paid the ultimate price for his valour. In those circumstances alone, Michael didn't expect Eugene to forgive him because he couldn't forgive himself, and he knew he would carry survivor's guilt with him for many years.

Aaron had said his father could be a cold fish and Michael was beginning to understand what his friend meant by that remark, as it was Leticia, when her sobbing had subsided under the disapproving scrutiny of her father, who did most of the talking, and even when Michael expressed how sorry he was that it had come to this, Eugene barely uttered a word.

'Well, you survived, didn't you? At my son's expense. Then again, you Landseers always possessed an *instinct* for survival. Ernest was always very particular about that.'

When Michael turned to Leticia to ask about her mother, who hadn't put in an appearance since he had arrived, she started to speak until a furtive look she caught from Eugene urged her to say no more.

'I am very sorry for your loss. Aaron was the best friend I ever had.'

Michael shook the hand that Eugene offered him after some hesitation and he saw the glimmer of a half-smile flicker momentarily across Eugene's eyes, but his handshake was loose and it lacked sincerity.

Leticia saw Michael to the door and she smiled. At one time she would have had a barbed comment or two to throw his way, and he would have given her it back as good as he got, but as Michael looked at her now, he could see that Aaron's sister looked dead behind the eyes.

How they were going to reconcile themselves to his death, Michael had no idea. He knew that he would miss his friend for the rest of his days, but as far as the Croziers were concerned he had done his duty by coming here – not that the gesture had been appreciated in the way that he had hoped or that it should have been – and now he would look to his future and endeavour to prove that his friend's sacrifice hadn't been wasted.

29

In Honoria's view Michael deigned to grace her with his presence three days after he returned to Melbourne. He told her of his excruciatingly difficult encounter with Eugene and Leticia, followed by the equally awkward meeting with the directors of Argate & Landseer, who much to his chagrin agreed all too quickly that he should carefully consider his future with the bank in light of what their audit had uncovered in his absence. Damage limitation is what they were interested in and Honoria didn't blame them.

Spencer Argate had assured her that whatever happened they would continue to trade as Argate & Landseer, as that was how their clients knew them, and although it saddened her that the direct link with the Landseer name was to be severed through Michael's departure, she would live with it. He was responsible for his own demise and he would have to live with the consequences.

'So it's a whitewash effectively. We agree that I go quietly with my investment intact and you can pretend this never happened.'

Spencer Argate had pursed his lips, steeping his fingers, resisting the urge to unleash his anger on Michael, because he doubted it would have any effect and he refused to give him the satisfaction.

'Indeed,' Spencer said as Michael struggled to his feet and limply shook the hand Spencer offered him.

It didn't strike Michael as ironic as it had Spencer that they had been rivals to the chairmanship of the bank. Michael had sown the seeds of his destiny long before he had volunteered for military action, which had been a commendable sacrifice given the injury he had suffered, but the downfall it had led to was attributable to *his* greed.

So sitting in the lounge opposite Honoria, as he nursed a glass of cognac and massaged the upper half of his left leg, she was torn between anger, which she couldn't bring herself to hold at bay, and sympathy, and for the time being the anger won.

'So there is no Landseer working at the bank your father established? I am glad he isn't here to see such a wretched outcome!'

Michael winced with pain but he refused to take her bait.

'Well, I have a lot to tell you, Michael. Most of which I suspect you probably won't like. I have had to repent for some of my transgressions. I only hope that recent experience has lent you the humility to do the same. There is one thing I expect from you and that is you won't contest Sarah's divorce.'

Michael was about to protest until Honoria held up her hand. 'You never loved the girl. She was a means to an end. That end is now voided, so you will do the decent thing by giving her freedom.'

'I am guessing there is some kind of trade-off which will be beneficial to me should I acquiesce?'

'Yes, the means by which you can locate Yolande.'

Michael nodded, intrigued that Honoria was inclined to encourage a relationship she had previously viewed as *abhorrent*.

'I understand a lot more about your grandmother now. Having read her letters and journals. I can see that prolonging her bitterness at Cyrus simply masked her true feelings towards the man she married – my father, whom her parents discouraged her from committing to. The journals told me that they would have liked to pursue Cyrus for breach of promise, but they lacked the funds and they saw no motive for her to rush into another liaison. Tom Chandler was as good a father as he had it within him to be for me, but Louise realised her mistake very swiftly and so Cyrus Calloway became the source of her bitterness which she never let go and passed on to me…'

Michael whistled and half-rose in his seat. Honoria watched him struggle for a moment and then said, 'What do you want?'

'I am guessing there is more you have to tell me, so I want another cognac. Better still, bring me the decanter.'

Honoria rose, walked towards Michael, took his glass and refilled it.

When he reached for the decanter, she shook her head. 'I have given Metcalfe the night off. There is more that I have discovered, some of which is going to unpalatable. So I thought it expedient that we had the house to ourselves.'

Honoria resumed her seat and Michael smiled. 'I am intrigued!'

'I hope when I have finished you will view Jensen Calloway differently. I certainly have since I visited him.'

Michael looked at her, askance, but he said nothing.

'I had no choice. The letter from the bank unnerved me. I thought they were going to prosecute… So I went to see Jensen. He resented my visit, which I guess was understandable, and he mistrusted my motives, but he did show me his copy of the loan application. The bogus one!'

Had she anticipated a reaction, she would have been disappointed, but she knew her son's inscrutable mask when she saw it.

'I challenged him about what he knew of his father and Louise, and he said nothing. I believed him. As far as Jensen was concerned there was nobody in Cyrus's life until he met

Jensen's mother and secured the mining concessions upon their marriage.'

Michael laughed mirthlessly. 'You believe Jensen! Why?'

'Because he had no reason to lie. A man like Cyrus was likely to have led an interesting life in his youth, but whatever he felt for Louise wasn't so strong that he couldn't throw her over, and those mining concessions would have been worth a fortune. They made him very wealthy. He built the mansion in Toorak on the strength of it and it likely set Jensen up for the future.'

'I wanted that mansion, you knew that! Now it will remain in Calloway's hands!'

'Be quiet! I know how much you coveted it and you were prepared to commit fraud to get it. How could the bank have filed default proceedings against Jensen on a fake contract? I always knew your greed would be your undoing. You are lucky to have escaped...'

Michael pulled a face and drained his glass, but Honoria ignored him.

'I can guess you are probably enjoying this tale, Mother, given how you are dragging it out, but is there any danger of you coming to the point? Or any kind of conclusion...'

Honoria pursed her lips. 'I was always intrigued by how swiftly and willingly Jensen responded to that blackmail letter you had someone send him. What could be so bad that he would go to such lengths to hide? Surely visiting a brothel a few times when his girls were young couldn't have been the extent of it. Most of Melbourne's businessmen would be hanging their heads in shame if that's all it took. There had to be more, so I hired an investigator and he did some digging...'

Michael smiled broadly, his curiosity piqued. 'And?'

'You would have been around ten or eleven years old and I came home early from some tedious committee event. I heard your father arguing in his study quite voraciously and then his visitor came storming out past me in a rage—'

'Jensen came to Father for money?'

Honoria shook her head. 'It wasn't Jensen he was arguing with. It was Eugene Crozier and their friendship was effectively over that night. My investigator uncovered the rest of what your father refused to tell me: that Eugene also frequented a brothel, but he wasn't as discreet and he sired a child. An illegitimate child with one of the girls. Her name is Zola Smith!'

Michael shook his head. 'So?'

'I went to see her and she confirmed that she was offered money by two different men. One likely to be Eugene offered her money to have the pregnancy terminated illegally by some back-street quack who would likely mutilate her and another man through a third party who offered her an alternative: to have the child in some rural setting and create a new life for herself. She took the money and did half of what he suggested, but returned to her life as a whore… The child was offered for adoption.'

'Is any of this relevant, Mother, or are you just talking nonsense? So Eugene sired a bastard and he wanted it gone. He wouldn't have been the first or the last!' Michael suddenly remembered Eugene's words from the other day. He had referred to Ernest's instinct for survival. 'And my old man wouldn't help! It explains a lot. Why Eugene wanted Aaron to sever our friendship and why he would still be alive today if he had heeded his father's advice.'

Honoria shook her head. 'You can't know that for certain. Aaron was very brave and he wanted to save you. Eugene is hurting… Grieving! He would feel the same whoever Aaron had tried to save.'

Honoria paused momentarily, then she continued. 'I showed Zola the photograph of Jensen taken at your wedding, and she denied he was the man who had sired a child, but she did say he could have been her benefactor, through a third party… That was the secret Jensen wanted to protect, that he had given money via a third party to a pregnant prostitute to have her child, but he couldn't ever be sure that she would do as he advised and he didn't want to risk prosecution for facilitating an illegal termination. That was why your letter worked. Why he *needed* the loan!'

Michael smiled. It was a lascivious, gleeful smile and Honoria sneered with derision. Had she thought that Michael wouldn't even now absolve Jensen of his sins or try to understand his vulnerability, then his look confirmed it.

'So you think your investigations are reliable? This Zola woman did she confirm whether she had the child?'

'I knew that she had the child before I went to see her. I went so she could fill in the last pieces of the jigsaw and she was very resentful and belligerent, but she gave me the answers I wanted. You will discover what she is like when you go to meet *her!*'

Michael had struggled to his feet and stood with the decanter in his hand. He poured another cognac and stared at his mother. 'Meet her? Why would I?'

Honoria looked him squarely and said, 'Because she is Yolande's mother!'

She watched Michael as he digested the news that the servant whore he professed to being in love with, who very likely caused his child to die when she pushed his wife downstairs, was the illegitimate child of Eugene Crozier.

'So Aaron is her half-brother?'

'Yes. Although Eugene must believe his money paid for the termination and that made the problem go away until Jensen's gift saved your lover's life!'

Michael looked ashen. He didn't know which part of it to believe, or whether he believed any of it. Yet so much of it fitted. It made sense!

He had felt the extent of Eugene's mistrust the other day and that it went deeper than grief. Eugene had expected *his* friendship with Ernest to amount to something when he had needed it most, but he hadn't received that reassurance and then, despite all his efforts to break their friendship, Aaron had offered *him* a hand in No Man's Land and paid for it with a sniper's bullet to the temple. The irony of it all was too great. He had confided in Aaron some of his plans for Jensen, although he never shared the truth about his lust for Yolande with anyone.

'Does this Zola know where Yolande is living?'

Honoria nodded. 'I suspect so. I believe she will receive you. For what it's worth she didn't appear surprised that Yolande had left my employ. As far as Zola is concerned, we are all part of the same arrogant, rotten class, so don't expect a warm welcome. Get what you need from her and leave!'

'Why are you helping me? I would have thought you would want to sever ties with Yolande by whatever means. Especially if you blame her for killing your grandchild.'

Honoria shrugged. 'I have tried to deter you from the ill-fated liaison with that wretched girl, but to no avail. So I surrender, on the condition that you keep your word and give Sarah her divorce?'

Michael bowed his head. She might have missed his nod, it was so brief.

'I have much to repent for, Michael, but I have reconciled myself to Louise's past. I should never have allowed her sense of hurt to subvert my judgement or to pass the desire for retribution on to you. It has become a corrosive legacy, so it could destroy you if you let it, so after I had read Louise's letters and journals, I consigned them to the ashes...'

Michael opened his mouth to speak, until Honoria halted him. 'It is done. We both need to move forward. So what are your plans...?'

Michael smiled ruefully as he didn't know how his mother would react to what he had decided to do. He knew she would struggle to believe it, as he could barely believe it himself.

'You remember the rural property Father bought near Hepburn Springs? I intend to move there and make a life with Yolande. Providing this…' he paused to thump his leg and winced, 'doesn't put her off. I can't stay in Melbourne. For the same reasons I readily accepted severing links at the bank, I don't want to visit the old drinking establishments that I shared with Aaron. His absence leaves too great a hole and I think that I can make a life with Yolande at the property where nobody will be aware of the nature of our relationship. I realise this won't be what you want to hear, but I didn't *want* to survive in No Man's Land when the bullet went into my thigh, nor did I care about the threat of gangrene they kept warning me about in the tented hospital on Lemnos after my tourniquet had been fouled up. I was ready to face up to any fears about death and to accept my fate. I could have had a hero's death…'

Honoria shook her head sadly. Michael was right that it wasn't what she needed to hear, but she doubted he was alone among the returning injured who felt that way. Yet he had been given a chance and he should accept it with grace and make the most of it, but Michael living a rural life on the land? She doubted he could endure that for very long.

'That derelict old homestead. I never understood why your father made that investment or that he set such store by wanting to retire there. I never wanted to. Even for the occasional weekend, it was my idea of torture…'

Michael laughed, rubbing his left thigh again; she watched him in silence for a moment. Yes, he had suffered, but she hoped he had learnt something from his experience of war. She hoped he had attained a little humility he had been sadly lacking when he went off to fight.

'I will have to check with our solicitors, but I suspect the property was left to you so you would sign the deeds over to me?'

Honoria nodded. 'Have it with my pleasure, but remember what I said, Michael, about settling the past. Old sins cast long shadows and I have been guilty for too long of holding on to Louise's past and letting it rule me…'

Honoria rose and made her way to the stairs as Michael poured himself another cognac before hobbling back to his chair. As he heard her footsteps ascending the stairs, he was in the trenches at Gallipoli again, with the sound of mortar fire all around him, as Aaron gripped his arm, trying to urge him to his feet, all the time ignoring Michael's pleas to leave him there and save himself, until the moment Aaron's grip slipped and he had fallen at his feet before other comrades pulled him out of danger. His hands shook as he put the glass on the table beside him and pressed his fingers against his temple, willing the images to recede. It was a disturbing dream that he hoped would fade in time, but as for the corrosive legacy of survivor's guilt, he feared he would carry that for the rest of his days.

30

Sarah was tired. It had been another gruelling shift. The toll of casualties was as relentless as it had been since she had arrived and her learning curve had been as steep as it had been swift.

Agnes had warned her in letters, but the reality of nursing close to the Front had been much starker than what Sarah had been told to expect.

The six-week voyage out from Port Albany seemed like a lifetime ago, but when she made the calculation she realised it was only eight weeks since she had reached Europe.

Her relationship with ambulance driver Ryan Mitchell had blossomed during the journey from Australia and she had also attracted the attention of Second Lieutenant Stuart Drayton, who made a point of introducing himself one evening as she had stood at the guard rail, the setting sun catching her hair as it blew in the sea breeze. She could hardly believe the attention she was receiving, and although she gently informed both men that she was married, she was trying very hard not to think about Michael. She did at rare quiet moments during a hectic shift wonder if Honoria had passed on the news that *she* wanted a divorce, striving to be as confident as her mother-in-law was that he would agree.

She pulled off her cap at the end of her shift, shaking her head so her hair fell free. Stretching, she was eager for her bed. Fatigue was a constant issue for her, never understanding how Agnes had grown accustomed to the daily toil during her time on Lemnos.

Many of the Australian troops who had survived the nightmare in the Dardanelles had been redeployed on the Western Front and she had been sent to the hospital close to the Gothic city of Rouen to tend them.

She slumped onto her bunk, trying to be quiet for a colleague in the adjoining bunk, and extracted Agnes's latest letter. Her sister was still nursing in Cairo and she seemed content to remain there for as long as her husband was deployed at the hospital situated in the Gezirah Palace Hotel. She would love to be reunited with her elder sibling, but she understood why Agnes wanted to remain close to Lennox.

For herself she couldn't rationalise why she was simultaneously attracting the attention of two eligible young men who could have their pick of other nurses. She had gently informed both Ryan Mitchell and Second Lieutenant Drayton that she couldn't commit to either of them because she wasn't free to do so and she wouldn't under any circumstances jeopardise her chances of securing a divorce. It was, however, the opinion of some of those serving under him that Drayton "*had it bad*" for her and this fact had been passed on, although they kept secret the fact that he had surreptitiously taken a photograph of her in uniform. They accused him light-heartedly of being lovesick for Nurse Landseer, a condition for which there wasn't a cure, and mostly he took their teasing well.

Although she liked both men equally, if forced she found Drayton a little too brash – and she'd had her fill of brash men, being married to Michael Landseer. Ryan was much quieter and modest, a characteristic which endeared him to her, but Drayton was dismissive of Mitchell as his rival, boasting Sarah couldn't possibly prefer that "boy" to *him*. Each night when the lights were out Drayton would smoke his last cigarette, gazing at the image of Sarah, confident that if any man was going to win her favour, it was him.

Cairo – Spring 1916

It was one of life's great ironies, which struck both Agnes and Lennox as poignant, that one of the last patients she treated in Cairo prior to receiving orders for transfer to France was Captain Tyson Mallory.

Agnes acknowledged that it was a demonstration of the measure of the man her husband was – given how he felt about Mallory – that he took her aside prior to her seeing him and told her gently that the prognosis wasn't good and that he appeared to be struggling with the reality. His injured left arm just hadn't healed swiftly enough and the wound had become infected, causing septicaemia, and he had a fever that was dangerously high when Agnes was first called upon to treat him.

She took a steadying breath and, squaring her shoulders, approached him.

Although she knew he wouldn't be imbued with whisky, she was always uncertain what mood Mallory would be in. Lennox stood back with his arms folded watching Agnes talk to Mallory. He looked bad and Lennox was conflicted. He never liked seeing a patient suffer and know there was little to be done to relieve the pain, but that was the reality. Mallory's septicaemia was too advanced. His body was shutting down and he would be lucky to survive the night. Lennox watched as Agnes laid a reassuring hand on Mallory's shoulder. She had always been too generous to that damned man than he had ever deserved. His expression remained grave as she approached.

'I am going to sit with him. Make his last hours comfortable. I am off-duty so it's not a problem and Matron Bryan is OK with it.'

Lennox shook his head. 'Well, I'm not. You should be coming home with me instead of being his private nurse for the night.'

Nurse Whitman stifled a giggle until the matron glared at her.

'I am staying, Lennox, and if it was any other patient, you would be commending me for my devotion to duty.'

Lennox's pride was hurt and he looked across at Mallory. He knew it was likely Mallory wouldn't survive the next few hours, let alone until morning. Agnes was right. He knew it in his gut. If it were anyone but Mallory, he would be commending her for her devotion. It was just that he had a blinkered view when it came to Mallory. Aside from the fact he laid his life on the line in the service of his country and, if not this night then another, he would likely pay the ultimate price for his courage.

He felt Agnes's hand on his arm, soft and encompassing.

'I need to do this. I cannot explain my rationale, but I ask you to trust that I *need* to do this. For him, yes – but also for myself...'

Agnes nodded gently at Lennox as she moved her hand and turned very quietly to return to her patient. She heard footsteps echoing in the uneasy silence which descended on the ward, and when she looked around again, Lennox had gone.

As Agnes approached Mallory's bed, he smiled. 'I'm guessing I have incurred your husband's wrath again? No matter, all bets are that I won't survive the night and then he will be shot of me... You, Sister Ashworth, you are made of quality stock and you are probably too good for both of us...'

'Ssh. Conserve your energy—'

Mallory snorted and said, 'For what, the battle to come? I am done for. All the medics say as much. This wretched blood poisoning has become my biggest enemy and I have lost!'

Matron Bryan approached her and said, 'You don't have to stay. I can sit with him at intervals and Nurse Whitman is on hand...'

Agnes looked at Matron and shook her head. 'He deserves better than her, even if he wasn't always *so* discerning...'

'I am still here... Besides, she's not so bad, just very young. What is a man to do, Sister Ashworth? Miles from home when all the best women are already taken?'

Agnes smiled as she mopped his forehead, the sweat saturating him as the fever took an even greater hold. His voice, always so booming, so authoritative, had grown weak and weedy, and Agnes offered him her hand, which Mallory gripped so tightly it caused her to wince.

'Will you be in trouble for staying at my side?'

Agnes shook her head. 'He will understand... Might take him some time and he will sulk for as long as he can get away with.'

Mallory smiled again. 'I don't blame him for being jealous...' He paused and she leaned in closer to him. 'Thank you, Sister. Because we both know this is more than I deserved...'

Although her experience taught her to expect it, they proved to be Mallory's last words. He drifted in and out of consciousness until just before dawn broke with a bright orange streak in the sky. Agnes was asleep and the first glare of sunlight woke her, and she knew in that instant as his hand felt cold and limp in hers that he had gone.

Within seconds she felt Matron Bryan's hand on her shoulder, but she felt strangely numb. Captain Tyson Mallory had rejoiced in being a difficult man when he chose to be and she had fallen victim to his worst excesses once, and he had been right when he said that her personal kindness in his final hours was more than he had deserved.

She hadn't done it just for him, or for some perverse motive to exert her authority over Lennox. She had done it for herself.

To know that she had finally forgiven him for his lapse of judgement when they first arrived in Cairo and to confirm that he was like every other patient in her care, who *deserved* her *utmost* professionalism to the very last.

Field Hospital, Rouen, France – Spring 1916

In Egypt trips to see the Sphinx became a popular pastime for the Australian nurses when off-duty. They would pair up with army personnel and in horse-drawn carts drive into the desert at dusk. In Rouen, however, the Gothic cathedral was the focal point of interest and when ambulance driver Ryan Mitchell asked Sarah to go with him the first time, she was hesitant, conscious of wanting to avoid antipathy between herself and Second Lieutenant Drayton, or between him and Ryan, whose company she was increasingly coming to prefer. After much deliberation, however, and some discussion with her colleagues, she politely declined, although sorry then to see the disappointed look on his face, as he had believed he was making some progress in his pursuit of her. She had overheard, however, some of the idle chit-chat between patients who were serving under Second Lieutenant Drayton, and while some would include her in whatever gossip they heard about her without feeling embarrassed, others would look away shamefaced if they were ever caught exchanging or repeating any of Drayton's boastful claims. So Sarah would bide her time, confident that Ryan would think she was worth waiting for and she would be ready to set the record straight if she heard Lieutenant Drayton being less than the gentleman that she would expect from someone of his rank.

As it was, she didn't have to wait too long to confront Second Lieutenant Drayton over his conduct or threaten to report him to his CO. Because he received the news of her decision to decline Ryan Mitchell's invitation into Rouen with too much gleefulness and word got back to her, that she must have realised it was a man she wanted to spend her precious off-duty time with, not a *"mere boy"*, as he so disparagingly liked to describe Ryan.

'I am intrigued, Lieutenant, that you imply you know me so well to know who I would like to spend my precious off-duty moments with.'

Second Lieutenant Drayton shrugged nonchalantly. 'I don't know why you would limit your options.'

'I am not aware that I am. Private Mitchell is very modest and respectful and kind, qualities that I am yet to find in you. I did decline him on this occasion, but I am sure he will ask me again and I will probably accept. I found your company equally amenable while we were on the ship, Lieutenant, and I was looking forward to spending some of my time with you also. Sadly you appear to have developed a habit for being overly brash and arrogant, and those are personality failings I suffered all too often from my husband to have now to endure them from you...'

Patients in adjoining beds smiled, until they caught the dark looks he was darting in their direction. Nurse Landseer might still be quite junior, but he was conscious she could still report him to Sister Gould, who would pass the complaint on to his CO. He would have to tread carefully.

Hers was a friendship still worth winning, but he swiftly realised he would have to be much more subtle than he was accustomed to being back home to win with her, and it was obvious the ambulance driver Mitchell was already stealing a march on him and he was *damned* if he would allow that.

Sarah had walked away satisfied with her calmness at dealing with Drayton, wishing she had possessed the same courage when dealing with Michael and his lover Yolande. Lieutenant Drayton wasn't the first man who considered himself irresistible to women, that he was the cock of the walk among some of his men. She had learnt that over-confidence usually came at a price and often in a war zone that could prove too high a price to pay.

In her next letter from Agnes she received the news she had been hoping for: that Lennox's deployment in Egypt was coming to an end.

He and Agnes would be sent to France; as yet Agnes had no confirmed details of where they might be deployed but was hopeful it would be jointly. Sarah begun to hope it would be at the same hospital as her, but she dared not hope too much.

Sarah discovered she had been correct in her belief that Private Mitchell would ask her for a second date and this time she accepted. It was only a half day's leave for both of them so Rouen was the only viable option and she wanted to see that its famous cathedral was as awesome in its splendour as she had been led to believe. When Second Lieutenant Drayton learned that she had accepted Mitchell's invitation, he was furious, to the extent that in a fit of pique he almost destroyed the photograph he had *so* slyly got of her but thought better of it. He still thought she was selling herself short with Mitchell, although he realised there wasn't anything not to like about the volunteer ambulance driver. He realised that his tactic for winning Nurse Landseer over wasn't winning her respect and he had to change.

When he asked her afterwards how the date had gone, Sarah had smiled as she took his temperature.

'How long have you been with us, Lieutenant Drayton? I was merely wondering as I would have thought you would be keen to get back to the action, so might I *suggest* you focus more attention to your recovery and less on my life outside this hospital. Unless…?'

He frowned at her as she made to leave. 'Unless what, Nurse?'

'You want to prolong your stay in here and risk being labelled a malingerer?'

The patient in the adjoining bed began to snigger until Drayton threw him a dark warning look as Sarah triumphantly walked away.

As the weeks rolled by, the fighting continued with an increasing intensity, and morale among the Allied troops dipped further. Sarah noticed how it was affecting Ryan Mitchell whenever their shifts coincided. They made a point of trying not to discuss the war on their days out, which were becoming rarer, but they inevitably always came back to the subject during the course of the day. As May gave way to June the sun shone brighter and warmer, as the resolve of the Allies was matched by that of the enemy. As the Somme offensive began on 1st July the casualties on the Allied side from the first day were colossal. News that valued colleagues had fallen victim to the relentless slaughter caused a pall of doom to descend on the hospital wards and the barracks while nursing staff had to reconcile themselves to the harsh reality that men they had treated and who were reported fit to return to action came back to them within days if not hours with even greater injuries than before or worst, names that were familiar to them were added to the roll call of the dead.

There had been a reconciliation of sorts between Sarah and Second Lieutenant Drayton, whose priorities had shifted in the heat of battle as many valued comrades fell in the first intense weeks of the Somme offensive. Further losses saw him being promoted very swiftly, to First Lieutenant and then to Captain, recognition that he welcomed, although the circumstances were far from ideal. As he was ready to leave the hospital ward, he held out the creased photograph to Sarah, realising it was overdue to admit that he had taken it surreptitiously, and as a newly appointed captain, he should show more maturity. He smiled as he offered her his hand, but to his surprise – and to some extent hers – Sarah kissed him lightly on the cheek, not caring if Sister Gould was watching.

'I know that I could have been kinder to you and Private Mitchell, and I am sorry for that. You deserve someone that can make you happy—'

'You showed me your best qualities on the ship coming out from Port Albany, when I felt more emotionally fragile than I do now, so I thank you for that, Captain Drayton.'

He smiled.

'Does it sound good to your ears?'

'It does, Nurse Landseer. Thank you.'

'I hope you can stay safe and be the leader your men deserve. Good luck.'

Sarah swallowed past the lump in her throat, conscious of how many men she had treated who had been subsequently lost in recent days.

The toll of Allied losses was weighing her down and she had felt her resolve weakening daily.

'I am not entirely pleased with how you came to have this image of me, but that said, I would like you to keep it. So turn around.'

He looked at her quizzically with raised eyebrows and she laughed. 'I want to rest on your back.' She snatched the image from his fingers and coerced him to turn his back on her as she signed her name across the creased image: *"From Sarah Calloway to Stuart Drayton with love."*

'You can turn around again now.' As he did she handed him the image. 'Take it with my blessing, Captain Drayton. Promise me that you will endeavour to make those who serve under you proud. Make your family proud, but above all, strive to become the best version of yourself that you have it within you to be!'

Captain Drayton took the image, his hand brushing hers momentarily as he pushed into his breast pocket. He smiled.

'You are a very remarkable young woman, Nurse Calloway… or Landseer?'

'Calloway is my maiden name. I guess I don't see myself as Sarah Landseer anymore. It is a part of my past that I have no wish to return to, no matter what my fate might be here…'

'You think that it could include Private Mitchell?'

Sarah shook her head. 'I don't think too far ahead about anything. Your recent promotions, however well-deserved, should have taught you that. I won't tempt fate, Captain. About you or him, even about myself.'

He nodded and, taking the last of his belongings, he left, with good wishes from fellow patients, orderlies and other nurses. Sarah smiled as he turned back once and she nodded gently then, very quietly and diligently, she turned her attention to her duties. There was, however, a slight heaviness in her heart that she had only begun to understand Stuart Drayton at the moment they were destined to part.

31

France – Autumn 1916

The weeks rolled on and in late September the rains came, incessant for days at a time, turning the parched earth to a quagmire into which cannons, horses and some of the men would slip, thus needing to be rescued. Sarah coped as best she could along with colleagues, many of whom were exhausted before the end of their shift as the fighting intensified. She received confirmation by letter that Lennox and Agnes were going to be redeployed at the field hospital at Etaples, so she would have to wait a while longer for a reunion with her sister and to meet for the first time the brilliant brother-in-law about whom she had heard so much.

Ryan was also struggling with the number of casualties he was transporting from the Front, with some of the injuries he was seeing first hand so horrific and the prospects for the victims seemed hopeless that he couldn't bring himself to look, let alone offer, words of encouragement.

There were some who, to their credit, knew when the game was up and were relieved that for them the fighting was over, while others hoped for the best-case scenario: to be passed sufficiently fit to go home and learn to adapt to a new reality. He had admitted to Sarah that seeing fit young men incapacitated in a matter of minutes had a profound effect on him.

Those images of some of the most horrific injuries would remain seared in his memory long after the war had ended. What struck Sarah and her nursing colleagues was just how young some of the volunteers looked. Australian, Canadian, New Zealanders, along with the British Tommies, many appeared younger than eighteen and she wondered how many recruiting sergeants' heads were conveniently turned as youthful hearts full of hope and sometimes a fragile courage signed up to be swiftly disillusioned by the harsh realities of war.

She knew the value, however, of appearing strong. The last thing that these boys – because essentially that's all that they were – needed to see were her tears as the stretcher bearers brought them into the ward. Especially those who were faced with the prospect of losing a limb. While others who clung on to the last moments of their young life remaining stoical, their suffering the hardest to bear, won the most respect.

Melbourne, Australia – Autumn 1916

Michael Landseer took some weeks to adapt to his new life. Although his bitterness at having the amputation against his wishes had dissipated a little, he grew morose, especially when what remained of his left leg gave him night cramps, and it was Agnes who bore most of his anger.

Honoria was surprised by his determination to make a new life outside the bank because it was all that he had known until he had volunteered for action, but she'd had no hesitation in signing over the property in Hepburn Springs to him as she had never shared her husband's enthusiasm for the rural property and she was surprised Michael appeared to be *so* enamoured of its potential. He knew that he would need a team of people to get the interior into shape before he started on the land.

What frustrated her more was his determination on staying in Melbourne until he had located Yolande. The wretched girl was hiding somewhere and Honoria was convinced Zola was duplicitous in whatever plan the wretched girl was hatching, but that was as far as her interest went. One of her conditions of giving Michael Zola Smith's address was that under no circumstances would he bring Yolande back under her roof, and reluctantly he had agreed, but reading between the lines she guessed Michael was convinced he could persuade Yolande to share the rural idyll that he envisaged them sharing in Hepburn Springs, and should that not prove to be the case, she didn't want to contemplate his reaction, nor could she guess at his "*Plan B*".

Michael's first trip to the tenement in St Kilda had been a disaster for him, culminating in a war of words on the doorstep with Zola, who he discovered was as bitterly resentful as Honoria had warned him she would be, and the incident had almost got him arrested after he angrily clutched Zola by the throat. She had claimed she didn't know where her daughter was living and that she wouldn't have told him if she had.

Michael was convinced Zola was lying and he promised he would come back, leaving her with the parting words that it was little wonder Yolande had turned out the way she had with her as a mother. Zola had merely smiled but he decided he would relay precious little of this altercation to Honoria, who, having met Zola Smith for her own purposes, could imagine how the scene would unfold. He knew that she had as dim a view of the mother as she invariably had of the daughter she had taken into her employ.

'Your old hag of a mother had me convinced you loved my daughter... Although I saw the cursory sneer on her lips as she said it. Although Yolande has assured me that you *do*. I said you were probably no different from the rest of them and it appears that I was right...'

244

Zola had blushed then, realising her error, as Michael pointed his finger at her. 'So she has been in contact? She has been here. Never mind, I will find Yolande no matter how long it takes me, and I will bring her back. I will lance the poison of your malevolent influence until she is ashamed to call you her mother...'

Zola had listened, her expression impassive as she looked down on Michael and sneered, just as Honoria had sneered at her, and said, 'As if my Yolande would look at you now...'

He had stormed off in a fit of anger, determined to set his investigator to unearth what he could at the next address. Yolande still occupied a special place in his affections so he couldn't bring himself to think too badly of her, but on meeting Zola Smith, his *gut* instinct was that her resentment went much deeper than the surface bitterness she displayed for what she had suffered at Eugene Crozier's hands and that much of her bile had been ingrained into Yolande over the years, despite his efforts to mould her into being more than just his lover.

France – Autumn 1916

Sarah was delighted when Agnes wrote to say that she had secured her first extended leave since deployment in France and she would be coming to Rouen in late November. She hoped the handsome ambulance driver Sarah had told her so much about in letters would be able to secure leave to join them. Although she wasn't yet sure whether Lennox would be coming, Sarah was delighted that the longed-for reunion with her elder sibling was to become a reality at last.

Sarah's sense of disillusionment was renewed when word got through to her that Captain Stuart Drayton had been killed in action some six weeks after he had been passed fit for duty and she had signed his photograph as a parting gift. She had reconciled her feelings for him as she had hoped he had come to accept that her future lay with Ryan.

So news of his death during the battle of Pozieres in the intense early weeks of the Somme offensive hit her especially hard.

When Ryan heard of Captain Drayton's death, he was saddened, but he misread the extent of Sarah's sorrow and challenged her on it, but she was only mildly resentful and she found his jealousy – if that is what it was – strangely reassuring and sweet, although she knew Agnes wouldn't have tolerated such a reaction to her grief, even from Lennox. She had stood outside the ward with Ryan at her side, nervously smoking a cigarette as he feared she was furious at him, until she smiled slightly.

'Stuart Drayton was very kind to me on the ship from Australia – just as you were – so yes, I am saddened to hear he didn't make it. It may surprise you to know that I have never been in love before. My relationship with my husband never went that deep. I know that I was just a means to an end with Michael. His mother has inferred that and so have my parents. However, I think I could get to experience that with you. I don't approve of jealousy, though, Ryan, and I certainly don't seek to inspire it in others. If Captain Drayton had feelings for me, then they were his own and I never encouraged them.'

Ryan smiled. He dropped the butt of his cigarette and trod it into the ground. He laid his hands on her shoulders but for once without wiping the dust onto his trousers first, and Sarah smiled at his boldness, although she knew Sister Gould wouldn't be happy to see her return to duty with a soiled uniform. He took a deep breath and he wanted to kiss her on the mouth with all the force and passion that he had in him. Sarah's intuition told her that this was in his mind, but she didn't see why she should always be the one to drive the initiative in their relationship, so she was inclined to let him take his time.

When he leaned in for a kiss, Sarah instinctively closed her eyes, but all she received was the perfunctory kiss on the cheek that Ryan usually gave her and her smile was warmly encouraging.

'I was a little embarrassed, truth be told, by my reaction to the news. I have feared the dam of emotion I have been holding on to would burst at some stage. I hope now that I have surrendered to all the pent-up emotion I will feel better... Hopefully stronger.'

Ryan nodded as he stretched an arm around her shoulder. 'It's natural for it to have an effect. I know you don't witness the injuries first hand in the field, but you are not far behind in seeing the impact. You shouldn't be *so* hard on yourself...'

Sarah nodded as he took his leave with a wave, then with head bowed she returned to duty. Another link – albeit very brief – had been severed with the loss of Captain Drayton and she knew for her own peace of mind she would have to learn to become immune to some of it to survive, because she knew there would be more losses for her to lament – some of which might feel very personal. There would be many more sad moments for her to endure before the war was over.

In late November, when the rain receded slightly and the air grew colder, Sarah visited the Gothic cathedral at Rouen once again. She realised now that she would never grow tired of seeing it or be over-awed by its splendour, and Agnes, who got to share it with her, said she had felt the same when Lennox first took her to see the Sphinx and the Pyramids.

Sarah was delighted to see Agnes again and although they were far from home, the old familiarity, the closeness they had enjoyed which seemed to alter the night of the pre-Christmas party in Toorak nearly three years ago, felt now as if it belonged to another time or that it had happened to other people and they had merely witnessed it first hand.

Sarah was disappointed that Lennox hadn't got leave to join them, but she had hugged Agnes close and they appeared to be locked in their embrace, oblivious to those around them, until Ryan coughed slightly and Sarah blushed as she introduced her sister to the man she wanted to share her future with.

'Hello, Ryan Mitchell. I hope you are doing right by my sister...'

Ryan laughed as he shook Agnes's hand; turning to Sarah, he whispered, 'As you said, *she* is very forthright!'

Agnes smiled. She could see immediately that Sarah was happy in this young man's company, and after all that she had *endured* in her marriage, she couldn't want more for her young sibling than that. They linked arms and made their way into the cathedral. Having absorbed its magnificent surroundings they went onto a café in the square for coffee and Agnes told them how she worried about Lennox not having had substantial leave in weeks and that she feared he was close to exhaustion. She elaborated on his plans to establish a hospital in rural Victoria.

'Not too far from the city?' Sarah asked as she took Ryan's hand in hers and smiled.

'Wherever there is the greatest demand. It has been his main ambition for years apparently. Within reasonable distance from Melbourne is what we are hoping for. So what are your work plans after the war is over, Ryan?'

'My family own a haulage business outside of Croydon that I was working in prior to volunteering, which is why ambulance driving was such a natural fit for me, so I could always go back to that...'

Agnes smiled but said nothing and Ryan wondered whether her silence was an indication of her disapproval at him for potentially taking her sister away from Melbourne.

'My first priority is to secure my divorce from Michael. I won't be thinking too far ahead until that has been secured...'

They sipped their coffee and chatted amicably for a while

until it was time for Agnes to depart. She looked across and saw Matron Bryan waiting for her, and Agnes waved in acknowledgement. She stood and embraced Sarah for what seemed like an eternity and felt the salt of unshed tears at the back of her eyes. She felt they had reached an understanding that was akin to what they had enjoyed growing up and she was glad to acknowledge that sibling closeness again.

'Stay strong, and you...' she poked Ryan gently in the ribs, 'look after her.'

Ryan nodded with a smile and then, without looking back, she joined Matron Bryan for the journey back to Etaples.

'So that is your sister?'

Agnes nodded. 'One of the best is Sarah.'

'It looks as though she has bagged herself a good-looking beau.'

Agnes thought for a moment and nodded. 'I make him nervous, I know that much, which isn't too bad if it ensures he treats my sister with respect.'

At which point the ambulance arrived to take them back to Etaples while they watched Sarah and Ryan order another coffee, looking cold and slightly isolated in the sparsely populated rain-soaked square. At one time Agnes had doubted she could share her leave in the company of Kathryn Bryan, but she had seen a softening in her demeanour since they had left Cairo and she had been content not to have made the journey to Rouen alone, but now she yearned to see Lennox. As the ambulance made its way across the cobbled square, she watched until Sarah and Ryan were specks in the distance and she could be content that her sister had found a man who was worthy of her trust.

32

It took Michael much longer than he had anticipated to find Yolande and to convince her to share his life in Hepburn Springs. Honoria had been reluctant to point out her fear that a reluctance to leave the city was the root cause for Yolande's stalling, because he wouldn't believe her and was likely to accuse her of causing trouble. It was when Yolande told him that under no circumstances would she return to Honoria's home that he told her about the rural homestead and persuaded her to at least take a look before dismissing it completely. He knew instinctively that she still loved him, but she had grown more confident since they had last met and a little more combative, and he knew that she wouldn't now be as easily swayed by his promises.

'It needs a lot of work and I will hire the labour firstly to get the house into a habitable state again and then to tackle the land.'

He hoped his tone remained neutral, because he couldn't convince her by sounding desperate or needy. She had to believe the homestead offered them a viable living whatever future plans he had for the land and on her first visit he could see the scepticism.

He had been tempted the first time they had seen each other again to ask her what she knew about her birth, but Yolande had locked him out, frowning deeply, and then she told him firmly that the subject was closed and she never wanted to hear him raise it again. All she knew was that she had been born in a convent in some rural small town miles from the city.

She then strolled across to the perimeter fence and, leaning her elbows on it, she scrutinised him. 'What about your wife?'

'Sarah won't be an issue. She has indicated she wants a divorce and I won't contest that. She wants her freedom. I want ours – I mean, mine.'

Yolande smiled at his slip and walked on, circling the property that had been neglected for many years. 'How did you acquire this place?'

'My father bought it, as an investment mainly, although I think he fancied living here part of the time after retirement, but my mother was never keen.'

Yolande nodded. 'That would be right. I couldn't see "Lady Bountiful" slumming it here.'

Michael suppressed a laugh, imagining his mother's sneer at being referred to in such terms, especially by Yolande.

'I think you have a right to know that I have met your mother… It was through Zola that I tried to find you.'

Yolande nodded. 'She said you had been. Made some threats, but she doesn't scare easily. Why did you believe that hunting her down was the best way of finding me?'

Michael shrugged. 'It was a lead, so I pursued it.'

'Well, you were fortunate we have mutual acquaintances who are willing to pass on a message, because I released myself from the shackles of her influence years ago and I have no wish to return. So Zola is out of bounds as well…'

Michael nodded, gripping his walking stick more firmly. It was ironic that Yolande was so decisively firm when it came to her feelings about *her* mother as she had regularly bemoaned

Honoria's influence on him as being too strong, thus urging him to break free.

Yolande turned and began walking back to the car.

'Well?'

'I will think about it. Now take me back to the city – please...'

Michael nodded, walking faster to catch up. He knew he had more convincing to do, but she hadn't given it an outright refusal as he had feared. That along with the fact that she hadn't rejected him because of the amputation – as Honoria had predicted she might – was a start.

It took fifteen months from the moment Michael took Yolande to the homestead to get it into shape, firstly for the house to be habitable to meet his needs, expanded outwards on one storey before the hired labour moved outside to excavate the land. Michael took charge of the project from the start and he spent days there alone, supervising his immigrant labourers – it was more economical to hire them and because several Australians had quit due to what they had described as his high-handed imperious attitude. To his surprise Yolande took a great interest in the men he had hired and Luca, an Italian who spoke the best English among them, was given the role of foreman so that he could communicate Michael's demands to his colleagues. Luca told Yolande that his family hailed from Southern Italy and that they had come to Australia for a better life. Michael tolerated Yolande's mild interest in Luca for a while until it became a distraction and then he made the error of challenging her on it.

'Why are you so interested in Luca's history?'

Yolande had shrugged nonchalantly; making a moue with her mouth, she smiled. 'It's good to see some strong muscle around the place. He's doing a good job, isn't he? You don't like getting your hands dirty, so let him. It doesn't hurt you to be civil.'

Yolande turned her back on him and he swung her round to face him.

'It's not civility you're treating him to, it's flirting, and I'm sick of it. I will be respected under my roof, Yolande!'

'You want me to return to the city? To forget this life you want to build for us here, to forget you and me having any future?'

'I won't be made a fool of. I have said I will put a ring on your finger as soon as I am free and I meant it, but if you want to pursue another option with the Italian do it. Just don't expect me to have to watch...'

Yolande stared at her him long and hard before walking out, slamming the door behind her. Michael sighed heavily. He didn't feel comfortable issuing threats because he genuinely feared that if pushed too far now, Yolande would leave him. Since leaving his mother's employment, she had learnt how to assert herself, to stand her ground to the point where he feared he might lose her forever.

Yolande stood with her arms folded firmly across her chest, an action which made her breasts taut against the outline of her shirt. She stood at the perimeter fence which the some of the labourers were repairing. Luca could see that she was upset and he approached her tentatively as she stood breathing heavily, trying to control her sense of fury at what she saw as Michael's growing but irrational jealousy. She knew she was at fault to some extent for feeding his fears, as she had been flirting with Luca even more since she had seen how it provoked a reaction. She recalled the time she had pleaded with him to get his mother or Grace Metcalfe to go easier on her, but he had negated her request by saying he tried not to get involved in domestic matters, so she had been left to feel increasingly isolated, no better than a drudge, until he had gone off to fight and she had been left to deal with accusations that she had pushed Sarah downstairs and contributed to his infant's death as a result.

Luca meant nothing to *her*. Aside from that, there was another immigrant girl from a neighbouring village in Southern Italy that he was keen on pursuing a relationship with now that they were both in Australia. She half-turned to the house and, seeing Michael standing at the door watching her and Luca, she decided that if he chose to be suspicious and insanely jealous when there was nothing for him to be jealous about, she might as well be accused and *damned* for something other than what was just in his imagination. So when Luca came closer, dropping the sledgehammer to the ground but hesitant about putting his work-soiled hands on her, she let her bottom lip quiver slightly. Although still hesitant, Luca sought to console her with an embrace. She looked back again to the house, expecting Michael to come storming out to confront them, but as he was no longer watching, either he hadn't seen Luca putting his arms around her or he had given up caring so much, realising perhaps that he just didn't have it within him to fight for her anymore and Yolande knew for her that that would be the worst outcome of all.

During the time he had been away fighting Yolande hadn't allowed herself to be tempted by other men; however, the first time that she had seen him with his left leg gone above the knee she had gasped with shock, realising the dynamic in their relationship had shifted and that she, like countless other Australian women welcoming their men back from the war, was confronting a new reality. After a few seconds she pulled away from Luca's arms and he apologised profusely. She knew she should feel a little ashamed that she could have got him into trouble with Michael, but she was aware also that her lover needed the labourers as much as they valued the work, so it would have been churlish self-indulgence if Michael acted rashly and fired Luca. However, it would still have been a gesture of a lover who *cared*. From the moment Yolande had agreed to come back to him, she had wanted Michael to understand that she had *changed*, matured, perhaps, and the slavish need that she'd had for him wasn't as great, but now she was beginning to fear she had pushed him too far and that the strength of his *lust* had also altered.

The Landseer Homestead, Hepburn Springs – September 1919

Sarah had been dreading the reunion with Michael for days. She didn't want to be confronted with Yolande under any circumstances, but as she feared that might not be possible, she had persuaded Ryan to accompany her. Ever since they had got engaged on the ship home from Europe they had made tentative plans for the future, although they agreed the first piece in the jigsaw was securing her divorce. She hadn't given any thought to how Michael would react to seeing her with another man, but she knew it was a sign of her inner strength now that she didn't care. He had lost any moral claim over her and now she had come to tie up the legal side of the issue to win her freedom from a union that she couldn't wait to consign to the past.

Honoria had taken the news of her engagement to Ryan better than Sarah had any right to expect, and while she didn't imagine Michael could display the same humility she did expect him to respect her wishes and sign. The previous evening she had thanked Honoria for all her kindness during the marriage and since, but she promised it wasn't goodbye.

Honoria had responded by taking Sarah's hands and telling her firmly to be happy as she went to secure her future.

They drew up outside the homestead on a dirt road mid-morning in the shimmering heat haze of a scorching day, and Ryan agreed reluctantly to wait by his truck, respecting her wish to confront Michael alone. She found her husband in a sombre mood. In fact, it struck her that there was a defeatist element to his entire demeanour that she had never witnessed before, although she cared less than she understood.

As she approached he stopped hoeing and leaned on the handle of the garden tool. She could hear humming in the background and guessed it was Yolande as she hung sheets on a line. She shielded her eyes from the glare of the sun as she took the divorce papers from the envelope, handing them to Michael.

'Hello, Michael.'

'Sarah. Isn't he joining you?'

Sarah shook her head. 'No. He knows I need to do this myself.'

Watching her walk towards him from the truck, he had seen how blissfully happy she had looked and he thought, *That is because of him. I never made her look that happy. Even on our wedding day she didn't look as radiant as she does now.* Michael knew he had treated her shabbily during their marriage and that was why she was so determined to secure her freedom now.

Michael bowed his head and reached for his shotgun, making a play of cleaning it, anything to make his hands look busy, to provide some distraction from the awkwardness of the situation and the fact he was acceding to her wishes, as Honoria had insisted he should. It was still for him the biggest admission of failure.

He could still hear Yolande's gentle humming, realising it was her method of making her presence felt, even though he had urged her to be out of sight when Sarah arrived. He could also hear male laughter and guessed she was distracting Luca or one of the other labourers from their work, because she knew how much it riled him.

'Do you have a pen?' he asked, and Sarah smiled as she produced one and he said, 'Turn around, so I can lean on your back to sign these…'

Hesitantly Sarah did as she was bidden and turned. Michael

wiped his sweat-smeared hands on his trousers and signed the papers that formally ended a marriage which had only ever been a means to end, which he had not been successful in achieving and now it was a *sham* that he was content to see the end of.

He handed them back as Sarah turned; looking down she saw his signature, and she blushed slightly that she felt the need to check.

'I am sorry, Sarah…'

She shook her head slightly and he wasn't sure whether it meant his apology was too little too late or that it just didn't matter, because she had moved on and he should do the same.

'Good luck…' he said as she turned to walk back through the heat haze to Ryan standing casually against the front of his truck.

She had known how to deal with Michael's anger and the sneering superiority that he had subjected her to so frequently, but this subdued version of her husband made her nervous.

Sarah clutched the envelope to her chest and walked back to the young man waiting to build a future with her. There was admiration and love in his eyes, and Michael knew he had done the right thing by Sarah.

Finally. He could still hear Yolande's voice and whichever of the Italian men she was chatting flirtatiously with in the background. As Sarah reached Ryan, Michael could see even from a distance as Ryan's arm snaked around her waist as he pulled her to him, claiming her as his, kissing her passionately. In the next moment, he raised his shotgun and Sarah, standing with her back to Michael, saw the sudden look of horror cross Ryan's face, and then she half-turned back to the farm as the awful reality dawned and then she heard one shot reverberating in the silence, then Yolande's piercing screams as Michael fell to the ground and the pristine white sheets were smeared with spots of blood.

EPILOGUE

Melbourne, Australia – October 1919

The inquest into Michael Landseer's death was short and the coroner's verdict decisive and straightforward. Only Ryan Mitchell and Sarah Landseer were called as witnesses to the scene and Honoria supplied testimony to his state of mind, as Michael had been uncharacteristically sharing his thoughts with her for weeks. Yolande was deemed too ill with grief to attend or deemed not to be a reliable witness. Honoria had sneered with derision at Yolande's claim to be grieving, but she was content that her presence was unnecessary. The coroner concluded that the victim had taken his own life, while his mind was unsound and the absence of any note ruled out premeditation. Honoria wasn't surprised by Michael's act, just very sad that her son's life should end in such an horrific way, and she came to her own conclusion – albeit reluctantly – that *he* should have had his wish fulfilled to die a hero's death on the battlefield alongside Aaron Crozier.

She had once said in anger that he didn't deserve a hero's death, but she deeply regretted that he had chosen this kind of death instead. She couldn't help thinking the futility of his action was systematic of his infatuation with the wretched servant girl Yolande Smith, that her long-held prediction, that his obsessive *lust* for Yolande would be to his ruin had borne out to be true.

Prior to the inquest she made one trip to Hepburn Springs after consulting with Sarah, who was still effectively his next of kin. She paid Luca and his team of labourers what they were owed and dismissed them with thanks, and then she issued notice for Yolande to find herself alternative accommodation within thirty days as the property Michael had seen as their future would now be sold. She could finally exclude Yolande Smith from her life.

After the inquest, she approached Sarah and took both of her hands, squeezing them. 'Thank you for coming. I am just sorry that lasting image of Michael should be so terrible... I *urge* you to erase it from your minds and claim the happiness you deserve...'

Sarah watched Honoria leave the courtroom and she smiled wanly at Ryan. 'I have never seen her look so lost. It's as if her life force was taken from her with Michael's act.'

Ryan Mitchell nodded. 'Let's go. Your parents are waiting, and I believe Agnes and Lennox are joining us.'

The Calloway Mansion, Toorak

Jensen Calloway was shocked to hear the news of Michael's death, but given how his former son-in-law had manipulated his situation to seize the family home, he wasn't inclined to show too much sorrow. He was just glad his family had come through so much turmoil intact, stronger and more content than they had been in many months.

He stood in his study waiting for Sarah and Ryan to arrive directly from the inquest. Having poured himself a small cognac, he raised the glass at the portrait of Cyrus and saluted him.

He anticipated Ryan and Sarah might set a date for their wedding soon and he knew Agnes and Lennox wanted to bless their union. He had come to a decision about his own future, with a plan to sell the brokerage as a thriving business and retire.

'Here's to you, Cyrus Calloway. The inscrutable old rogue.'

He heard additional voices in the vestibule and he opened the study door as Agnes embraced her sister and shook hands with Ryan.

'How was it?'

'Functional, but very bleak,' Sarah said with a shudder.

'I can't believe Michael would ever commit such an act. I know how much he struggled after the amputation and how much he resisted having it, but I could never have predicted this.'

Jensen shook his head. 'Ssh. From now it should be happy thoughts, focused upon the future. Lennox has seen that his hospital is being built and it's going to thrive, and you two are ready to commit to your future together. I cannot tell you how grateful I am to be spared the grief that so many Australian families have suffered. Both my daughters have emerged from the carnage of this war with promising nursing careers ahead of them. So I think it fitting that we raise our glasses and propose this toast: to Agnes and Sarah: the Calloway sisters! May happiness be with you always...'

Agnes looked at Sarah and winked conspiratorially. They had come through so much and had found their way back to each other, and in a private moment they had vowed never to be divided again.

SELECT BIBLIOGRAPHY

John Grehan and Martin Mace, *Gallipoli and the Dardanelles*, Pen & Sword, 2014.

Peter FitzSimons, *Gallipoli*, Bantam Press, 2015.

Peter Rees, *The Anzac Girls*, Allen & Unwin, 2008.

Thomas Keneally, *The Daughters of Mars*, Sceptre, 2012.

ACKNOWLEDGEMENTS

Firstly I would like once again to thank the staff at Crawley Library for their assistance in finding the titles listed in my select bibliography.

I also thank family and friends for their continued interest and support in various writing projects.